"Sorry,"

Cass mumbled.

"For?"

"Acting like a weepy broad."

Blake nuzzled the top of her head, his chuckle in her hair as soft and seductive as a summer breeze. "*Broad* seems apt, at the moment," he murmured, gently patting her belly.

She turned away, couldn't back up quickly enough from the flash fire his touch ignited.

"Cass." When she refused to turn toward him, he touched her again, this time gently hooking two fingers underneath her chin. "Cass, look at me."

She glanced up, blinking, and saw the remnants of all the hope and promise of so many years ago. Was she seeing what was in his eyes, though, or a reflection of what was in hers?

"Whatever goes on here goes way beyond the wreck we made of our marriage," he said. "I never stopped caring about you. About what happens to you. Even now, if there's anything I can do…"

Dear Reader,

Well, we're getting into the holiday season full tilt, and what better way to begin the celebrations than with some heartwarming reading? Let's get started with Gina Wilkins's *The Borrowed Ring,* next up in her FAMILY FOUND series. A woman trying to track down her family's most mysterious and intriguing foster son finds him and a whole lot more—such as a job posing as his wife! *A Montana Homecoming,* by popular author Allison Leigh, brings home a woman who's spent her life running from her own secrets. But they're about to be revealed, courtesy of her childhood crush, now the local sheriff.

This month, our class reunion series, MOST LIKELY TO…, brings us Jen Safrey's *Secrets of a Good Girl,* in which we learn that the girl most likely to…*do everything* disappeared right after college. Perhaps her secret crush, a former professor, can have some luck tracking her down overseas? We're delighted to have bestselling Blaze author Kristin Hardy visit Special Edition in the first of her HOLIDAY HEARTS books. *Where There's Smoke* introduces us to the first of the devastating Trask brothers. The featured brother this month is a handsome firefighter in Boston. And speaking of delighted—we are absolutely thrilled to welcome RITA® Award nominee and Red Dress Ink and Intimate Moments star Karen Templeton to Special Edition. Although this is her first Special Edition contribution, it feels as if she's coming home. Especially with *Marriage, Interrupted,* in which a pregnant widow meets up once again with the man who got away—her first husband—at her second husband's funeral. We know you're going to enjoy this amazing story as much as we did. And we are so happy to welcome brand-new Golden Heart winner Gail Barrett to Special Edition. *Where He Belongs,* the story of the bad boy who's come back to town to the girl he's never been able to forget, is Gail's first published book.

So enjoy—and remember, next month we continue our celebration….

Gail Chasan
Senior Editor

Please address questions and book requests to:
Silhouette Reader Service
U.S.: 3010 Walden Ave., P.O. Box 1325, Buffalo, NY 14269
Canadian: P.O. Box 609, Fort Erie, Ont. L2A 5X3

MARRIAGE, INTERRUPTED

KAREN TEMPLETON

Silhouette

SPECIAL EDITION

Published by Silhouette Books

America's Publisher of Contemporary Romance

SILHOUETTE BOOKS

ISBN 0-373-24721-4

MARRIAGE, INTERRUPTED

This edition published by arrangement with Harlequin Books S.A.

® and TM are trademarks of Harlequin Books S.A., used under license.
Trademarks indicated with ® are registered in the United States Patent
and Trademark Office, the Canadian Trade Marks Office and in other
countries.

Visit Silhouette Books at www.eHarlequin.com

Printed in U.S.A.

Books by Karen Templeton

Silhouette Special Edition

Marriage, Interrupted #1721

Silhouette Intimate Moments

Anything for His Children #978
Anything for Her Marriage #1006
Everything but a Husband #1050
Runaway Bridesmaid #1066
†*Plain-Jane Princess* #1096
†*Honky-Tonk Cinderella* #1120
What a Man's Gotta Do #1195
Saving Dr. Ryan #1207
Fathers and Other Strangers #1244
Staking His Claim #1267
**Everybody's Hero* #1328
**Swept Away* #1357

Silhouette Yours Truly

*Wedding Daze
*Wedding Belle
*Wedding? Impossible!

†How To Marry a Monarch
*Weddings, Inc.
**The Men of Mayes County

KAREN TEMPLETON,

a Waldenbooks bestselling author and RITA® Award nominee, is the mother of five sons and living proof that romance and dirty diapers are not mutually exclusive terms. An Easterner transplanted to Albuquerque, New Mexico, she spends far too much time trying to coax her garden to yield roses and produce something resembling a lawn, all the while fantasizing about a weekend alone with her husband. Or at least an uninterrupted conversation.

She loves to hear from readers, who may reach her by writing c/o Silhouette Books, 233 Broadway, Suite 1001, New York, NY 10279, or online at www.karentempleton.com.

Dear Reader,

After writing nearly twenty books for Harlequin/Silhouette, *Marriage, Interrupted,* is my first for Special Edition...and I cannot tell you how thrilled I am to be included in this group of wonderful authors. For those of you who have read and enjoyed my family-oriented, down-home stories for Intimate Moments, trust me—nothing's changed. For those readers who might be sampling one of my stories for the first time, I hope you enjoy this tale of second chances, of good-hearted people who, being human, have made mistakes...and learned from them. And of course, about the kind of love strong enough, and stubborn enough, to withstand those mistakes.

I truly feel as though I've come home, and I hope, as you laugh and cry along with Cass and Blake and their anything-but-ordinary *family,* that you will, too.

* * *

Dedication

To Gail, still and again, for your constant support and encouragement. Not to mention giving this book a *second chance* and finally, a home.

I literally couldn't have done any of this without you.

And to my family, who may yet learn what the Do Not Disturb note on the office door means... although I'm not holding my breath.

I couldn't have done this without you guys, either.

Chapter One

On the other side of her swollen belly, Cass was reasonably sure she still had legs. Under normal circumstances, which these definitely were not, she would have waited until after the baby's arrival to become reacquainted with her phantom appendages. However, in less than two hours, she had a funeral to attend. In a dress. Which meant pantyhose…which meant she had to shave her legs.

Through the eight-foot-tall yucca standing guard outside the window, the low-angled Albuquerque spring sun cast a spiky shadow across the master bath as she stood considering her options, her bellybutton straining the snaps on her cotton robe. They weren't pretty, any of them. If she got in the tub, she'd never get out. If she attempted it in the shower, she'd probably break her neck. And if she sat down, she could neither bend down nor get her foot up.

Which left the sink. Cass dimly remembered performing

this little trick when she'd gone into labor with Shaun a million years ago, while Blake dashed around the house doing whatever it was that had kept him out of her hair until she was ready to leave for the hospital. So this was doable. Or at least it had been when she'd been twenty and a lot looser-hipped than she was now.

Cass filled the sink, shoved the belly to one side, and heaved, grabbing at the towel rack before she toppled over. Her balance regained—physically if not mentally—she pretzled herself in order to perform her task, furious tears pricking her eyes.

God help the next man dumb enough to ask her to trust him.

First leg mowed and once again consigned to oblivion, she hauled up the other one, nicking herself above the ankle with the first swipe of the razor. Swearing, she wadded up a piece of toilet paper into a little square and smacked it against the wound.

For more than ten years, she'd resisted remarriage. To anyone. Between raising a child on her own, holding down a succession of retail jobs and finishing up her marketing degree, there'd been no time, let alone interest or enthusiasm. Loneliness, when she acknowledged it at all, was that nameless, faceless stranger standing on the corner as she zipped from day care to work to school, forgotten before the image even had a chance to fully register. Then she meets a charming, respectable, seemingly sane man at a chamber of commerce dinner, they hit it off, they start dating, she hears him offering her the few things she still occasionally allowed herself to believe she needed. Wanted.

Safety. Security. A full-time father for her son, drowning in adolescent angst. And the opportunity to have another child. Unbridled passion hadn't been part of the deal, but, frankly, that had been fine with Cass. She no longer had the energy for passion, unbridled or otherwise, she didn't think. Let alone all the garbage that went along with it.

Fool me once, shame on you. Fool me twice…

The bleeding had stopped. Cass quickly finished up before her hips permanently locked in that position, then, on a groan, lowered the second foot to the floor. The baby kicked; her hand went to her tummy, soothing and stroking.

Well. She'd gotten the child, at least.

Copious, angry tears surged from what she'd thought was a dry well. She slammed the heel of her hand against the sink, then dropped onto the toilet lid, stifling her sobs in her stinging palm. How could she have made virtually the same mistake a second time? *How?* Other women could see beyond the surface, past the charm and the promises and the compliments. Why couldn't she?

"Cassie, sweetheart—is everything all right?"

Cass yanked off a yard or two of toilet paper to blow her nose. Talk about your major ironies. Despite everything, Cass adored Alan's zany, exuberant mother, who had been in residence long before the marriage. Not even the louse's deception could change that.

And to your left, folks, we have the grieving widow.

Yeah, well, she somehow doubted she was the first woman since Eve to link the words *louse* and *dead husband.*

Cass swiped at her face with the heel of her hand, willing her voice steady enough to call out, "Yeah, Cille. I'm fine."

"And I'm one of the Olsen twins," she rasped through the closed door. "So open the door before I break it down."

At four-foot-something, and maybe ninety pounds after a full meal, eighty-year-old Lucille Stern would be hard put to break down a doggy gate. Cass struggled to her feet, then waddled over to the bathroom door, opening it to a sight guaranteed to obliterate self-pity.

Reeking of mothballs and Joy perfume, Lucille stood with fists planted on bony hips swallowed up inside a hooker-red satin dress, complete with a mandarin collar and side slits. A tilt of her head made rhinestone earrings the size of manhole covers flash in the streak of sunlight knifing down the hall. She squinted up at Cass through stubby, mascara-clumped lashes.

"Don't take this the wrong way, sweetheart, but you look like hell."

Cass was still blinking from the dress. Not to mention the rhinestones. "Gee, thanks," she finally managed as they moved into her bedroom. "But, hey—my legs are shaved."

The old woman fiddled with a red satin bow jutting out from the nuclear-blast-resistant whorls of short, improbably red hair. "Terrific. So we'll tell everyone to look at your calves." Then she turned around, jabbing one thumb over her shoulder at the open back of her dress. "This meshugah zipper and my arthritis are a lousy combination. Zip me up, there's a dollbaby."

"Cille." Cass weighed her words carefully as she zipped the dress over a black lace bra. Even for Lucille, this was extreme. "You don't think this dress is a little—" *Gaudy? Flamboyant? Tacky?* "—bright?"

That got a phlegmy sigh. "This is not exactly the best day of my life, you know?" Futzing again with her hair, the former Brooklynite turned, lifting disillusioned green eyes to Cass. "So I could use a little cheering up. So I'm wearing red. So what are they going to do, kick me out of the funeral home?"

Cass scraped her lip between her teeth. Alan had been Lucille's only child, dutiful in his own way, she supposed, but not exactly a joy to his mother's heart from what Cass had observed over the past year or so. If Lucille was mourning anything, most likely it was for a relationship that had soured long before the man's death.

And Lucille didn't know the half of it.

But they were tough broads, the pair of them. They'd both

get through this. "No one's kicking you out of anywhere, Cille. Not without getting by me first—"

"Mom?"

Sweeping her uncombed hair away from her face, Cass shifted her gaze to the doorway, where her son stood awkwardly attired in some friend's sports jacket and khakis—a startling contrast to his normal uniform of frayed jeans and oversize T-shirts. What a stunner to glimpse the adult Shaun would one day be. If she didn't strangle him first. She supposed their mother-teenage-son relationship was no more fraught with problems than usual—and probably less, if she thought about it—but there were times...

Times she wondered if he'd ever understand.

"My God!" Cille craned her neck to look up at him on her way out of the room. "The boy has ears."

With a self-conscious grin, Shaun touched his right ear, revealed by dint of the ponytail into which he'd pulled his shoulder-length blond hair. Even though all his friends wore their hair short, he had to do things his own way. Including the trio of open-ended loops in one ear, courtesy of some galpal with a hot needle and an ice cube a few months back. The only thing keeping Cass from killing him that time was the nasty infection that had nearly done the job for her. "Cool, huh?"

"Literally," Cass agreed, deciding to be grateful Shaun had shown no desire to pierce other body parts. Or dye his hair chartreuse. "Now that they've made contact with the air...what?"

Shaun had held up one hand, angling his head into the hall. When the door to Lucille's bedroom clicked shut, Shaun turned back, fidgeting with one of the jacket's pocket flaps. The grin had vanished, replaced with an expression of uneasy concern. "How're you doing?"

He'd asked her that a hundred times since Alan's death. She'd yet to be truthful. "I'm managing—"

"Dad's here."

"What?" She dropped, hard, onto the edge of her bed. "Why?"

A mixture of defiance and guilt flashed through all-too-familiar hound dog eyes. "I called him, yesterday morning."

Shock jolted a million nerve endings, leaving her slightly dizzy. "You asked him to come down?"

"I…uh…" He wriggled his shoulders underneath the jacket, stuck his hand in the coat pocket. Took it out again. "I just told him what'd happened, is all. I didn't know he was coming."

But he obviously knew that's what Blake would do. Cass swallowed her immediate reaction—that none of this had anything to do with her ex-husband and why the hell was he here, invading their privacy?—when she remembered that Shaun had been jockeying for his father's attention all his life. Why should it come as any surprise, then, that he should want Blake here now? Especially when this past year had turned out to be such a colossal disappointment.

"Mom?"

Cass's head jerked up, her heart aching for the child still hovering underneath the fragile, easily punctured surface of new adulthood. She'd done her best, had only wanted something better for him when she'd married Alan. That it hadn't turned out the way she'd hoped wasn't anyone's fault, but still—and again—her son had gotten the short end of the stick.

"It's okay? That I called Dad?"

In his frown, she could still see the toddler seeking Mommy's approval. She pushed herself off the bed and crossed to him, slipping her hand into his. How odd, she thought, to be pregnant with her second child when her first was already several inches taller than she. "Of course, honey.

You…he…" Her shoulders raised, then dropped. "It just took me by surprise, that's all."

Underneath the unfamiliar clothes, the boy's entire body let out a sigh. "Okay. Well. I think he wants to talk to you."

Just when you think things can't get any worse…

"Tell him I'll be out in a minute," she said.

They say it takes a big man to admit when he's made a mistake. In which case, Blake thought as he sensed more than heard Cass enter the room, he should be at least twelve feet tall by now. His feigned interest in the ostentatiously large impressionistic landscape over the stone fireplace immediately abandoned, he pivoted, his breath catching in his throat.

He'd never seen her look worse.

Her gold-tipped bangs catching in her lashes with each blink, she stood at the edge of the step leading down into the brick-pavered living room, one hand propped on her lower back. Despite her above-average height, she seemed dwarfed by the tedious expanse of chalky white wall, soaring fifteen feet to the beamed ceiling overhead. A bank of clerestory windows slashed the top of the wall, choking the air with sunlight, but even so, the room seemed cold. Inhospitable.

A smile flitted over her lips, as if she wasn't sure what was appropriate, under the circumstances. "Well. This is a surprise."

His pulse involuntarily quickened at the sound of that crème-de-menthe voice. He used to tell her she could make ordering breakfast in a truck stop sound like a seduction. And she would laugh, right before she'd give him a smile that made the laugh seem childlike by comparison.

She wasn't smiling now. Instead, she'd obviously been crying. Well, what did he expect? She'd just lost her husband, for God's sake—

Breathe, Carter. Breathe.

There was nothing he could say that would make any sense, or make things any easier. He hadn't been sure, when he'd decided to come down from Denver, what he thought he could possibly do. What a shock to discover that all he really wanted was to pull her into his arms. "How are you holding up?"

She carefully stepped down into the room. "I'll let you know when the Prozac wears off," she quipped, just as he would have expected. For a second, irritation prickled his skin. Cass had always used humor as a cop-out to mask what was really going on in her head. Blake had never been sure what, exactly, had destroyed their marriage, since Cass had too often substituted wisecracks for honesty. Oh, the obvious reasons were, well, obvious enough. What fed those reasons, however, was something else again. Now, twelve years later, the relationship was undefined, ambiguous. Not friendship or love or hate or even mutual disinterest colored their forced conversations. At least with good old-fashioned animosity, you knew what you were dealing with.

With an unmistakable grimace, she lowered herself onto a ladderback chair in front of a bare window, next to a carved table littered with carefully arranged knickknacks. Blake remembered the posture well—legs apart, one hand still on her back, the other absently rubbing against her thigh. The memory slashed through his heart, catching him off guard. He didn't let on. "I thought Shaun said the funeral was at eleven?"

"It is."

"But you're not dressed yet."

Tropical blue eyes lifted to his, more weary than sad, he thought. Hoped. "I didn't expect company this early on the day of my husband's funeral."

Point to her.

Cass cocked her head at him, her hand wandering over her

swollen middle, instinctively massaging the child within. Another man's child.

Another slash. Irrational and petty as it was.

"You didn't have to come down," she said.

"I got the feeling Shaun was asking me to."

She nodded, then looked away, letting a silence slip between them so profound it was practically visible.

For a second he scrutinized her. She'd lightened her hair a little, he thought, the shag cut softly framing those high cheekbones, her long neck, in wispy strands of shimmering red-gold. Her smooth skin, pulled taut across model-worthy cheekbones, a square-edged jaw, was nevertheless etched with a tracery of worry lines, around her mouth, her eyes, between her brows. She seemed thinner, too, despite the pregnancy. That, he didn't like. Her eating habits had always been atrocious; when she'd been pregnant with Shaun, they'd nearly come to blows over her diet. Olives for breakfast, he remembered. And French fries. But only Burger King's, no one else's. The one time he'd tried to sneak a package of McDonald's fries past her…

Blake forced his attention elsewhere, again fighting the insane urge to hold her, to comfort her. As the friend he'd once been, if nothing else.

"Did you drive down?" The question echoed in the vast room.

"Yes. Figured I'd rather have my own car."

She nodded again, slipped back into the silence.

She reminded him so much of the overwhelmed college freshman who'd tripped up his heart seventeen—no, eighteen—years ago. He'd been a senior, working part-time in UNM's bookstore, when she'd come in, all huge eyes and tremulous smile, and he'd fallen so fast he didn't even feel the bruises from landing for weeks afterward. A soft ache accompanied the memory of how hard she'd fought not to let him, or anyone else, know how petrified she was that first day. She wore exactly that expression now, overlaid with an edgy exhaustion that brought out a keen protective streak—for himself almost more than for her.

Hands in pockets, Blake's eyes flicked again over the living room he'd never seen before today. Hadn't been able to face. Shaun had flown up to Denver a few times since Cass's marriage, but Blake hadn't once returned to Albuquerque. His business had provided a convenient excuse.

Oh, yeah. She'd done well. The house, set high in the Foothills on the east side of the city, screamed money. Fairly new money, Blake thought, tempered by good taste. Sleek, contemporary furniture in blacks and grays, richly patterned Navajo rugs, gallery-quality artwork. Impressive. And not a trace of the Cass he'd known—or thought he'd known—anywhere.

"Nice place," he managed.

A slight wince preceded her shifting as she tried to find the mythological, more comfortable position. She had narrow hips; the final months of pregnancy weren't easy for her. Irrationally—again—Blake hated this guy, for being her husband, for making her pregnant. Even for dying on her. For leaving her with that frightened-little-girl look in her eyes. Hell, not even Blake had done that.

Or had he?

"Thank you," she replied at last. "The view at night—" he followed her gaze to the expanse of glass that led out to an upper level deck "—is really something. You can see the whole city from up here—"

Her voice caught. He was intruding, he knew. But leaving wasn't an option. Not until…

Until what?

Cass was watching him, he realized with a start. "What?" he asked.

"Is it me, or is this incredibly awkward?"

His lips cracked a little when he tried to smile for her. "Probably not all that unusual, though. With so many step-families nowadays…" His heart rate kicked up as her brows hitched underneath her bangs. "I'm still our son's father. That didn't change because you remarried."

Heeling one hand on the end of the table, she pushed herself out of the chair. "The limo's coming for us at ten-thirty," she said, her words clipped. "Now I do need to get dressed." She seemed to hesitate, worrying her knock-your-socks-off solitaire with the fingers of her right hand. He found himself wondering what she'd done with the plain gold band he'd given her. "Do you…you could ride with us, if you want."

"Thanks, but no." He smiled, a little. "That *would* be awkward."

That got a quietly assessing look for a moment. "Yes, I suppose so." She started out of the room, then turned back. "I didn't thank you for coming."

"Please, forget it. You're a little preoccupied, I'm sure."

Understandably, there was no joy in her smile. "I hope I don't reach the point where I ever forget my manners, Blake. No matter what the circumstances. Besides, I know how busy you are, with your business and all—"

"This is still family, Cass. That always takes precedence."

Accusation flared in her eyes, reminding him of his less-than-sterling reputation in that particular area, before she finally left the room. It struck him, as it had so often since the divorce, how badly he'd failed her.

"Dad?"

And that he'd failed his son even more.

Like tangled barbed wire, guilt lodged in Blake's chest as he glanced over at the unwitting victim of his own pain and disappointment, standing on the opposite side of the room.

The boy's grin seemed shy. "You look really weird in that suit."

As in, Shaun had rarely seen Blake in anything other than jeans. With a grin that was in all likelihood equally timorous, Blake reciprocated. "Not nearly as weird as you do."

"Dork-city, right?"

"Hardly. Just different. Good different, though."

In the mildly uncomfortable silence that followed, Blake thought again how much he'd missed his child every day they were separated—far too many days for his comfort. But stuff got in the way, didn't it? If only…

A sharp gasp of realization caught in his throat, as even the blood chugging through his veins came to a screeching halt. Blake wasn't a religious man in the traditional sense, but he liked to think he knew an epiphanous moment when one smacked him upside the head. And this one was a pip:

He wanted his family back.

And if that didn't earn him a deluxe, all-expenses-paid trip to the booby hatch, he didn't know what did. As if…what? He could somehow pick up the widely scattered pieces from the last dozen years and glue them back together, good as new? As if Shaun—as if *Cass*—would *let* him?

Well, you could scratch that epiphany right off the list, boy, 'cause this one had No Way in Hell written all over it.

"So, anyway," Shaun tried again, as if Blake had been the one to let the conversation die, "Towanda wants to know, you wanna cup of coffee?"

His brain buzzing, Blake covered the distance between them, drawing his son into a quick, one-handed hug around shoulders at nearly the same level as his. "Coffee sounds great." If there was ever a Maxwell House moment, this was it. "But who's Towanda?"

Catching the startled "What the heck is this?" look on

Shaun's face, Blake released his grip. After they both tugged at their jacket hems, neither seemed to know where to look or what to do with their hands. "You'll see," Shaun said, still eyeing Blake with suspicion.

As he followed Shaun down a short, tiled hall to the kitchen, a series of revelatory aftershocks rattled his skull (since clearly his brain hadn't gotten the memo about scratching the epiphany off the list). *It isn't too late,* came the thought. At least, there might still be time to forge a relationship with his son, to repair the inadvertent damage inflicted by total cluelessness.

But the epiphany had said *family.* Not *son.* Family. As in *Cass.*

Forget it, Blake mentally yelled at whoever was in charge of these things.

Uh…no, Whoever calmly replied. Which is when Blake came to the mildly depressing realization that there's apparently an iron-clad No Return policy on epiphanies. Who knew?

All well and good. Except how the hell was he supposed to heal a breach with someone who regarded him as though he were carrying a contagious disease, hadn't even buried her second husband yet, and—oh, yeah—was pregnant with said dead husband's child? The timing wasn't exactly ideal here.

Tough. Deal with it.

Yeah, well, there was also the minor detail of his still, to this day, having no idea how to fix something that had at one time seemed so right and yet had gone so horribly wrong.

Then maybe it's high time you get off your lazy butt and figure it out.

Right about now, Blake thought as they reached the kitchen, a lobotomy wasn't sounding half-bad.

"Well now…" The generously bosomed black woman in the monochrome kitchen, her prodigious figure encased in a geometric-pattern shirt and polyester pants with permanently

stitched-down creases, rose from a stool behind the granite island and walked over to Blake, clapping a firm hand on his arm.
The dark eyes that met his were warm and fearless and una-
pologetically judgmental. "I take it you're this boy's daddy."

Blake met her confident grin with a slightly less certain one
of his own. "Last time I checked."

"Well, I'm Towanda, and the rule around here is don't give
me any guff and we'll get along just fine." With that she returned to whatever she'd been doing, her crepe-soled oxfords
making no sound on the gray-tiled floor. "Coffee's over there,"
she said with a twitch of her head, her dark blond waves remaining suspiciously rigid. "Help yourself."

In business, Blake mused as he filled a mug, he'd gloried
in a succession of triumphs. In life, he'd bombed, big-time.
After the divorce he'd dated, some, when he could fit it in,
but none of the budding relationships ever caught fire. Nor had
he cared overmuch that they hadn't. No other woman had ever
gotten to him the way Cass had, and he suspected no other
woman ever would. And if that sounded sappy and overly sen-
timental and improbable, so be it. He hadn't purposefully
closed himself off to loving again, but since it hadn't happened, or even come close, in all this time…

Blake took a sip of the best coffee he'd ever tasted, mulling this over.

For way too long, he realized, he'd dwelled on what had
gone wrong with his marriage, an exercise which had done
little more than leave him with a nagging, burning sensation
not unlike chronic heartburn that he'd somehow let the ball
drop. That he'd given up too easily. Well, now…maybe, just
maybe, it was time to remember what had been right. And
with time—lots of time, considering the woman's husband
had just died—with patience, and with a lot of prayer, maybe
Cass would remember, too.

Of course, there was also the definite possibility that he was on the brink of making a total ass of himself.

He took another sip of coffee, then grunted.

Which would make this not exactly a venture into new territory.

By midafternoon, the crowd had begun to thin, as more and more people slipped out the front door and back into the stream of their normal lives. The funeral, the burial, 1001 nameless condolence givers had all—mercifully, Cass decided—become an indistinct blur.

Except for Blake.

She sat on one of the sofas in the living room, Lucille next to her, close enough for the older woman to occasionally squeeze Cass's hand. That is, when she wasn't talking off the ear of whoever came over to offer his or her sympathy. Cass didn't know ninety percent of these people, a fact that made it much easier to keep her emotional cool.

Except about Blake.

His nearness, both through the services and now, back at the house, tormented her no less than the too-hot-for-March noonday sun that had seared her skin through her black silk maternity dress. Had she been deluding herself these past dozen years? Cass really had believed she'd broken Blake's almost mesmeric hold on her heart, her mind. Her soul. But the truth was, she now realized with a mixture of embarrassment and horror, the attachment had never truly been severed. Like stretching a rubber band thin enough to give the illusion of separation, if you increase the tension even a little too far—*twannnng!* Right back where you started.

Like now. Her mental and emotional resources stretched to the max, all it took was Blake Carter's reappearance in her life, and…*twannnng!*

And, boy oh boy, did it smart.

"I'm so sorry for your loss," said yet another pleasant-looking middle-aged stranger, grasping Cass's hand. Cass gave the woman a brave little smile and murmured her thanks, wondering which one of them was more relieved at having gotten through the requisite contact. That done, now whoever-she-was could scarf down the catered hors d'oeuvres with a clear conscience, while Cass could return to obsessing about her ex with anything but.

All she knew was this absurd attraction was inappropriate at best and sheer, stark-raving, just-lock-me-up-now-and-throw-away-the-key idiocy at worst. All she knew was, whatever was going on in her head had to stay there, where no one could see, or know how seriously flawed she was. All she knew was, she was a brand-new widow, almost seven months pregnant with her second husband's child, but she would have spilled state secrets to feel her first husband's arms around her. So damn Blake Carter for reappearing in her life to remind her of what she'd lost, of what she'd missed, of what she would never have again. Not with him, at least. And judging from her abysmal track record thus far, not with anybody else, either.

Speak of the devil. Cass glanced up to catch Blake approaching her, his brows dipped in an undecided expression somewhere between pity and confusion. His nearly black hair was still too long, she noticed, the threads of silver at his temples the only thing making him look any older than when they'd been married. She knotted her hands together at the memory of gliding her fingers through those thick waves when they—

The tiny moan just sort of slipped out. Yet someone else she didn't know gave her a funny look. "The baby kicked," she said with a shaky smile.

The woman smiled back and returned to her conversation while Cass went back to studying the only man who'd ever rocked her world. In rapid, profound and heart-stopping succession.

Okay, she *really* had to stop this.

Mercedes Zamora, one of her business partners, had snagged him with a tray of something or other. Blake politely took one, obviously trying to extricate himself from Mercy's rapid-fire monologue. Thank God for small favors, Cass thought, trying to shift her weight on the sofa. Maybe by the time he made it over here, her heart rate would be back to normal.

Right. Now she noticed the fine webbing at the corners of his eyes, which made him look more distinguished, as did the creases bracketing a mouth she remembered with a clarity vivid enough to make her squirm in her seat. And not because of the baby, either.

Having escaped Mercy's clutches, Blake was back on course toward Cass…and the fantasies vaporized in the heat of those hound-dog eyes, eyes that seemed to plead with her to explain what had happened between them. On the surface, the answer seemed simple enough—that he'd broken one too many promises for her to ever be able to trust him again. But in truth, the answer was anything but simple. God knows, she would have given anything to untangle the myriad reasons why their marriage had sizzled, then fizzled, at least enough to lay them out in order of importance. But the more she tried to sort out the jumble of disappointment and heartache left in the wake of their divorce, the less she understood. Two things, however, she was absolutely sure of: She could never forgive him for virtually abandoning their child, and she could never forgive herself for still, after all this time, wanting him so much.

Even now, as he lowered himself onto the sofa beside her—since, after loudly announcing she had to pee like a race-horse, Lucille had abandoned her—where she sat staring at a plate full of food she couldn't get past her throat if she tried, she *still* yearned to feel his touch, to hear his soothing voice when he'd kid her out of a bad mood or comfort her when she was legitimately upset. For so long, he'd been her best—and often, her only—friend. That their marriage had destroyed their friendship hurt almost more than anything else.

"How're you holding up?" she heard at her elbow.

She shrugged, shook her head. Refused to look at him, to react to that soft, Oklahoma-tinged voice that had always turned her insides to warmed honey.

There had to be a logical reason for this. Hormones. Exhaustion. Misdirected grief.

Insanity.

Yes, let's go with that, shall we?

Blake seemed to hesitate, then cautiously took her hand in his, sending trickles of warmth to places she'd just as soon forget existed. Yep, she was seriously messed up, all right. As if to compensate, a shiver slalomed down her spine.

"You're freezing," he said, his brows taking a dive. "Here…" He pulled an ivory wool throw off the back of the sofa, tried to spread it over her lap. But she pushed it away, as if accepting his ministrations somehow indicted her.

"It's just my hands," she insisted. "I'm not cold. Really."

"But you have been under a helluva lot of stress, ho—" She watched as he swallowed back the endearment. "Maybe you should go lie down."

"I will. Soon," she promised before he launched into his Poppa Hen routine, before she remembered far more than she wanted to. Before she forgot the one thing she most needed *to* remember. Finally she met his gaze, only to immediately wish she hadn't. "I'll rest in a bit. I just don't want to be alone right now."

His expression was unreadable. "I understand."

But he didn't, of course, since she barely understood herself. She didn't want to be alone, to think about her situation, to worry about how she was going to get through this mess, to wonder why Blake's presence was so thoroughly discombobulating her, especially after all this time. Especially today.

She hadn't noticed when he'd risen. He now stood in front of her, his hands slouched in his pockets as usual, although the navy jacket and tie were anything but. However, unlike her son, who looked about as natural in his get-up as he might have wearing chicken feathers, Blake seemed right at home. But then, she supposed these days he wore suits, even formalwear, pretty regularly. After all, Blake Carter was a millionaire now, an entrepreneur who'd beaten the odds and rocketed to the top of his industry. Idly, Cass wondered if money and success had changed him.

"Well," he said, "I guess I'll get back to the hotel—"

"Like hell you will," Lucille squawked right behind Cass, making her jolt. The woman had a habit of popping up, prairie-dog fashion, at remarkably inconvenient moments. She sidestepped the arm of the sofa to snag Blake's forearm in red talons. "With six bedrooms, you should stay at some hotel?" She vigorously shook her head, the rhinestone earrings flashing like a blitz of paparazzi flashbulbs. "Forget it."

"Cille, really, I don't think that's such a good idea—" Cass put in, but Lucille had pressed her crimson lips together in her you-can-talk-but-I-won't-hear expression.

"The man should be with his son. And the son should be with his mother. So maybe this isn't the most ideal situation in the world, but since when does life play along? Besides, sweetheart…" She nailed Cass with her green gaze. "I know you wouldn't push my buttons at a time like this." Tarantula lashes swallowed up her eyes as she squinted. "Would you?"

"I believe this is called emotional blackmail, Cille."

"Whatever works. Besides, Blake would be happy to stay." The tarantulas veered in his direction. "Right?"

After a moment—a very long moment—Blake replied, "If you're sure it's no trouble."

"Listen to him. Like it would be trouble to put up my stepgrandson's father. Besides, have you looked in the kitchen recently? There's enough food to feed Yonkers in there. All these people on these weird diets…nobody eats real food anymore. Towanda's been kvetching for the last half hour about how the hell is she going to stuff it all in the Fridgedaire. We won't have to cook for a week."

"This has got to be a bad dream," Cass muttered, but Lucille pretended not to hear her.

"This is no time for Cassie and me to be sitting around, depressing each other. So, for a few days, you'll stay. Be a father to your son. Regale us with stories about the ice cream business. Keep our spirits out of the toilet."

Apparently convinced the matter was settled, Lucille left to see out the last of the guests, except for one set of distant cousins, who seemed to have bonded with the buffet. And Mercy was still here, too, having a set-to with Towanda, if the raised voices coming from the kitchen were any indication. Suddenly, the argument stopped—which led Cass to wonder whether the two women had come to terms or killed each other—leaving the house ominously quiet.

Blake hesitated before asking, "Is this okay with you?"

"Oh, right. As if I have any say in the matter."

His mouth tilted. "I'm not afraid of an old lady."

"Yeah, well, I am. And if you had any sense, you would be, too."

"Nope, sorry. Although Towanda's another story entirely."

Cass glanced away before she was tempted to smile. "In any case, please don't feel obligated to stay if you don't want to."

"Actually…I wouldn't mind hanging out more with Shaun. While I'm here."

"I'm…sure he'd like that."

They could have hung laundry on the tension strung between them.

"Well, then," he said, jangling his car keys, "I suppose I'll go back to the hotel, get my things. If that's okay."

Propping her elbow on the arm of the sofa, Cass let her head drop into her palm, her eyes drifting closed. "Blake, please. Don't make me think. Or make decisions. Or even react. Just do whatever you need to do, okay?"

"Only if you're sure…"

Now her eyes popped open. *"Blake!"*

The ambivalence in the gentle brown eyes that met hers tied her insides into a million little knots. And she knew, at that moment, that he hadn't changed. Not really. Not enough to matter, at least.

Why, God? Why are you doing this to me?

She straightened, folding her hands primly in what was left of her lap. "I'm going to be miserable, no matter what you do. So if it makes Lucille a little happier right now…" Her breath gripped her throat, and she realized how perilously close she was to falling apart. "And I'm sure Shaun really would appreciate your being here," she got out. "He's got some activities planned I'm not going to be up for. If you could stick around and take him, I'd be very grateful."

At that, she saw some of the tension ease from her former husband's shoulders. "I'd be happy to help," he said with that smile that used to…

Never mind what that smile used to do. She couldn't let it

do it now. Or ever again. And that's all she needed to remember, she thought as she watched Blake leave the room, recalling how she used to cuddle up to those broad shoulders on chilly mornings....

N'uh, uh-uh...

All she needed to remember was that remembering was not an option.

Chapter Two

Blake found Shaun doing a bad impression of a skateboarder in the cul-de-sac in front of the house. The kid had changed into a pair of droopy jeans with shredded hems, topped by three layers of shirts in varying degrees of grunge. For a split second, Blake considered whether he even wanted to be seen with the kid.

"I'm going back to the hotel to get my stuff," he called over. "Wanna come?"

The skateboard went flying in one direction, Shaun in another, as he came to a halt. Panting, he took off his hat—its original color anybody's guess—shook out his now-unconfined hair, then pushed the hat back on his head. Backward. "You staying here?" he asked as he snatched the skateboard up off the pavement, then ambled toward Blake, board dangling from his knuckles.

"Appears so." Blake waited until the boy reached him before continuing. "Lucille's idea."

Shaun nodded, a half grin tugging at his lips as he hissed out a breath. "What'd Mom say?"

"Not much," Blake said cautiously. "Although she did mention that you had some plans for the next few days and maybe I could play shuttle service."

Another nod. "Yeah, that'd be cool. I s'pose." Now he gave Blake's Range Rover the once-over. "Not bad," he pronounced, skimming one hand over the hood. "New?"

"The Bronco gave up the ghost last winter." For some reason, Shaun's nonchalance was making Blake antsy. "So. You want to come with me or not?"

"Yeah. Sure. C'n I put the board in back?"

"Yeah. Sure," Blake echoed, opening the door.

The skateboard duly deposited, they both climbed into the car. Shaun immediately asked if he could turn on the radio; Blake, assuming the kid wasn't thinking along the lines of an easy listening or classical station, not so immediately agreed. Two button clicks later, the glove-leather interior of his car pulsed with mind-numbing, quadrophonically enhanced hiphop. Blake glanced over at his son, who was drumming the dash in time to the…music. He sucked in a deep, deep breath, then let it out very, very slowly.

It was a start.

Cass blew a puff of air through her bangs and considered the plate of food in her hands, still uneaten, still unwanted. Right on cue, reminding her she wasn't the only one who needed to eat, the baby delivered a swift kick to her right kidney. With a sigh, she lifted something unrecognizable to her mouth and began to nibble, only to quickly dispose of it in her napkin. Whoever had put the chicken liver on her plate had an obvious death wish. Liver, in whatever form, from whatever animal, was still something's innards, and Cass did not eat innards. Ever.

Tears sprang to her eyes.

"Hey, honey…you okay?"

Cass immediately reined everything in as Mercy plopped herself down beside her, wiping her sapphire-blue-tipped fingers on a napkin. The nails were a perfect match to the petite woman's fitted suit. Her lips, thankfully, were not.

"Sure," Cass answered. "I'm fine."

"Uh-huh."

"So if you'd already made up your mind how I was, why'd you ask?"

"Because that's what friends do."

"Ask? Or predetermine the answers?"

"Whatever works."

Cass settled farther into the sofa, the plate precariously balanced on top of the mound that contained her unborn child. "Well, consider this. If I *was* okay, they probably really would come take me away."

"Good point," Mercy said. "But with the baby coming and everything? Dana and I are just worried about you, you know?"

Dana Malone, the third partner in their business venture, was—thank God—not in evidence at the moment. "Don't be. Please. You know hovering makes me crazy."

"Tough. If we didn't bug you, you'd probably starve to death." Yards of ebony corkscrew curls, only minimally tamed by a narrow, blue velvet headband, tangled with the collar of her suit as she shook her head. "For someone so savvy about running a business, you're pathetic when it comes to taking care of yourself." Teak eyes settled on Cass's plate. "Why didn't you eat the liver?"

"Because I'd rather cut out my own. So live up to your name, Mercy, and show me some."

"Liver's a good source of iron, which you need for the baby—"

"So bring me a bowl of Total. Get off my case."

Mercy humphed, then scanned the room and the dwindled-to-almost-nothing crowd. "Your ex left?" she asked, making Cass jump.

"Only temporarily," she said, trying to sound blasé. "Lucille got her claws in him and invited him to stay over."

"Stay over? As in, *here?*" One sapphire nail jabbed downward. "In this house?"

The soft leather cushioned Cass's aching neck muscles as she leaned back against the sofa and faced her partner. "Does that mean I'm not the only one who thinks this is a little strange?"

Her brows now dipped, Mercy leaned over and snitched a taquito off Cass's plate. Crossing her legs, she propped her elbow on her knee as she munched, waving the truncated taquito around for emphasis. "I think…I think I don't know what I think. Except… *Dios mio,* he's a hunk and a half. Oh, God—" Five long fingers clamped around Cass's wrist. "That was really stupid."

"Forget it. Besides, you're right."

Up went the brows again.

"Oh, for crying out loud, Merce. Look. If someone lets you borrow something—like, I don't know, a beautiful piece of jewelry or something—it's no less beautiful when you have to give it back, right?"

Mercedes considered that for a moment, then said, "Well, all I have to say is, what you gave back is serious Harry Winston material." She shook her head, then picked a cheesy something or other off Cass's plate and popped it into her mouth. Mercedes Zamora, Cass had decided a long time ago, epitomized the word *spitfire*. Petite, pretty, vivacious, adorable figure, just quirky enough to keep you on your toes. "So what happened? Why'd you two break up?"

And deadly.

"Geez, lady. Anybody ever tell you your timing stinks?"

Mercy pinned her with a look that could intimidate a Mafia goon. "Maybe. But you have this nasty habit of holding things in, and that's not good, you know? Very bad for the blood pressure."

Cass closed her eyes, hoping against hope the woman would go away. "I'd rather think of it as keeping my personal life, well…personal."

But going away was clearly not on Mercy's to-do list. From two feet away, Cass could hear her chewing. "The guy's history, right?"

The mantel clock chimed during the several seconds that passed before Cass replied, her eyes still closed. "Ancient, even."

"So?"

"So…" So she would toss her friend a scrap and maybe *then* she'd go away. "We got married too early. We couldn't handle it. End of story." The baby squirmed again; Cass absently rubbed the little elbow or knee or whatever it was. And through the anger and the confusion and all the dreck that threatened to turn her into a raving nutso, floated the love she felt for the little guy who knew nothing of any of this.

"And…you're not going to say anything more."

Tired as she was, Cass opened her eyes, looked her friend straight in hers and lied. "There's nothing else to say. Really." She shrugged. "Just one of those things."

Mercy rolled her eyes and stuffed another taquito into her cute little mouth.

* * *

Blake's head was still softly buzzing, like overhead power lines, from his far-too-close encounter with current pop culture. More than his humming head, however, he'd regretted that the noise had precluded conversation. Now, as he tossed his overnight bag into the car before returning to the house, he decided to get the conversation going before his son made any musical requests.

"So…how's school?"

The sardonic smile seemed far too old on a fifteen-year-old's face. "Dude—" he buckled up, adjusted his shoulder strap "—you sound like every lame father in every lame movie, you know, when the father is, like, trying to 'relate' to his estranged kid."

Blake tried not to tense. Or get defensive. Or ask if Shaun wanted the music back on. "I see. Well, unfortunately I really am interested in how you're doing in school. Lame though that may be."

"'S'okay," the kid allowed, and Blake felt a muscle or two relax. "I made Honor Roll last nine weeks." He leaned forward, index finger poised to send Blake over the edge. Blake caught his wrist.

"Forget it. My brain cells are still staggering around in my head, thudding into each other. They need some time to recuperate, okay?"

Shaun was giving him that odd, pitying look again. Then he scrunched down in his seat, his arms folded over his chest. "Yeah. Whatever."

They pulled out onto I-40, headed back toward Albuquerque's Far Heights. "Good for you. About the Honor Roll, I mean."

"Yeah, but like, Mom is still on me about *everything*." The words tumbled out in a rush. "Where am I going? Who am I going to be with? Crap like that."

The reprimand fell out of Blake's mouth before he could catch it. "Watch your mouth, Shaun."

"God." The word came out on a groan. "Not you, too."

"Yep. Me, too." Blake checked his side mirror before pulling into the left lane to pass a truck. "A regular tyrant. In any case, your mother has every right to know where you are and what you're doing. In case you missed it, you're not legal yet. She's responsible for you. If you screw up, she gets blamed."

Shaun shifted in his seat, his brow beetled. "Why does everyone assume I'm going to screw up?"

Remembering what it was like to be his age should have helped. Instead, thinking about the Dark Ages of his youth only made Blake feel old and tired and woefully inept. For a split second he envied his partner, Troy, and his three-year-old twins. Three-year-olds, even those three-year-olds, he could deal with. A Happy Meal and the zoo and you were good to go. Teenagers…?

His heartfelt sigh earned him yet another of Shaun's looks. "No one does," he said quietly. Hopefully. "But kids do mess up, you know. And she—and I—just want you to be careful."

"Geez, man…" The lanky arms twisted more tightly across his chest. But there were no further comments. Blake wasn't sure if this was a good sign or not.

"So…" Fool that he was, Blake refused to let the silence gain a foothold. "Next lame question…" That got a sideways glance and a cocked eyebrow. "Any girls in your life?"

"You mean, like a girlfriend?" Shaun gave a sharp, short laugh. "Uh, no. Chicks are *way* too expensive. Besides, with no wheels, it's like, pointless. I mean, whuttami s'posed to do? Ask Mom to drive me on a date?"

He decided not to go anywhere near the "wheels" topic. "Whoa. *Chicks?*"

Bam! Up went the wall again. "Hey. Lighten up. It's not like they care or anything."

"Well, I care. And your mother would probably boot you clear into next week if she heard you say that. Let me fill you in, if you expect to get anywhere with the female sex, ever. '*Girls*' is okay until they reach about seventeen. After that, they're '*women.*'"

Silence. Then, "You going to criticize everything I say?"

Damn.

"That wasn't my intention, Shaun. Look, I didn't come down here to argue with you—"

"Why did you come down, anyway?"

Puzzled, Blake flicked his son a glance. "Because I thought you wanted me to."

"Oh, right. Like that made any difference before."

Careful...

"Meaning?"

"Meaning..." The kid hit the automatic window button, lowering the tinted glass. Raised it again. Lowered it. Slouched even farther down in his seat. "Meaning how many times did I ask you to come down this past year, and you were too busy? Now, suddenly, Alan's dead, and look who's here." The boy punched his knee with his fist. "Oh, hell, man...this really, really sucks."

His own stomach churning, Blake spoke without thinking. "Shaun. Language."

"Oh, come *on,* man. This is way kids talk nowadays. Get with the program, geez."

"I'm not naive, Shaun," Blake snapped, angry that they were skirting the issue. Angrier because he wasn't sure what the issue was. "This is the way kids have always talked.

Around each other. Not around their parents." He leveled his gaze at his son. "Got it?"

A sullen glare was his only response.

Several seconds passed before Blake spoke. "I apologize. I didn't come all this way to hassle you about your language. But I guess…I'm not very good at this."

He caught Shaun's frown. "Good at what?"

One hand on the steering wheel, Blake gestured ineffectually with the other. "Knowing what to say when someone dies. To make them feel better." At the boy's blank stare, Blake pushed on, "About Alan's death. I imagine you're upset about it—"

Shaun's harsh laugh startled him. "Why would I be upset about that? I mean, yeah, it was a shock and all, but upset?" He shook his head.

Now it was Blake's turn to look blank.

The kid blew a disdainful "pffh" of air between his lips. "The man didn't care Jack about me. Oh, he made noises at first like he was going to, I don't know, fill some gap in my life or something…" Shaun propped one foot up on the dashboard, banging his fist against his knee. "Give me a break."

Blake didn't know what to say to that, although a vague anger suffused his thought. "I had no idea. I'm sorry."

Shaun rubbed his hand over his thigh, then picked at a loose thread from a hole in the denim. "It had nothing to do with you. No big deal."

"But it does have something to do with *you,* which makes it a very big deal."

The boy's sad shrug made him feel like slime. But his confession sparked more than a few other questions in his brain, all of which centered on Cass's relationship with her second husband, none of which were any of Blake's business.

He told himself.

"I really am sorry I wasn't able to come down before," Blake said quietly, needing to justify himself somehow while still skirting the truth. "But it wasn't as if we didn't see each other. Besides, I thought you enjoyed coming up to Denver. Getting way from the house." He glanced over. "Going to Broncos games."

The boy went through his hat-off, shove-fingers-through-hair, hat-back-on routine. "Yeah, I guess. It was okay." *Since that's what you want to hear, Dad,* his expression said, *that's what I'll give you.*

"But it wasn't what you wanted."

That merited a grunt.

"I told you," Blake persisted, "I was busy. Getting away this past year wasn't easy. The business—"

"You *own* it, for crying out loud. You can do anything you want."

"It doesn't work that way, buddy." At Shaun's not-buying-it glare, Blake added, "Just because I don't punch a time clock doesn't mean I have more free time. If anything, I have less. And this year was a killer in terms of expansion—"

"Dad, please. You make *ice cream.*"

Blake's hand squeezed the steering wheel, hard. Anger hissed through his veins, at Shaun for his insolence, at himself for creating the situation that created the insolence to begin with. "Yeah. I make ice cream. By myself, in my kitchen, one gallon at a time."

Again, no response.

"Maybe this doesn't seem like a big deal to you, but in ten years Troy and I have set up three processing plants around the country and sold more than a 150 franchises in thirty-seven states. That didn't happen by working nine-to-five."

He could feel duplicates of his own deep-brown eyes scrutinizing the side of his face. "And was it worth it?"

"What do you mean?"

"I mean, you're rich, right?"

Wondering where this was heading, Blake carefully replied, "Let's just say it's been a long time since I've worried about meeting the monthly bills."

"And, like, what has all that gotten you, exactly?"

Ah. They'd pulled into the wide driveway fronting the three-car garage at the side of Cass's house. Blake cut the engine, then leaned back, one hand on the steering wheel. Typically for this time of year, the wind had picked up, hazing the air with dust and pollen. But the clog in his throat, he guessed, had little to do with the sudden jump in the pollen count. "I've been able to provide jobs for a lot of people, Shaun. You won't have to worry about college—"

"Dammit, Dad! Can't you give a *single* straight answer?"

His heart pounding, Blake met his son's angry gaze. "Give me a straight question, and I'll see what I can do."

"Fine," Shaun retorted. "Are you happy?"

Blake squinted out the windshield, jabbing a hand through his hair in a gesture that echoed his son's. "No. Not really."

"So what's the freakin' point?" Shaun said with such vehemence Blake whipped his head back around. "What is it with grown-ups and their fixation with success? So you've, like, buried yourself in this business. And now you've got all this money, right? But, what else do you have?"

An early season lizard darted up the adobe wall as Blake stared out the windshield, trying to figure out what to say. "Are you talking about us, Shaun?" He turned to face his son. The lowermost earring in Shaun's lobe glinted dully. "About my not being here for you?"

"Man, you just don't get it, do you? Dude—I'm not talking about you and me! I'm talking about—"

"Oh! Oh! Come quick!"

They both looked up to see Lucille frantically waving from the second-story deck, the fringed ends of a gold-and-purple scarf she'd tied around her head plastering to her face in the wind. "It's Cassie!" she yelled, clawing at the scarf. "She fell, now she's having contractions, and she won't let me call anyone—"

Blake was out of the car like a shot, aware of Shaun's car door slamming a split second behind his as he bounded across the driveway and up the stairs into the house.

Her mouth set in a grimace, Cass adjusted the pillows behind her back, then leaned up against the black lacquer headboard. "They're just Braxton-Hicks. They'll pass."

No sooner were the words out of her mouth than Blake saw her lips thin even more in an attempt to mask the contraction. He instantly leaned over, placing his hand on her abdomen. Obeying an instinct for which he'd long since had no need, he sneaked a glance at his watch, breathing out a small sigh of relief when he felt her muscles relax after barely twenty seconds. He caught her glower, the bright-blue eyes faded to almost the same gray as her sweater and maternity pants. In that outfit, she was practically invisible against the muted-plaid bedspread covering the enormous bed. She swatted at his hand, which he posthaste removed.

"If I'd needed my midwife, I'd've called her."

"I doubt it."

She shot him a look, then levered herself higher up, lacing her hands together over her middle. "I'm not having this baby, Blake. Not today, at any rate."

He gave her thigh a friendly pat. "That's my girl. As much of a pain as ever."

Her eyes flitted briefly to his, then away. But he saw the

smile twitching her lips. "A gal's gotta maintain her reputation, after all."

Blake sat on the edge of the bed, carefully palming the knot her hands made over her tummy. "What happened?"

He could see her struggle to remain aloof as she contemplated their layered hands. "I can't see underneath me," she said softly, like a child trying to downplay an errant deed. "I was on my way into the living room and misjudged where the step was, that's all. And my sandal twisted out from under me." One shoulder hitched. "So Mommy went boom."

"And then the contractions started—"

That got a sigh of pure exasperation. "I told you. They're not contractions. Not real ones, anyway. I've been having these for the last month." A fierceness out of all proportion to the situation blazed in her eyes. "They do seem to come on when I'm particularly stressed. And I think the last few days would qualify, wouldn't you?"

He gently squeezed her hand, then removed it, tamping down the irrational, absurd surge of jealousy. He'd left her, for God's sake—what did he expect? That she'd stay alone for the rest of her life?

"Yes," he finally said. "I imagine they would."

"You okay, Mom?"

They both looked over at Shaun, who'd come a few feet into the room, wearing that hopeful, frightened look of a kid desperately seeking reassurance.

"Yes, honey, I'm fine," Cass replied with a tired smile. "Lucille just went a little nuts, that's all."

"A pregnant woman lands flat on her tuchus four feet in front of me, I'm going to go nuts," came from the doorway. "It's an old lady's prerogative." Lucille stomped into the bedroom—or she would have stomped if she'd weighed more than a feather and the room hadn't been so thickly carpeted—

sweeping the scarf's tails over her shoulders with a gesture worthy of Greta Garbo.

"Well?" she directed at Blake, though her eyes remained pinned on her quarry. "Did you talk some sense into her?"

Reluctantly, Blake stood. "I…" He caught Cass's warning glare. "Actually, I think she's probably fine. The contractions seem mild and short and she's not in any pain." He frowned at her. "Are you?"

She shook her head. Blake lowered his voice, although he decided against wagging his finger at her. Since he wasn't really keen on the idea of having it bitten off.

"But she will stay in bed. *Won't she?*"

On another sigh, she nodded, then said, "Only if everyone will quit obsessing about me."

A brief tremor of familiarity swept through him. At about the same point in Shaun's pregnancy, Cass had slipped off a ladder while hanging curtains in the nursery. She'd started contractions that time, too. And she'd refused to get herself checked, just like now. And Blake had bullied her into staying in bed, just like now.

That time, though, she had accepted his railroading with good humor, love shining in her eyes. Now her acceptance seemed tainted with bitter resignation. She clearly didn't want him here. Yet her very resistance had set off a faint, persistent alarm—illogical though it was—way at the back of his brain that her not wanting him around was exactly why he needed to stay.

"You want something to eat, sweetheart?" he heard Lucille ask, jarring his thoughts. "Some juice, maybe?"

"Nothing, thanks," Cass said with a hint of a smile. She slid down into the pillows, then over onto her side, shoving one pillow underneath her bulging middle. "I think maybe—" she yawned "—I'll just take a little nap…"

Her eyes closed the instant the words were out of her mouth. Blake looked up to catch Shaun looking from one of them to the other, and he instantly surmised what Shaun had been about to say when Lucille's screams had interrupted him. No, he hadn't been talking about Blake's relationship with him. He'd been talking about Blake's relationship with *Cass*.

Oh, God, he thought on an exhaled breath after Shaun and Lucille left the room. Blake wasn't the only one who wanted his family back. Which meant—maybe—he had an ally.

Of course, this also meant that Cass had an adversary—since somehow he suspected she'd rather give birth while riding a galloping camel than get back together with him—but, hey. Sometimes the odds are in your favor, sometimes they're not. Such is life, right?

On his own way out, though, he glanced around the bedroom his wife had shared with another man, at the mottled tan walls and thick taupe Berber carpet and lifeless chrome-and-glass nightstands. He caught himself wondering if the baby Cass carried had been conceived in that bed, then sharply reminded himself he was being juvenile.

Just as he reminded himself that she didn't owe him a damn thing. And certainly not a shot at something he'd forfeited so long ago.

His gaze once again swept the room. For all its lack of charm or warmth, nothing in here had come cheap. A study in minimalist extravagance. And again, very un-Cass, who adored chintz and frills and lace. And cats. The woman was crazy for cats, he remembered suddenly. When they'd been married, they'd had four, not counting the outside strays Cass would "secretly" feed.

He looked back at her, then crossed over to the beige tweed chaise in the corner of the room, pulling a gray mohair throw off of it. That's what was wrong, he decided, gently covering the obviously unhappy woman who still held his heart in her hands. There were no cats in this house. No goofball kittens, no swaggering toms, no prissy longhairs to climb up in your lap and leave a veritable fur rug in their wake. He skimmed one knuckle over the soft pile, shaking his head.

No wonder she was so miserable.

Finally.

Once she was positive Blake was gone, Cass opened her eyes, tucking one hand underneath her cheek, only to choke with the effort not to cry when she smelled his scent on her hand.

This wasn't going to work, his being here. She wished he'd go away, leave her alone to sort out what was left of her life in peace. Okay, sure, when push came to shove, he'd made a rotten husband and father. And yet, she mused as she hitched the throw higher on her shoulders, she'd never known a kinder human being. When he was around, anyway. And she didn't need, or want, kindness. Kindness was dangerous, made you believe in things that shouldn't be believed in.

And pity was even worse. And that's what it would become, wouldn't it? When he found out? She didn't think she could stand that. So what was this nearly overwhelming, idiotic urge to beg him to stay and make it all better?

Well. Apparently, she hadn't changed any more than Blake. At least, not as much as she'd wanted to believe. Not on the inside, at least. But then, perhaps growing up wasn't as much about conquering your weaknesses as it was about seeing them for what they were. And then never, ever letting them get the upper hand.

She was exhausted was all, she told herself. And the contractions had given her more pause than she'd let on. Still, her sadness had gone beyond weeping, to a sort of not-quite numbness a millimeter short of despair. She'd like to think it was nothing more than hormone-induced moodiness, exacerbated by recent events, but she'd given up lying to herself for Lent. And for however many days on earth she had left after that.

In all this, the baby was the only thing that seemed to make any sense. Not that Cass loved this child more than Shaun—as if that would have been possible—but by virtue of Shaun's being first, she spent so much time worrying about him and fussing at him that sometimes love got lost in the shuffle. She'd made lots of mistakes with Shaun, more than she liked to admit. So maybe she was being a Pollyanna, but somehow she hoped this child would give her an opportunity to make things, if not right, at least better. Even if, once again, she was doing this all on her own.

Such was obviously her lot in life, one with which she should have long since made peace. Because being on her own was good for her, made her stronger. Lord, she thought on a tight smile. The life-as-spinach philosophy. Hey—she could write a book, go on Oprah.

She lay there, feeling the little one squirming inside her, watching the pine tree outside her window shudder noiselessly in the wind—the triple-glazed windows allowed no sound. After a year, she still hadn't adjusted to the airless silence. But Alan couldn't stand outside noises. Or dust.

Weenie, she thought irritably, clutching the pillow. How would he have dealt with the noise and mess and dirt of a child?

Well. Moot point now, wasn't it? Fifty years old, no spare tire, no predilection for junk food, no history of heart disease, and the man drops dead while jogging. Major coronary, gone within minutes, the paramedics assured her. He didn't suffer, they said.

No. He wouldn't.

Her eyes squeezed shut again as she realized she couldn't

move. Didn't want to. Her brain felt cluttered—so many decisions to make so quickly, none of them easy. But there was one thing, if nothing else, Cass knew—fish would play strip poker before she'd ever marry again. Not for her sake, not for the child's sake, not for anyone's sake. Two unmitigated disasters were quite enough for one lifetime, thank you. Especially as she'd be paying, literally, for the second mistake for the rest of her life. So from now on, she was relying on nobody but herself. God knows, she wasn't perfect, but at least she wouldn't give herself a broken heart She didn't think, anyway.

A tear dribbled down her cheek, tickling her nose; she irritably swiped at it, despising herself for feeling like a whiny toddler who couldn't have a cookie before dinner. But after all, she reminded herself, cookies weren't good for you.

Spinach, however, was.

She should write that down.

Chapter Three

Since Shaun missed his bus the next morning, Blake drove him to school. To his combined relief and annoyance, the boy wasn't in a talkative mood, yet Blake still felt as though someone had played basketball with his brain by the time he returned to the house to find Lucille on the second-story deck, madly planting pansies in assorted pots and tubs. Still, the sight—the *idea*—of someone planting flowers was reassuring somehow. And at this point, he'd take whatever tidbits of reassurance he could get.

"Got enough flowers, here?" he asked the industrious little figure whizzing about like a dazed parakeet.

"I bought them before—" She cut herself off, shaking her head, then shoved her sunglasses back up onto the bridge of her nose. "If I don't get them into the dirt, they'll all die."

His eyes narrowed, Blake scanned the horizon, waiting for

the awkward moment to dissipate on its own, like an unpleasant aroma. "Cass still asleep?" he asked after a moment.

"Far as I know." Speaking of unpleasant aromas, enough perfume for an entire chorus line wafted over to him on the stiff breeze. Blake casually moved upwind of her, squinting from the glare bouncing off the rhinestone trim of her electric-blue sweatshirt. She lifted her head, peering at him from the south side of a floppy-brimmed straw hat with chiffon ties securely anchored beneath a wattled chin. "You get Shaun to school okay?"

"We just made it," he said to mirror-coated sunglasses. "If I'd known he was supposed to catch a bus, I would have hustled him out a lot sooner."

Crimson lips spread out into an amazingly wide smile. "Wouldn't have done you a bit of good, cutie. Kid misses the bus every single day. And every single day Cass chews him out for it." The hat quivered as she nodded toward a white wrought-iron patio chair with a plastic floral cushion lashed to it. "So sit. Enjoy your coffee while I putz."

So he sat, occasionally offering a comment in response to one from Lucille as he nursed a cup of Towanda's miraculous coffee, staring toward the west at white-capped Mt. Taylor glittering against an endless sky. As warm as it had been yesterday, the temperature had dropped again overnight; he flipped up the collar of his denim jacket against the breeze. At least the March sun still listed southward enough to splash a few welcome rays across the western-facing deck, taking the chill off the air. Still, it was a magnificent spring morning, at such odds with the understandable tension in the house.

Suddenly aware he was being eyed, he smiled. Her brow knotted, Lucille didn't return it. Tension coiled at the base of Blake's neck, as if he sensed what was coming.

"I shouldn't have insisted you stay here," she said, returning to her task. Silver gecko earrings swung in dizzying circles as she poked and prodded in the soil, a three-inch-wide silver-and-turquoise cuff smothering a wrist that looked far too frail to support it.

His fingers tightened around the mug's handle. "What makes you say that?"

"Because you still have feelings for Cassie."

Blake allowed the breeze to carry away a brittle chuckle. "You don't mince words, do you?"

"At my age, what's the point? So, am I wrong?"

He tapped a finger against the edge of the mug. "No," he admitted quietly.

"And does Cassie know?"

"What do you think?"

The old woman sighed, her expression unreadable behind the huge sunglasses. Then she heaved herself to her feet, clumping in red plastic gardening clogs over to the tempered-glass patio table where she'd left the rest of the flowers.

"So tell me something…Cassie and Shaun have been living here for more than a year. How come this is the first time I've seen you?"

The swallow of coffee in his mouth turned acrid. "It seemed the more prudent course of action, considering Cass was married to another man and all."

"Yeah, but your *son* wasn't." Before he could figure out what, if anything, to say to that, she said, "Which would lead to one of two conclusions. A, that you're a slimeball. Or B, that you didn't want to risk seeing her. So which is it?"

"You forgot C. All of the above."

She batted at the air. "Nah. Believe me, I know from slimeballs. You don't even come close. So I'm going with B. Okay, next subject—I suppose you're wondering why I don't seem more broken up over my son's death."

Blake doubted he had enough caffeine in his system to keep up with the woman, but as she didn't appear interested in slowing down, the best he could do was hobble along behind. "I hadn't… It isn't my place to…"

But she wasn't listening. Now kneeling on a bright yellow foam pad, she gouged the soil with probably more vehemence than necessary. "You bring a baby into the world," she muttered to the dirt, "you think nothing can go wrong…"

She jerked her head up to Blake, several strata of makeup insufficient to mask the mixture of bafflement, anger and profound sorrow etched in what had once been, he decided, a beautiful face. "Why am I telling you this? A stranger? Except, maybe, who else can I tell?" she went on without waiting for a reply. "To keep all this locked inside…" She pressed one fist to her sternum, wagging her head. "Maybe this is why you're here, so an old lady can vent her spleen."

Blake leaned forward, gently removing the sunglasses to see turquoise-lidded green eyes shimmering with tears. "Vent away."

She removed a tissue from a pocket tucked into the sweatshirt, then dabbed with extreme care at her eyes. "You sure?"

"I'm sure."

Lucille let out a great sigh, then said, more to the pansies than to Blake, "Before Cassie, Alan had never married. Dated, yes, but never married. When he hadn't settled down by thirty-five, his father and I, we figured maybe he was…well, you know."

She lowered her voice, as if the neighbors might hear. "It was a disappointment, but what could we say? A person's gotta follow his own path, right? Anyway, after Alan's father died—we'd been out here ten years already, we couldn't take those awful winters back east anymore—Alan asks me if I'd like to move in with him, so I wouldn't be alone. So I figure, why not? I mean, Wanda came in to do for me, sure—I've got a bunch of medical problems, you don't want to know, Wanda's a practical nurse but she doesn't like telling people 'cause then they all start asking her for medical advice—but being by myself at night didn't sit so well, it was true.

"But then, once I move in? He barely talks to me. Acts like I'm invisible or something. Always too busy, always away on some trip or something, especially once he sold his dry cleaning business, four, five years ago. So I ask you, what was the point of my being here, since I was alone at night, anyway? Or worse, when he was around…" Her lips pursed. "He'd get this look in his eyes, like I was some kind of huge embarrassment to him, like he couldn't figure out how I was his mother. Nothing but criticisms, every time he saw me. I didn't talk right, dress right, think right. All I was, was some stupid old woman.…"

Her sentence left hanging in midair, she dug in her sleeve for a tissue, then blew her nose, while Blake felt as though someone had stepped on his chest. "And it finally dawns on me," she continued, "this is why my meshugah son never married. Never in my life did I see a man more wrapped up in himself! So I figure, the hell with this—I'm outta here, as the young people say."

Blake couldn't hold back a smile. "And?" he prodded.

"So I make up my mind to move out into one of those whaddyacallits, those gated communities—except it's criminal how much they want for rent in those places, so I wasn't going anywhere—when suddenly Alan brings home this lovely young woman and announces they're getting married. Out of the blue, just like that, with him pushing fifty, already. Me, I'm thrilled, thinking maybe my son's finally got his head on straight, that this woman's performed some kind of miracle. So now, maybe, things will be better." She hunched her shoulders in a helpless gesture. "I should have known, right?"

A frown pinched Blake's brow, waiting for her explanation. To his chagrin, however, she veered off on one of her tangents, leaving her thought in the dust.

"That Cassie is a keeper, let me tell you," she said instead. "Always treated me like gold. And at my age, listen—a daughter-in-law I could get along with…what more could I ask? Oh, sure, it would have been nice if she'd been Jewish, but you can't have everything, right? But you know something, I love that girl from the bottom of my heart, like she was my own." She went back to stabbing the dirt. "If anybody deserves good things, it's her."

A draft of cold air wriggled up Blake's jacket, making him shiver.

"Lucille," he said, "I don't mean to push, but…what do you mean, you should have known? About Alan?"

It took her a second to find the dropped thread, but then she said, "Oh. That it couldn't last. That Alan could no more be a real husband than I could fly to the moon."

"You mean, he *was*—?"

"No, no. Not that. I told you. Alan only loved himself." Her lips drew into a tight line, like a vivid, fresh scratch across her face. "But he did want a child. And Cassie, for reasons known only to her, God bless her, agreed."

Several moments passed before the pieces fell into place. "Are you saying…this was a marriage of convenience?"

"On my son's side, at least," Lucille said, rearranging a pansy she'd just planted. "I frankly don't know…well, Cassie and I never discussed things, exactly…" She hesitated, while Blake's heart played racquetball inside his chest.

"What?"

Lucille got to her feet again, then clomped closer, perching on the arm of the chair across from his, near enough to lay her hand on his wrist. "Cassie doesn't know that I know this, so don't say anything, but, see, I had figured out a couple months ago that things weren't exactly hunky-dory between them. So I wasn't all that surprised when Cassie seemed more stunned than grief stricken when Alan died. But then, the day after he dies, after the lawyer leaves the house…" One eye squinted shut as she wagged a gardening-gloved finger. "*Then* she's upset. Like someone had yanked the rug out from under her. So I call the lawyer myself, only he starts giving me this song and dance about how there's nothing to worry about. As if I wouldn't know telling me there's nothing to worry about is always the first clue that there is. So I told him to cut the bull, already, and tell me what the hell was going on." She shrugged. "So he did."

Maddeningly, she chose that moment to have a sneezing fit that ate up the better part of two minutes. Finally, after another minute of indelicate nose blowing, amid profuse apologies about it being pollen season, she turned to Blake. "To cut a long story short, my son decides, a month after his marriage, to liquidate almost his entire estate and invest in some little up-and-coming computer technology company that, unfortunately, up and went." She sneezed again, then sighed. "On top of that, there were credit cards. Had he lived, maybe he would've landed on his feet. But he didn't. Which means his estate is worth, as that little Mercedes would say, *nada*—"

"*Lucille!*"

They both spun around—Blake snagging Lucille's spindly arm before she fell off the arm of the chair—to catch Cass standing at the French door, her face ashen but her eyes sparking with embarrassed fury. Every instinct he possessed told him to get his butt out of there and let the two women duke it out. But one look from Cass told him if he so much as moved an eyelash, she'd knock him clear to the Arizona border.

* * *

Her cheeks stung with humiliation. This was her problem. *Hers.* The only thing in this whole stinkin' mess she'd been able to control had been who knew and who didn't. Now, thanks to her mother-in-law, she didn't even have that.

"Cille, how *could* you?" Huddled into herself against the morning chill, Cass crossed to the older woman, refusing to look at Blake, to see the pity in his eyes. The baby was kicking her mercilessly this morning, so hard she felt bruised in spots. "How could you go behind my back, discussing family business—" She pressed her hand to her mouth, then lowered it enough to push out, "This was *personal,* for God's sake. Is that so hard to understand?"

"And if Blake isn't family, I'd like to know who is." Never easily buffaloed, Lucille wagged the trowel at her. "He's Shaun's father. Anything that affects Shaun will ultimately affect him. So I thought he should know. And God knows we'd all be taking vacations to Mars before *you* got around to it."

The lack of even a hint of remorse in her mother-in-law's eyes made Cass's voice—and undoubtedly, her blood pressure as well—rise several notches. "Well, I'm Shaun's *mother,* and what and who I tell is my decision. Not yours."

"*Bubelah,* calm down. It's not good for the baby…"

"She's right, Cass. You're getting yourself in a state—"

"*You* stay out of this!" She hurled this in Blake's direction quickly, so she didn't really see him, then back at her mother-in-law. "Oh, for pity's sake, Cille. I'm pregnant, my husband just died, and, as most of Bernalillo County probably knows by now, I am, as they say, financially embarrassed. A little hissy fit isn't going to raise my blood pressure any more than it already is." She looked around, saw the flowers. For some reason, that nearly took her over the edge. "And why are you planting flowers? It's still freezing at night."

"They're just pansies, Cass," Blake said in that even, reasonable tone of voice used on people who live in padded rooms. "They can live through cold weather, remember? We used to plant them in March all the time. So they'll be fine. Which is more than I can say for you."

"I *am* fine, Blake," she retorted, wrapping her sweater more tightly around her protruding midsection. Her teeth were chattering, the baby was kicking, and right now life was about as far from good as she ever wanted it to get. "B-back off."

"No, Cass. I'm not going to back off." Stunned, she met an expression in those deep brown eyes she knew only too well. The this-is-for-your-own-good look. "You just admitted how much stress you're under—"

"That doesn't mean I can't handle it."

"Why are you being so hardheaded, woman?"

Because my very survival depends on it. "Because I didn't ask for your interference, Blake," she said, thinking that only a crazy person would attempt to reason with one being so unreasonable. Except, at the moment she wasn't too sure which one of them was which. "Besides, after all this time, why are you suddenly so hot to stick your nose in my business?"

"Because maybe I can help, for crying out loud!"

"I don't need or want your help! So you can tell that idea to go take a hike!"

Inside, the phone rang. After a moment Towanda stuck her head out the door. "It's for you, Miss Lucille. Your sister in Florida."

With a sigh, Lucille took off her gloves and tossed them onto the tempered glass table, along with the trowel, which landed with an overloud clatter. "Well. The comments I could make about what I just heard.... All I can say is you should be grateful I'm the kind of woman who knows when to keep her thoughts to herself." She started into the house, then hesitated, looking from one to the other. "You think you two could manage not to do each other in while I'm gone?"

After a moment they both nodded. Curtly.

For a full minute after Lucille's departure, neither spoke. Still seething, Cass walked over to the edge of the deck, unsuccessfully ignoring the buzz of energy behind her. She grasped the railing, wincing at the sting of cold metal against her palms as she sucked in several deep breaths, trying to calm down. Trying to think, to ready herself for Blake's attempt to take charge, to play macho man coming to the rescue. It would be just like him to try to exploit her current situation as a means to appease his own guilt for giving up when she'd really needed him. Wanted him.

Well, too damn bad, she thought sourly. A day late and a penny short, as they say.

And dammit, she thought on another tidal wave of emotion, why was it always all or nothing with this man? Why hadn't he ever been able to find that middle ground between suffocating her with his protectiveness or ditching her completely?

Brother. Could she get herself in deep, or what?

The house. She would think about the house. Under other circumstances, she might have loved it, with its sweeping views of the city, the way the rooms seemed to endlessly flow into each other. But it was huge and a pain to keep up, and the idea of a baby toddling around with all these stairs scared the hell out of her. Selling it wouldn't be such a horrible thing. As long as she could unload it before the bank foreclosed on the loan....

Her fingers found their way to the crease between her brows. Almost immediately, she felt Blake's arm slip around her shoulders.

Not good. Especially for someone whose grip on her emotions was as precarious as a car hanging off the edge of a cliff in some action movie, the seagull perched on its end the only thing that kept it from going over. With Blake's touch, the seagull flew away.

And she crashed.

With a soft sob, she turned into the chest that had sheltered her when she was young, that she'd believed would always shelter her. Her bad, most definitely. Still, he smelled the same, felt the same, stroked her back as he always had, his fingertips massaging that spot between her shoulder blades that always tensed up. Like magic, the baby quieted as Blake stroked and soothed and gently rocked her.

It felt too familiar, too right and, consequently, all wrong. She dug into her sweater pocket for a tissue, pulling away to blow her nose.

"Sorry," she mumbled, looking back out toward the city, shoving her hair out of her face. A nagging wind blew it right back.

"For?"

"Acting like a weepy broad."

His arm possessed her shoulders again as he nuzzled the top of her head, his chuckle in her hair as soft and seductive as a summer breeze. "*Broad* seems apt at the moment," he murmured, gently patting her belly.

She couldn't back up quickly enough from the flashfire his touch ignited, spitting out the only words guaranteed to make him retreat. "I loved Alan!"

A long second passed, during which his features seemed to ossify, his normally luminous brown eyes turn the color of dried mud. "I'm sure you did."

Once again she turned away. That Blake was enough of a gentleman not to point out that the man she *loved* had just screwed her to the wall, only made her angrier. And more confused.

"Cass." When she refused to turn toward him, he touched her again, this time gently hooking two fingers underneath her chin. "Cass, look at me." Finally, as if facing a painfully bright light, she glanced up, blinking, and saw the remnants of all the hope and promise of so many years ago, tattered and battered and bruised beyond recognition. Was she seeing what was in his eyes, though, or a reflection of what was in hers?

"Whatever's happening here goes way beyond the wreck we made of our marriage," he said. "I never stopped caring about you. No, it's true," he added at her snort of disbelief. "About what happens to you. Even now, if there's anything I can do—"

"There isn't," she said flatly. Even less than his pity, the last thing she wanted was insincere lip service about how much he cared about her. Please. Maybe he had, at one point, on some level. But instead of facing their problems, working with her to figure out how to solve them, he'd run. That she'd repeated her mistake with Alan…

Not once, but twice, she'd placed her trust in rainbows. She'd really be an idiot to let it happen again.

"I've already got it all figured out," she said. "I'll sell the house, and we'll get a smaller place. Lucille has some income of her own, and I've got the shop." She lifted her chin. "God knows I've had a lot less, Blake. This was a shock, true, but it's not a disaster."

"You are Woman, you are Strong, you can handle it, right?" he said with a slanted smile that, a lifetime ago, had repeatedly hoodwinked her into bed and out of facing reality. For Shaun's sake she'd regretted, even been angry, that Blake hadn't been around more since their divorce; for her own, she'd been immensely grateful he'd stayed away. Because, rather than their strengths complementing each other, their weaknesses had only dragged each other down. Even letting him touch her—especially letting him touch her—was like doing a jig on the edge of a snake pit. Blindfolded.

"Something like that, yes," she agreed, then started back inside, needing to tear herself away from the insane yearning to seek comfort in Blake's embrace. After all, there was more to Woman than being strong enough to field all the crap life flung your way.

"What about the charge cards?" she heard behind her.

Turning back, she managed a smile. "Lucille probably made things sound worse than they are. It's only two or three. I can manage the payments. No problem." His eyes snagged hers, just long enough for her to realize what she had to say. To do.

"Okay, look, you're welcome to hang around, for Shaun's sake. But I really think it's best if we…well, if we stay out of each other's way as much as possible. I've simply got too much garbage swimming around in my head to deal with anything more."

A breeze blew a strand of inky hair across his knotted brow. "I thought we were still friends, Sunshine."

She bit back a curse. He hadn't called her that since the early days of their marriage, when some group or other had resurrected the old song. Blake used to sing it to her—really, really badly—usually while dancing around the apartment with her. He was a really, really bad dancer, too, she recalled, the memory like a bittersweet poison.

"Be real, Blake—our friendship died with our marriage, and you know it."

The frown turned into a full-blown scowl. "My fault?"

"No. No, Blake. Nobody's fault." That much she did believe. "But the only reason you're here is for Shaun. Not for me, remember? There is nothing between us. Not anymore. And there's not going to be. If you really want to help me, you'll remember that and respect my wish to be left alone."

With that she quickly went into the house, before Blake could see how badly she was shaking. It would be so easy to accept whatever he had to offer—his friendship, his help, even his concern. But "easy" came with a price, one she'd already paid too many times. With this last time, she was going to pay enough for a thousand women.

She stopped just inside the door until a contraction passed, then continued into the granite-and-chrome kitchen and poured herself a glass of orange juice. Towanda said something to her, but Cass only vaguely responded, and the woman went on about her business without further hassle.

She eased herself up onto a bar stool and palmed her forehead, her bangs spiked between her fingers. Lucille didn't know the whole truth, thank God. Cass had threatened the lawyer within an inch of his life if he ever let on the extent of Alan's—and now Cass's—debt, let alone the nature of it. There had been no bad investment in some start-up company. True, the insurance had been borrowed against, his portfolio trashed, the equity in the house virtually tapped out. But there were more than three charge cards—each with a maxed-out credit limit greater than some people paid for their cars. *Luxury* cars. The truth was, no matter how hard she worked, she had no idea how she'd ever pay it all off.

Nor was she about to tell an eighty-year-old woman with a dicey heart that her son—her quiet, unassuming, ultraconservative son—had had a wee problem with gambling. That on his business trips, ostensibly to check out potential investments, he went instead to gambling meccas around the country. A string of good luck a few years back had made him far wealthier than his dry cleaning chain ever had, with the unfortunate effect of convincing Alan he was invincible. What Cass hadn't known when they'd started dating was that his luck had begun a downward spiral—until he met her. He'd told her—after they were married, of course—that he liked to "dabble" in the market, and that since they'd started dating, he'd been doing very well. He called her his good luck charm; she hadn't taken it seriously.

He must've thought she was one helluva rabbit's foot.

And she must've been more worn-out than she'd thought to have taken him at face value, to have missed the signs of his sickness. Not to mention his true personality. He'd been a damn good actor, she'd give him that. Still, weren't people who wore masks of their own supposed to be more adept at seeing through others'? In her case, apparently not.

The lies, the empty promises to get help, that came later, however—those, she couldn't have missed if she'd been in a coma. If it hadn't been for Lucille…

Cass kicked back the rest of her juice and slipped off the stool, then perambulated over to the sink where Towanda snatched it out of her hand and washed the glass, before hustling back to the other side of the kitchen. When Cass turned around, her heart somersaulted into her throat.

Blake blocked the kitchen doorway, his forearms bracing the frame. His right foot was thrust forward, the knee bent, accentuating the way his soft, worn jeans clung to thighs as muscled as they were during his college-track-team days. She forced her attention north, past his trim hips and waist, his chest, his shoulders, to a face locked in a determined grimace. The eyes fastened to hers glinted with anger and concern but not, she realized, pity.

She opened her mouth to say— Well, actually, she had no idea what she was going to say. Not that Blake was about to give her the chance.

"Now, you listen to me for a moment, Sunshine," he started in, quietly, unaware of Towanda's presence not ten feet away. "I know we've had our problems. And, God knows, we still do. But I've spent far too long taking out our differences on our son, staying away from him so I wouldn't have to deal with you. I know what you're going to say, so you can save your breath and let me fill in the blanks—yes, I took my sweet time figuring this out. And yes, I know I've screwed up big-time, especially with our son. No sense calling a skunk anything else. But I figure I can either let things go on the way they have been—and risk losing him altogether—or see if Shaun will give me a shot at coming up from behind. And since you're Shaun's mother, my trying to fix things with him and ignore you isn't going to work. Which means you and I are both gonna have to finally grow up, decide exactly where we stand with each other and go from there."

He shifted to cross his arms, still leaning in the doorway. "So this is how it's gonna be. If you still choose to avoid me these next few days, that's up to you. But while I'm here, I'll be damned if I'm going to tiptoe around, pretending I don't exist. Just remember, though, any tension between us is going to affect the boy, and I think he's been through enough without having to deal with our old battles, don't you?"

With that, he pushed away from the door, his boots clomping down the tiled hallway as he retreated. After a moment Cass realized she'd never closed her mouth from when she'd opened it before Blake said his piece. She snapped it shut, trying to figure out what she felt. Ticked off, naturally, was right up there at the top of the list. Right along with affronted and indignant. But…but…there was something else.

Deep down, way past the anger and the confusion and the pain inflicted by a pair of Husbands Past, by the unsettling suspicion that her choices in that regard had been somehow preordained and therefore unavoidable, glimmered a tiny flame of something she thought she'd never feel again: the thrill of having a man care enough to risk making a total idiot of himself.

She dropped like a rock onto the nearest stool.

"You okay, baby?" Towanda asked, amusement tingeing the dark voice.

Cass nodded, then speared the housekeeper with the fiercest look she could manage. Towanda was really intimidated, she could tell.

"One word out of you," she said, "and you're fired."

"Uh-uh," was the woman's only response. But the second Cass left the kitchen, the other woman started to laugh so hard Cass feared she might pull something if she wasn't careful.

Chapter Four

Blake shifted in his seat behind the steering wheel in the parking lot, waiting.

He'd already done the footwork, made a few preliminary choices. And he knew Cass'd probably have five fits. At first. Women tended to do that when you sprang things on them they're weren't expecting. Cass, especially, if memory served. But ever since yesterday morning, when he'd finally put his foot down, Blake couldn't erase the image of her flummoxed expression.

Laughter rumbled in his chest. Oh, before he'd launched into his speech, he really had been PO'd. And he'd meant every word he'd said. But damned if she didn't look like she'd been goosed with an ice-cold cattle prod. And with that, Blake—in his continuing series of epiphanies—realized the only way to win his lady love back was to keep her off balance. Keep her guessing.

Keep her so engrossed in trying to figure out his next move she wouldn't worry too much about all the mess she sure seemed to be in. It was sorely tempting to think that if this Alan person hadn't been already dead, Blake might've been sorely tempted to kill the bastard. What sort of man shoots his whole wad on a single investment, when he's got a family to provide for? And a baby on the way, no less. Didn't make a lick of sense.

The school bell rang. Instantly, a thousand teenagers poured out of doors, down steps, over the sidewalks; the boys barely distinguishable from the girls in their unisex outfits of jeans and hoodies.

Squinting, Blake wondered how he was supposed to find his son in the adolescent swarm. Suddenly one of the swarm seemed to be bearing down on him, loping along in a way that was beginning to become familiar. With a wide grin, Shaun bent over, peering into the driver's-side window. "Sweet. My ride didn't come today. And the bus is, like, the pits."

"So I gathered," Blake mumbled as his son bopped around to the passenger side and got in.

"So why'd you come?"

Blake started the car, shooting a bemused half smile in Shaun's direction. "I have to have a reason?"

"I guess not," the kid acquiesced as Blake pulled out between a late-seventies Tercel packed with an indeterminate number of giggling girls, and an iridescent-red pickup that was basically a boom box on wheels. "Actually," he shouted over the din, "I do have an ulterior motive."

"Figures."

"Oh, I think you'll like this. I need your help."

That got a pair of raised eyebrows. "Does it involve lifting anything heavier than I am?"

He pretended to consider for a moment. "Nope. Nothing heavy."

The boom box turned left when they hit the street, zipping toward the intersection as if the hounds of hell were after it. Blake stuck a finger in his ear, wiggled it around.

"Wuss," Shaun said.

Blake turned to his son, catching the grin. He'd take teasing over scowling anyday. "Call me crazy, but I'd like to keep my hearing past forty, thank you very much."

Shaun grunted, then said, "So where are we going? And can we stop and get somethin' to eat? My stomach was growling so loud last period the kid next to me complained I was keeping him awake."

Blake chuckled, as something suspiciously like contentment trickled through his chest. "You'll see. And, yeah, I suppose we can feed you on the way."

"Sweet," Shaun said.

It took them a half hour, but they finally decided on a pair of littermates, a ginger female and a little black-and-white boy. Ten weeks old, more fluff than substance, and both of them purring at full throttle in Shaun's lap on the way back, Blake's plea to put them back in their carrier having fallen on deaf ears.

"It really sucked when we had to give our cats away when Mom got married again," Shaun said, looking pretty damn close to purring himself.

"I imagine so. Your mother's always been crazy about cats."

"Yeah, I know." The kid cupped the black-and-white kitten against his chest. "Me, too." Then his eyes slanted to Blake. "You're sure this is okay with Lucille? And Wanda?"

"I'm not a total idiot. I checked first." With them, at least. "Lucille said Alan was allergic, so he couldn't have them in the house."

"Oh, right. I remember. What about the dog, though?"

Ah, yes. The dog. Blake glanced over his shoulder at the

three-month-old retriever-shepherd mix with the size-sixteen paws snoozing in the back seat. That hadn't been part of the game plan. But one look at his son's face when he saw the pup, and Blake had melted.

"Your mother's probably going to kill me."

"Cool. Can I watch?"

"Anybody ever tell you you're a smart-ass?"

"Dad."

His son's suddenly serious voice got his attention. "What?"

"I don't care what kind of language you use around your friends, but please. A little respect, okay?"

Blake grinned. The kid was okay. The grin faded, though, when he remembered how little he had to do with it. So, yeah, it might take more than a pup and a pair of kittens to undo twelve years of neglect. In fact, the minute they pulled up in front of the house, Blake had an acute attack of second-thoughtitis.

As in, springing a pup and a pair of kittens on a many-months-pregnant woman who already had issues with his maturity—or lack thereof—might not exactly go a long way toward convincing her he'd grown up.

Now he thinks of this.

Both kittens slung in the hem of his T-shirt, Shaun bounded out of the car and up the steps, leaving Blake to bring the pup, who, having sensed Something was About to Happen, was giving him a toothy grin and thumping his tail against the back of the seat.

"C'mon, boy," he said, and the dog clumsily threaded assorted limbs and tail and body through the opening between the bucket seats, planting twenty solid pounds of hot-breathed excitement in his lap. He snapped the leash on to the dog's new collar, then shoved the car door open with his foot, scrambling to get him and the dog out of the car before a well-placed paw turned him into a soprano. As if he knew where to go, the dog immediately yanked him in the direction of the stairs.

Blake followed, a bead of sweat trickling down his back.

"Mom! Mom! Come quick!"

Cass turned to the real estate agent with an apologetic smile. "My son. For some reason, he has difficulty grasping the concept that 'hello' is the word civilized people use when they come home."

C. J. Turner, the broker Cass's partner, Dana, had recommended—since a cousin of hers had worked for him a while back and seemed to think he knew his stuff—flashed her the kind of smile women should be immunized against. "Go ahead. I'll keep poking around, if you don't mind, so I can get that market analysis done up." He glanced around, his deep-blue eyes not missing a thing. "This is a beaut, though. And the fact that there aren't other houses jammed right up next to it makes it even more remarkable."

"Alan bought up three lots before he built, just so that wouldn't happen—"

"Mo-om!"

With a long-suffering sigh, she left C.J. to tour the bedrooms on his own, then leaned over the railing looking down into the great room.

And nearly fell over it.

She looked from Shaun to Blake. Then at the kittens. And the dog.

The *dog?* The dog whose feet were bigger than hers? The dog with the big, itchy teeth that would chew everything in sight?

"Blake Carter...what did you do?"

She saw the goofy smile momentarily fade, only to flash even brighter.

"You didn't have any cats," he said, as if that explained everything.

For a moment she was so struck by his remembering how much she loved cats she forgot she was supposed to be mad. Then the pup let out a single, piercing, "Yarp!"

"And how does that explain the dog?"

"Dog's Shaun's," Blake said with an unconcerned shrug. "So. You gonna come say hi or just stand up there looking pretty?"

Oh, what she would have given to have been able to stomp down the stairs. As it was, all she could manage was an indignant waddle, which didn't go anywhere near giving the impression she wanted to give, which was that her son and her husband—she sucked in a sharp breath: ex-husband—were shortly going to die at her hands. And here she'd been feeling better about things, for reasons she didn't even know and wasn't any too keen to go yanking apart to figure out the whys and wherefores, since trying to figure things out only led to more trouble, she'd found.

"Now you listen to me, Blake," she said, slightly out of breath, irritated when a Braxton-Hicks stopped her in midrant. She breathed deeply, waited for it to pass, then continued, "I'm about to put the house on the market. The last thing I need is pets. So you can take them back right now—"

She jumped when a soft, wet tongue lapped across her fingers. Then—and here's where she made her first mistake—she looked down into a pàir of the sweetest, sorriest, please-ya-gotta-love-me eyes she'd ever seen. Next to Blake's. And her son's. Both sets of which were plastered to her face.

"Blake, this is not going to work." She crossed her arms over her middle so the puppy couldn't get to her hands. So, being an obviously bright dog, he threw himself down across her feet and bared his spotted pink tummy to her, his entire back end squirming as he wagged his tail, making down-soft fur tickle her ankles. A laugh tried to surface; she swallowed it back.

God. She'd never had a puppy in her entire life. Being an Air Force brat had precluded that idea, and she'd never considered it, for some reason, once she was grown. Maybe because she'd always thought of herself as a cat person.

As if on cue, Blake thrust the ginger kitten into her arms, who immediately curled against her collarbone and started to purr.

"Blake," she said, more softly. "You're not playing fair."

He handed her the second kitten, who followed the first's example.

"At all."

"I generally don't," was his ingenuous reply, accompanied by The Grin.

And she was here to tell anyone who'd listen, that grin and her hormones were a seriously bad combination. Always had been, always—she sighed—would be.

Totally flummoxed, she backed up to the sofa, plopping down with the kittens to let them crawl over her distended tummy. The pup started chasing his tail, yipping at it when he couldn't catch it, finally tripping over his gargantuan feet in a flurry of limbs and ears.

Again, the laugh tried to get a foothold. Again she tried to squelch it. Then one of the kittens crawled up her belly at the precise moment the baby kicked hard enough to send the little thing shooting a foot into the air, instantly puffing up to twice its size…and that did it. The laughter came, hard and strong, wave after wave of uncontrollable giggles. And damn, it felt good, she realized, wiping tears from her eyes. It had been so long since she'd laughed. Really laughed. Had anything to laugh *at*.

She glanced up at Blake and her son and knew she'd lost the battle.

Still chuckling, Cass let out a sigh, then shook her head. "Pets take so much work—"

"The cats don't." Blake sank into the sofa beside her, scooping the black-and-white kitten into a hand larger than the entire cat.

"Their pans still need to be cleaned, which I can't do while I'm pregnant."

"I'll do it, Mom."

"And he will," Blake said with a nod in their son's direction. "And take care of the dog, too. Or they go back." She caught Blake's searing look at their son, which is when she realized his arm had slipped up onto the back of the sofa, behind her head. She shifted forward, as old fears and memories and disappointments tried to ruin her first moment of real peace in years.

"And take care of the dog," the kid said, that little-boy look back in his eyes. "I always wanted a dog, Mom."

"You did?" Without thinking, she'd brought the ginger kitten up under her neck, reveling in the tiny purr. Trying to recapture the fleeting magic of only moments before. "You never said anything."

"I never thought you'd say yes."

But she'd shut her eyes, not really hearing him. She held the fluffball more closely, realizing how much she'd missed her kitties. She'd been down to two when Alan had asked her to marry him; she'd had to give them away. They had good homes with Mercy's mother, but she'd still missed them. She could feel her blood pressure lowering, her fears at least somewhat receding as she continued cuddling the tiny beast. Still, she had to make it look good.

"I am not taking care of this dog, Shaun, you hear me?" she said, opening her eyes. "You feed him, clean up after him, exercise him. And the first time you blow it off, he goes straight to the pound. Or up to Denver."

"Yes, ma'am," they both said at once, which made her smile.

"Mrs. Stern?"

"Oh, shoot. I'd forgotten about the agent. Here—" She shoved the second kitten at Blake, then struggled to get out of the sofa, shivering at Blake's touch on her back to help her up. "Coming!" she called, then threw over her shoulder as she made her way to the stairs, "Put the litter pan in my bathroom, between the sink and the tub, and get the dog outside. And if Wanda gives you grief, don't coming bellyaching to me."

"No. I don't know how quickly I can move the property for her."

Not that Blake had expected any guarantees, but since he wasn't up on the market situation in Albuquerque these days, he didn't figure there was any harm in a little judicious information gathering.

C.J. leaned back against his silver Mercedes, apparently unconcerned about what it might do to his pricey wool slacks. Or his bad-ass leather jacket, which gently squeaked when the agent folded his long arms across his chest. "It's a jewel, though, the way it's set on the lot and all. But—" the intense blue eyes clouded slightly "—being at the upper end of the price range, even for this area…that might be a problem. And Mrs. Stern seems adamant about setting the initial asking price high, at least at first."

Mrs. Stern. He still couldn't wrap his head around that being Cass's name. Shaking off the pointless thought, Blake instead wondered how much he dared divulge about Cass's situation. "You think she's asking too much for the house?"

"*That* willing to let a client call the shots, I'm not. No, it's not out of market. Just pushing it." He scraped a knuckle along his jaw, then said, "I take it…she needs to sell?"

Blake hooked his thumbs in his back pockets. "Are you asking as seller's broker or buyer's?"

C.J.'s smile relaxed otherwise angular features as the breeze ruffled his short brown hair. "The only information I'm duty bound to share is what affects the property itself. Not the owner's personal reasons for the sale. I can hint that the seller's motivated, but…" He squinted up at the house. "She told me the house was too big. And all the stairs, with the baby coming, worried her." Now he faced Blake, sharing a conspiratorial grin. "That's all a potential buyer needs to know."

After all of three seconds' consideration, Blake fished in his back pocket for his wallet, from which he extracted a business card. "I'd appreciate it if you'd keep me…informed."

"You saying you want to put a bid on the property?"

"I'm saying…I have a personal stake in the outcome."

The man fingered the card, then asked quietly, "How long does she have?"

"I don't know, really. She hasn't been much more forthcoming with the details with me than she has with you. But I'm guessing a couple months, tops."

"I did wonder. Never heard yet of a woman that far along in her pregnancy moving unless she absolutely has to. Because someone's transferred, maybe, something like that." C.J. shook his head. "So I figure one of two things. Either she's greedy, or she's in trouble." He propped his briefcase on the hood of the car, popped it open, pulled out his Daytimer. As he slipped Blake's card inside a plastic compartment, he glanced at Blake. "And my hunch is she's not greedy."

"No. She isn't."

They talked about nothing of consequence for another minute, maybe, before C.J. left and Blake returned to the house, his boots crunching the sandy surface of the outside stairs as he approached the massive carved front door. Cass was waiting for him, a kitten tucked against her chest.

"Getting a little cozy with my agent, weren't you?"

"Just guy stuff," he said lightly, trying a smile. "We're both Broncos fans."

"You are such a liar."

Blake held up his hands in mock surrender. "Fine. You got me. But the guy's no fool, honey," he said, now gripping the doorjamb as he nodded toward Cass's stomach. "It doesn't take much to figure out a woman as pregnant as you are must have a damn good reason for wanting to move. And since you didn't give him one, he came to his own conclusions."

"Oh? And what conclusions might those be?"

"That you need to unload the house. That's all."

"Which you didn't deny, I assume."

"Well, no, since he'd already figured it out—"

She stalked off into the living room. Sort of.

"Oh, for crying out loud, Cass…don't go gettin' all crazy on me again—"

She spun back around, eyes ablaze. "If I go crazy, it'll be your fault, Blake Carter." Her voice shook, but her eyes were dry. "I feel like…like everywhere I turn, there you are. Being…whatever it is you're being. Dammit, I dealt with everything myself for all these years, I sure as hell don't need you horning in now!"

Refusing to rise to the bait, Blake let himself fall into a club chair a few feet away, propping one foot up against the edge of the glass-topped coffee table in front of him. He saw Cass's eyes zip to his booted foot, then to his face. He didn't budge. "And I have no intention of interfering," he said. At her raised eyebrows, he added, "Unless I see you about to really screw up."

He'd forgotten how fast a pregnant woman could move if

she was angry enough. She flew at him with both fists raised, raw fury emanating from her throat. He easily caught her wrists before she could inflict any damage, throwing her off balance so that she landed neatly in his lap. Even in her present state, he doubted she weighed more than 130 pounds, which felt like nothing, even as she flapped about like a bird caught in cherry tree netting.

Towanda—her hair a deep auburn today—picked that moment to walk through the great room. Black eyes calmly assessed the situation before she said, "You need any help, Mr. Blake?"

"No, thank you, Wanda. I seem…to have…everything…under—" he finally got his arms around Cass so she couldn't squirm as much "—control." He offered the housekeeper a smile. "But thanks for asking."

"Anytime," she said, then continued on through the room and out the other door.

"Let me go," Cass said under her breath. Considering what was happening to his anatomy underneath that skinny little rump of hers, letting her go was probably the wisest choice. But he was just as stubborn as she was.

"Not yet."

"For God's sake, Blake." If he were to fall into her eyes right now, he'd freeze his butt off. "This isn't funny, despite that cute little exchange you and Wanda just shared. It's…unseemly. What if Lucille should walk by?"

"I'll tell her the truth. That I said something that got your hackles up, you came at me hell-bent for leather, and I caught you before you fell and seriously injured yourself. I'm sure she'd understand."

She wriggled again, but he held fast. Suddenly her eyes filled with tears. "I don't want to be sitting on your lap, Blake. It's not right, it's not funny, and if you think this is some sort of a game, it's one I have no interest in playing. Please let go of me."

He immediately released her. She shot up so quickly she nearly toppled over again. This time, however, she caught herself before she fell.

"I asked you this once before," she said, her voice somehow steely and shaky at the same time, "but apparently it didn't take. Please stop getting in my way. I don't want you doing things for me. I got into this mess on my own, and I'll get out of it the same way." She flushed slightly, then said, "At least I know I can count on myself. Which is more than I can say for some people in this room."

Blake leaned forward, scrubbing his hands down his face. She had every right to say what she had. *Every* right. Still… "I've changed, Cass. I swear."

Her expression softened. Slightly. "Maybe you have. But you can hardly expect a handful of words to overturn more than twelve years of indifference."

She might as well have slapped him. "I've never been *indifferent,* Cass!"

"Oh, yeah?" Her arms linked over her belly. "Could've fooled me."

And again, she was right. Because for damn sure his actions since their divorce hadn't gone far toward proving otherwise. And even he knew that trying to fix a problem that went back to before their son's birth with a single declaration—no matter how sincere—was like trying to close a four-inch gash with a Band-Aid.

"Blake," she said more gently, making his eyes cant to hers, "I've no doubt you mean well. But your track record stinks. And I'm sure you can appreciate that I'm no position to take your, or anybody else's, word on anything right now. It's just safer this way, okay?"

On a long sigh, Blake leaned back against the cushions, rubbing his eyes. Words were useless. Even he could see and understand that. She needed proof that he'd changed, that he wasn't the same man who'd run out on her all those years ago. The question was…how, exactly, was he supposed to go about that? 'Cause God knew the kitten thing sure hadn't worked.

He stayed quiet for several seconds, then opened his eyes and crossed his arms over his chest, looking at her. "If you really don't want the animals, I'll take them back."

That got a bit of a smile. "I'm sure the pup and Shaun are blood brothers by now. It would be easier to get gold out of Fort Knox than to get that dog away from him."

"And the kittens?"

"You mean Fred and Ginger?" At his raised brows, she said, simply, "Lucille," and he nodded. She hesitated, and he could see the turmoil bubbling behind those sweet blue eyes. "You took a big chance, doing that. And…" In went a huge breath. "And I thank you," came out on an equally huge sigh. "But it still doesn't change the fact that I need…space. From your good intentions. To figure things out on my own." She glanced down, then back up at him. "If you really do care, please give it to me."

When she walked away this time, he didn't follow her. The black-and-white kitten jumped onto his knee—Fred, he guessed—the tiny claws hooking clumsily into his jeans. He gathered the little critter to his chest, where he curled up into a ball and promptly conked out.

No matter, he thought, scratching the kitten's head. He had a couple days yet before he had to go back. She'd come around.

He frowned at the loud *Ha, ha, ha!* reverberating inside his head.

Chapter Five

She wasn't going to come around.

And that he'd thought she would only went to show exactly how far down on the growing-up ladder he still was.

With a shudder of irritation, Blake set his fork and knife on his dinner plate. He was leaving tomorrow, and the wall was still up. And topped with barbwire, no less. He sighed heavily, plucking a roll from the basket in front of him and sopping up a puddle of Towanda's silky beef gravy (you can only eat leftover buffet food for so long, after all) from his otherwise empty plate. Between her cooking and his frustration, Blake wouldn't be at all surprised to discover he'd gained five pounds in the four days he'd been here.

For one thing, he was about to go insane wondering about Cass's marriage, he thought as he surreptitiously observed her across the granite-topped dining-room table, picking at food she wasn't eating. Again. The light from the black iron chandelier above the table glistened in her hair, made that ridiculously ostentatious diamond flash like…like a ridiculously ostentatious diamond. What the hell had the guy been trying to prove? And what if Lucille's ramblings were true? What if the marriage had been on the rocks?

His eyes slipped to her rounded belly, peeking above the table.

Yeah, well, even if there had been problems, there was nothing worse than a spouse grieving over unresolved issues.

And Cass had had every right to fall in love again. To move on with her life. That he hadn't done either had nothing to do with her. And if he truly cared about her—which he certainly *thought* he did—then he should be feeling bad for her. Gloating, temporarily satisfying though it might feel, wasn't gonna cut it.

Blake glanced down at his hands to see he'd been shredding the roll into dust. He quickly dropped the mangled bits onto his plate, covering them with his napkin.

Maybe he'd been a damn fool to let Cass get away, but where'd he get off thinking he had a gnat's chance of winning her back? Not to mention why he wanted to in the first place, but he could only handle one pressing question at a time. He had time, he had patience, but there had to be a window here. And so far the only one he'd glimpsed had been firmly slammed shut in his face. If it hadn't been for Shaun…

Shaun. Now his gaze shifted to his mercurial-tempered son, scarfing down his third helping of roast beef and herb-roasted potatoes as if he wasn't sure when he'd see his next meal. And slipping the occasional piece of meat underneath the table to the pup when he thought no one was looking. Blake wished he knew how he was faring in that department, since his son wasn't giving any clues. No surprise there, though. After years of his being a sometimes father, Blake could hardly blame the kid for not simply handing over the keys to his psyche, just like that. Yeah, things had been cool right after the Great Animal Escapade, and there'd been a few good conversations here and there. But the kid still knew, come tomorrow, Blake would be gone again. In Shaun's mind the situation was probably like the old adage of not becoming too attached to the dog who followed you home, in case you had to give it up. So his son's reaction to him had ping-ponged between acceptance and wariness since the funeral. Where it had ended up, though, Blake wasn't sure, despite his hunch the kid hoped to see his parents reunited.

But then, he probably wouldn't mind seeing a Porsche land in the driveway with his name on the title, either.

Towanda suddenly appeared at the table, wiping her hands on a dish towel, which she then slapped across her wide shoulder. Blake had decided the sixtysomething housekeeper-slash-nurse had been a rottweiler in a past life, one fiercely loyal to her family—she'd been with Alan's parents for nearly twenty years, and more or less regarded Lucille, and now Cass and Shaun, as her own. Blake had quickly learned which was Wanda's good side, and then how to do everything humanly possible to stay on it, the alternative being far too scary to contemplate.

"You finished with your dinner, Miss Lucille?" the housekeeper boomed, hands parked on hips broader than a mobile home. "And did you remember to take your pills beforehand?"

"Yes, Wanda, to both," Lucille meekly replied, backing up slightly so the woman could take her plate.

The empty dish clunked onto a tray, Towanda's sleek black 'do glistened like mink underneath the chandelier. In the five days he'd been here, Blake had yet to see the same wig twice. Same style—a short, conservative cluster of soft waves—just different colors. "And what about you, droopy drawers?"

"Yeah, me, too." Shaun wiped his mouth on a napkin, then bounced up from the table. "Me and a couple of the guys—"

"A couple of the guys and I," Cass automatically corrected.

"Yeah, geez, whatever…anyway, we're gonna go up to the park and skateboard while it's still light."

Blake saw the frown cross Cass's features. "Just stay out of the arroyo, okay?"

He immediately understood her concern. The flood-control ditches, with their straight, smooth surfaces, were a favorite venue for skateboarders. Unfortunately, they could also be deadly, occasionally filling up with sudden, unexpected floodwaters which swept down to the valley at speeds up to forty miles per hour after a storm. While there hadn't been a drowning in a couple years, that didn't diminish the danger.

Only try explaining that to a fifteen-year-old.

"Mom, for Pete's sake, there's not a cloud in the sky. And you can't have a flash flood without rain. Lighten up, wouldja?"

"Shaun," Blake warned. "First off, you don't tell your mother to *lighten up,* and, second, you stay out of those ditches, like she said. And I don't care what the other kids do, before you huff out one of those 'what do grown-ups know?' sighs. There've been clouds over the mountains all day. Besides which, you *could* get hurt."

"That's right," Cass said. "You remember how Billy Sandersen broke both his wrists skating in the arroyo last year?"

"And you do that," Wanda said, juggling dishes, "don't be looking to *me* to be wiping your butt when you have to go to the bathroom. That was the one thing I sure did hate about nursing, always having to wipe people's butts."

That was enough to provoke a horrified expression on the kid's face. Not to mention slightly stunned looks on everyone else's. "Okay, okay…I'll stay out. I promise," Shaun added at Blake's glare, backing out of the room.

"Apologize to your mother first."

"Blake, it's okay—"

"No, it isn't," Blake said mildly, his attention never wavering from his son's face. He saw resentment flare in the coffee-colored eyes, then fade.

"Sorry, Mom," he mumbled.

"It's okay, honey." She pressed her napkin to her mouth, then smoothed it back on her lap. "We're just concerned about you, that's all." A smile flirted with her unlipsticked mouth. "That's why we get the big bucks."

"Geez, Mom—I'm not stupid, okay? Believe it or not, I can take care of myself. After all, it's not like I haven't had enough practice," he pushed out, then left the room before anyone else could get on his case.

Cass, however, was immediately on Blake's. "Why did you do that?"

"High time somebody sat on that child," Towanda pronounced without the slightest compunction. "Ain't that right, Miss Lucille?"

Lucille raised her water goblet in a mock salute of agreement.

However, a crease roughly the size of the Grand Canyon marred Cass's brow.

"I apologize," Blake said quietly, aware of the other two women's trenchant gazes taking all this in. "You've been handling Shaun just fine without my interference up until now. I should've stayed out of it."

"The hell you say," Towanda said, punching Blake none too gently in the shoulder. "Look at her!" She flapped in Cass's direction as if she couldn't hear. "The woman is in no fit condition to be handling no ornery teenager whose brain is lost somewhere in those baggy pants of his."

"Well, thank you, Wanda, for those words of support," Cass said dryly.

"You're welcome, baby. Now, are you finished?" she asked without missing a beat. But before Cass could reply, Towanda clucked in the direction of Cass's virtually untouched plate. "Honey, if you don't start eating more than that, that child you're carrying's going to come out looking all tired and scrawny, like some chicken nobody'd want. And you know you don't want two skinny-assed kids driving you crazy, now, do you?"

To Blake's surprise, Cass smiled. "God forbid. Although, for your information, the midwife assured me the baby's a perfectly decent size." But she picked up half a roll and began nibbling on it.

When Towanda rolled her eyes in clear disbelief, Blake said, "If it makes you feel any better, she didn't eat worth a damn when she was carrying Shaun, either. And he ended up weighing nine pounds at birth."

"Get out of here! Nine pounds?" She snatched Cass's dinner plate off the table, then the roll out of her hand. As she toted the dishes out of the room, they could hear her muttering something about big babies and getting stuck and going in after them with the Jaws of Life.

"A real charmer, isn't she?" Cass asked, looking down at the table.

He looked up sharply at the deadness in Cass's voice, then caught the worried look on Lucille's face, as well. He glanced around, then asked in a low voice, "Are you going to have to let her go?"

That got a wry smile. "I already tried. She won't leave." A glimmer of actual humor warmed her eyes. "Says she won't be able to sleep nights, worrying about us trying to cook for ourselves. Or that Cille won't take her meds."

"Like I can't read a label," Lucille said.

"Never mind that I cooked just fine for years before I came to live here."

Blake cleared his throat to cover up the smile. Cass had many talents, but cooking had never been one of them, certainly not when they'd been married. And according to Shaun, things hadn't improved much in the intervening years. "I take it Alan was footing the bill for her wages?"

Lucille snorted. "Even paying her as much as she'd get in any hospital, my son knew he was getting a bargain. As opposed to putting his father and me in one of those assisted-living facilities," she said at Blake's questioning look. "I've got my Social Security and what's left of Sammy's pension, but there wouldn't be a lot left over."

"Then let me help," Blake said immediately. "I'd be glad to pay her salary—"

"Blake, don't start," Cass said on a sigh, rubbing the space between her eyes. "I told you, this is my problem to deal with."

"You can't let the woman work for free, for crying out loud!"

"I have no intention of letting her work for free!" Cass said, clearly appalled that he'd even think such a thing. "I'll find the money, somewhere."

"Oh, for God's sake, Cass—"

"And on that cue…" Lucille stood up, plucking at the seat of her pants. "The static electricity in this dry climate, it's enough to drive you crazy. Well, I've got a hot date with an old movie on AMC, so I'll excuse myself, if you don't mind."

Blake watched as the old woman practically sprinted away from the table, then returned his attention to his former wife. Who was sitting with her head in her hands, her shoulders slumped. And he thought, for someone determined to put on a show of being able to handle everything on her own, she was doing a piss poor job of it. Still, his heart ached for her, for the burdens he'd placed on those slender shoulders when he'd walked out, for the ones she refused to let him help her with now. There wasn't even any point to his wondering why Cass was being so stubborn. Because she was absolutely right, his track record stank. After all, if he were in her shoes, would *he* trust him not to screw up?

"He's right, you know," she now said on a long sigh.

"Who's right? About what?"

"Shaun. About being basically left to his own devices."

Blake decided it was the better part of valor not to point out that, judging from her newfound penchant for switching subjects at the drop of a hat, Cass had clearly been living with Lucille too long. "I hardly think that's true," he said. "Kids shoot off at the mouth, honey. You know that. Besides, if anyone's to blame for that, it's me. Not you."

She gave him an obviously exhausted smile. "I never said it wasn't."

He grimaced. "I walked right into that one, didn't I?"

"Yes, you did."

It might not have been exactly a sweet moment, but it was better than a stick in the eye. So he decided to run with it. But he'd no sooner said, "Okay. Explain something to me…" than she rose from the table, shaking her head.

"Not now, Blake. I'm too tired."

He reached across and snagged her hand in his. It was cold. Too cold for a pregnant woman. "I'm leaving in the morning, Cass. A few minutes' conversation isn't going to kill you."

The blue eyes warily met his. Then she sat back down. "Fine," she said. "So talk."

"Oh, yeah. You sound real receptive."

"This was your idea. Not mine."

"Are we ever going to be able to have a normal conversation again?"

"Have we *ever* had a normal conversation?"

"Okay, maybe not," he admitted. "But could we at least try now? For Shaun's sake, if nothing else?"

She seemed to regard him thoughtfully for a moment, then again pushed herself up and away from the table, wandering out toward the great room. Blake followed suit, staying a careful few feet behind her. Coming to a halt in front of one of the windows, she stashed her hands in the pockets of her pale-green maternity jumper, apparently entranced by the blazing tangle of persimmon-and plum-colored clouds in the west. Below that, lights from the sprawling city twinkled weakly.

"Why can't I stay mad at you?" she said, apparently to herself. She scraped one hand through her feathery hair, then held it there, shaking her head. "I try and try…but it's like trying to hold rain."

After a moment Blake said, "I'm not sure what to make of that."

She almost laughed. "Neither am I. Although don't get too excited. I still don't trust you as far as I could throw you."

"You know, somehow I got that message." He was close enough to take in her scent, a blend of magnolias and citrus. Close enough to lay his hands on her shoulders, to stroke, if he had a mind to, a cheek as soft as a baby's breath. To keep from touching her, he picked up a framed photo from the mantel, realizing he had no idea who the person was. "If I ask you something," he said quietly, "will you be honest with me?"

"If this is about why did I married Alan," she said, "I already answered that."

Her perception didn't surprise him, although her words slammed into him like an ice-cold wave.

"Is it rally so incomprehensible , she asked softly in the wake of his silence, "that I'd fall in love again?"

Blake arefully set the photo back on the mantel, leaning

one elbow up against expanse of stone. Cass's face glowed in the deepening, ruddy light as she looked at him. How many times he'd held that face in his hands, kissed that mouth. Watched her face glow, almost like this, when they made love. And he understood, in that instant, how deeply he was still in love with her. And since twelve years apart hadn't dampened either his interest or his ardor, if his body's current state was any indication, it was pretty damn likely he would always be in love with her.

Was he a fool or what? "No," he said at last. "Of course not. You had every right to move on."

"Thank you" she said quietly, then added, "does it bother you? My talking about him? Because if it does, I won't."

Does it bother me that another man watched what I watched, did what I did?

Does it bother me?

"Hey," he replied, evenly. "I brought it up. But I guess I hoped you'd married him for his money."

Her brows flew up, then she laughed, a metallic, hollow sound. "You really think I'm that shallow?"

"Of course not."

"Then why'd you ask?"

"To yank your chain."

Cass actually smiled, then sighed. "No, Blake, I didn't marry Alan for his money. I didn't need it. Oh, sure, he was far better off than I was—or at least that's the impression he gave—but I was doing okay. Between your child support and what I took in from the shop, we weren't in dire straits, by any means. And I don't need a lot." She glanced around. "Most women would probably have engaged a decorator before the ink was dry on the marriage certificate, but I frankly didn't care. This was Alan's house—his and Lucille's—and I saw no reason to turn his world upside down on a whim—"

Her face clouded as she sucked in a breath.

"Contraction?"

She nodded, her mouth drawn. "They're so much stronger than they were with Shaun." Massaging her lower back with the knuckles of one hand, she walked over to one of the sofas, leaning against the back so she could bend over, taking some of the pressure off her spine. When she straightened again, she didn't seem to be talking to him as much as pointing out something to herself. "The ironic thing, of course," she said, backing up to rest against a stool in front of the wet bar, "is that financially I'm now worse off than I was before I married him." She gave a startled laugh. "Isn't that a kicker?"

"Are you angry with him?" he asked, selfishly.

He could tell nothing from her expression. "I'm not exactly thrilled that he left me with a boatload of debts. But he left me with some good stuff, too."

"Such as?"

Her gaze was cool, steady. "The baby, for one thing. Bear of a pregnancy though this has been. And Lucille. And I'm glad I can give the old girl the grandchild she always wanted. There's good in every situation, if you're willing to see it."

Blake pushed himself away from the fireplace and back to Cass, clicking on a lamp by one of the sofas as he did. "But…"

"What can I tell you?" she said, her voice flat. "The man who died last week wasn't the same man I married. Or thought I was marrying, at any rate. Any more than the man I thought I was marrying at nineteen was the same one who left me three years later."

Blake turned away, wondering if he'd ever be able to breathe normally again.

"Alan was very…gallant," he heard behind him. "And considerate. All the time we were dating, and even the first few months of our marriage, he was *there* for me. Especially about the business. In that respect, at least, I can't fault him—he gave us some damn good advice, advice that I have no doubt helped Babies, Inc., come as far as it has in such a short time."

"And?" Blake said quietly, turning to face her.

Her mouth curved slightly. "And I was tired. Tired of being alone. Of *doing* it all alone. Alan happened into my life at the right time, I guess."

He opened his mouth to protest. Her raised hand stopped him. "Taking your son one weekend a month and a couple weeks in the summer isn't the same as being responsible for a child day in and day out." She didn't sound angry yet, although he could hear the edge in her voice. "And neither does money make up for that. Not that you haven't been generous to a fault about providing for Shaun, but there's more to supporting a child than making sure he has shoes and clothes and the latest game system."

And how dumb was it to feel pissed when he'd come to the same conclusion himself just four days before? But there it was, fangs and all. "Now, wait a minute, Cass. I gave my son more than stuff, and you know it, even if we couldn't be together all that much. I've always loved him."

"I don't think Shaun's been so sure about that," she said softly. "It's hard to know when you're loved if the person simply isn't around. And that was one of the reasons, when I met Alan and we seemed to hit it off, I reconsidered marriage. I needed someone who'd be there for my son, too. Someone other than his neurotic mother for him to talk to, if he needed. At least, that was the plan."

He barreled right over the deadness in her voice, not hearing what she was really saying. "And was that part of your plan, too?" Blake bit out, unable to quell his bitterness as he nodded toward her bulging middle.

She angled her head at him, clearly not believing what she

was hearing. "Yes, I had sex with my husband, Blake. After about a million years without. So, you know, I figured I'd more than paid my debts to the celibacy gods. And please don't expect me to believe that *you've* abstained all this time."

He had nothing to say to that. Nothing she'd want to hear, at any rate.

"We both wanted this child very much," she went on. "My getting pregnant wasn't an accident."

"Unlike Shaun."

The sudden coldness in her eyes instantly corresponded with the heat flaring in his own face. "Well," she said. "That explains everything, doesn't it?"

"Oh, hell...that's not what I meant—"

"Isn't it?"

"No." He took in a breath. "No, Cass. Not the way you're taking it, anyway. But Shaun *was* a surprise. We hadn't planned on having kids so young."

"But he happened, anyway, didn't he? And some of us had a tougher time adjusting than others."

Trying to gather up the pieces of his brain scattered all over the room, he crisscrossed the floor, tunneling his fingers through his hair. "Dammit, Cass, why is it every time we get together, we end up having the same argument? Why can't you just let the past go?"

And didn't *that* catapult him right to the top of the list for Idiot of the Year? Her hand on his arm reeled him around so fast she was out of focus for a second. "Because I was the one who was abandoned, Blake. Because I was the one who had a kid to raise, virtually on my own. Because I was the one who was made to feel that the pregnancy was my fault, and therefore my responsibility—"

"That's not true—"

"Of course it's true! You *left* me."

"You asked me to, if memory serves."

Her eyes—huge, angry, hurt—shimmered with tears she wouldn't shed.

And behind the tears, something more. Something he'd never seen before, couldn't define now. Something that jolted him into the realization that this wasn't about him. Not solely, anyway.

"No," she said at last. "All I asked you to do was remove your things. You had already gone months before that." She then pushed past him. "If I don't see you before you leave tomorrow morning," she said over her shoulder, "have a safe trip."

"Cass!" He went after her, pulling her back around, desperate for another glimpse of whatever it was she was keeping locked up inside her. Because suddenly he had no doubt, none, that whatever was going on here went far deeper than a simple—albeit totally justified—reaction to his betrayal, all those years ago. And that until he shook whatever it was loose, he didn't have a chance in hell of fixing whatever had gone wrong between them. "I screwed up, okay? I know that, I readily admit it…why won't you give me a chance to at least try to make it up to you?"

Old wounds gaped raw in her eyes. "Because I trusted you once, and you let me down. Because I trusted Alan, and damned if he didn't let me down, too. That's why I'm being so anal about standing on my own! Because every time I've let myself believe in someone else, I've gotten the shaft. Now would you please let me go so I can get some rest?"

He stood frozen for a long time, staring at her retreating back, now more than ever understanding that what came out of Cass's mouth didn't necessarily match what she kept locked inside that unfathomable head of hers. But damned if he knew where she kept the key.

The slight noise, off to the right, startled him. Towanda

stood in the shadows of the dining room, obviously ready to leave. Instead, she clunked her purse on the dining table and made for the wet bar.

"You driving anywhere tonight, Mr. Carter?"

He shook his head. She banged open the bar doors, pulling out a decanted bottle of something undoubtedly expensive and potent.

"You drink?"

"On the rare occasion."

With a nod, she grabbed a shot glass off the shelf above the sink, poured a drink, then handed it to him. "This definitely qualifies as an occasion," she said. "Scotch, by the way. The good stuff. Enjoy it. I imagine Miss Cassie will be getting rid of all this in a few days. No sense dangling temptation in front of a fool teenage boy."

Blake studied the drink for a moment. "Drinking as a way of avoiding problems is a cop-out."

"I couldn't agree more. And if I thought you were the type who used booze to avoid your problems, I wouldn't've given you the drink. But sometimes, baby," she said softly, "it don't hurt to take the edge off. Long as you know that's all you're doing."

He tossed back the drink, trying hard not to grimace as the fiery liquid seared his insides. Now he remembered why he wasn't much of a drinker.

"So," he said, handing her back the empty shot glass, trying hard to focus through his watery eyes, "you heard."

"Not that much, and not on purpose." She sighed. "You two got one helluva mess to sort out, don't you?"

"Noticed that, did you?"

That got a soft chuckle. "Forgive me if it sounds like I'm speaking out of turn…but Miss Cassie strikes me as one of those people who has no trouble letting you know how she feels, but cluing anybody in to what she's *thinking* is something else again."

"That's Cass, all right," Blake said with a tired smile. "Even when we were married, she never talked much about her past, her family. I knew she'd lived all over the place, since her father was career Air Force, but she never even talked about that very much. Would you believe she was almost painfully shy when we met?"

"Actually, that doesn't surprise me." He saw a flash of white in the darkness when she smiled. "She sure got over that, didn't she?"

"Yep. She sure did."

Blake could hear Wanda's polyester-encased thighs abrading each other as she walked back to the table to pick up her purse. She hesitated a moment, then said, "I got one thing to say, and now that Mr. Alan is gone, I don't much care who knows it." Her dark eyes darted toward the hall, anyway, and she lowered her voice to a discreet rumble. "Now, I think the world of Miss Lucille, and that sweet lady you were just fighting with, and even that fifteen-year-old conglomeration of confused hormones you brought into this world, and I'd've stayed on as long as they needed me. But, well…things just wasn't right around here. I never could put my finger on it, exactly, but I always felt uneasy around Mr. Alan."

"Uneasy? In what way?"

"Hell, honey, I couldn't explain it if I tried. Just chalk it up to intuition, I s'pose. But I'll tell you one thing, and you can ask anybody who knows me—when my hackles go up about somebody, you better believe they're up to no good, somehow, someway. And my hackles shot up like nobody's business, every time that man walked into the room. There was something…slippery about him. And you want to know something else?"

He figured she'd tell him whether he gave her leave or not. "What?"

"I really *don't* think Miss Cassie knew who she was marrying, 'cause that man…huh. He could lay on the charm thicker'n Miss Lucille's makeup, when he wanted to. In fact, he even had me fooled for a while, he was being so nice to her, and that's goin' some. Only, I guess it didn't take. So all I can say is, I just hope that child she's carrying turns out to be a chip off her block, and not his. You know what I mean?"

He didn't, not really, but she'd done a superb job of planting about a million questions in his already overloaded brain.

"You want her back, don't you?"

Startled, he met the calm gaze with a sheepish grin. "Nuts, isn't it?"

"Probably. But it's the crazy people in this world who get what they want, I've always found. Besides, I like a man with gumption. Not many of those left nowadays." She picked up her purse again, rummaged around in it a few minutes for her car keys. "Well now, you have a good trip back. And we'll see you again soon."

She was out the door before he could reply. But then, she obviously didn't expect one, since the sentiment hadn't been a wish but a statement of fact.

Chapter Six

"Hey, lady." Mercy rapped her knuckles on the desk in front of Cass. "Have you heard a single word I said?" At Cass's blank stare, her partner said, "Yeah, that's what I figured. I told you, you shouldn't have come back yet."

"Please." Cass pulled over a recently dropped-off stack of baby clothes and began sorting through them. "Staying in the house would drive me nuts. Especially as the real estate agent keeps dragging people through. Oh, look at this." She held up a tiny white romper with red roses embroidered across the smocked yoke. "Isn't this cute?"

"Adorable. So…your ex is gone, I take it."

"Speaking of driving me nuts." *Which you're doing nearly as well as he was.* Cass placed the romper in a pile of things to be marked, then quickly rejected the next three items, all of which were stained. Honestly…did people think they were blind or what? "He left this morning."

As in, gone but definitely not forgotten.

"Oughta be a law, man having a mouth that sexy," Mercy said dreamily, stirring her coffee.

As she was saying.

Cass breathed a sigh of gratitude when the ringing phone snagged Mercy's attention. Her partner had never made any bones about how little she thought of Alan—a club that had seemed to recruit new members daily. She wasn't even sure his own mother had liked him very much. Lordamercy…what kind of woman gets taken in by a man even his own mother had reservations about?

The same kind of woman, she wryly observed, who had thoughts of her first husband stuck to her brain like lint to polyester.

She decided to blame it all on the pregnancy. Logically she should be relieved that Blake had finally left, that she no longer had to see the way his mouth crooked a little higher on one side than the other when he smiled, no longer had to catch a whiff of him fresh from the shower, when his damp hair curled the way it did at his nape, no longer had to avoid looking into eyes that threatened to drag her under. Staying out of his way hadn't helped one bit, especially as he handled the kittens as much as she did, so every time she picked one of them up, she could smell his aftershave in their fur.

And she sure did have a thing for that aftershave.

Geez, were stress and horniness a deadly combination or what? Throw in an obviously contrite, handsome-as-sin ex-husband who still knew exactly what rang her chimes, and she was doomed. Thank *God* he was gone.

Now if only she would stop missing him so much, everything would be just peachy-keeno.

On the horniness/stress front, anyway.

"Hey, y'all—look what I got!"

A dozen wallpaper books whacking everything in her path, Dana wedged herself into the already jam-packed office, grass-green eyes wide, dimples aflashin'. As usual, her shiny chestnut hair was pulled up into a topknot, which added a whole inch to her five-three frame. And, as usual, half of the hair had slipped out, framing her face in wispy, sexy tendrils. Cute as a button, sweet as honey, with enough energy for five people and the brain capacity of about twenty, Dana was the shop's number cruncher, as well as the one who'd suggested they expand the used-furniture area to include some real antiques and a nursery decorating service.

Cass adored Dana. Most days. Today, however, the woman's enthusiasm made Cass feel old and tired. She met the dimpled smile with a grimace. "And where, pray tell, are we going to put those?"

"I'll find a place," Dana declared, plunking the sample books on the floor so she could remove a half-dozen baby-furniture catalogs off the chair to the corner of Cass's desk, which she couldn't do until she'd shoved over the pile of Cass's pile of baby clothes.

"Hey!"

"Oh, hey, yourself." Tugging her emerald green tunic over hips that refused to kowtow to constant dieting, she retrieved her "real" cup—the kind that looks half-dressed without its companion saucer—from the cabinet beside the coffeemaker and filled it. The cup and saucer tinkling precariously in one hand, she swished delicately through the stacks of stuff on the floor, then plopped her round bottom into the chair with a satisfied huff, disseminating a burst of some subdued but pricey fragrance. She took a sip of coffee, then somehow found a spot to place cup and saucer on the corner of the desk. "Oh, how sweet!" she said, swiping the romper off the top of the pile. "And we're running low on twelve-month things, too."

"The only thing we're running low on," Cass mumbled, scanning the tiny, cluttered office they all shared, "is sanity. And floor space."

Her call finished, Mercy jumped back into the conversation without a hitch. "Which is why we need to be thinking relocation." She fished a bagel with gooey red stuff slithering out of it from a white paper bag from the deli two doors down, then chomped down on it. "And soon."

"Mercy's right," Dana put in. "It's long past time. And we could easily afford it, Cass, so don't even go there."

Somewhere behind the constantly squirming mound that was her second child, Cass felt her stomach clench. A week ago, they *could* afford it—if all three of them plowed back an equal share of their profits into expansion. Now, however, Cass couldn't do that. Alan's debt would eat up every penny she could scrape out of the business, without even so much as a smell left over. In fact, if she didn't figure out some way to at least make the minimum payments on those credit cards, she might have to sell out her share of the business. Five years of her life had gone into this enterprise. The thought of having to unload it now made her sick.

Her face flushed as angry tears bit at her eyes. She blinked them back, surreptitiously sucking in a long, steadying breath. "We could also consider not trying to do everything that pops into our heads, guys," she said evenly. "This was originally supposed to be a consignment shop, remember? Used clothing and furniture. No hassles, low overhead."

"We also agreed we'd let things blossom." Dana smoothed her skirt over her knee, her taupe T-strapped foot bouncing in front of her. "So we're blossoming."

"Yeah. Right out the front door."

Her bagel dispatched, Mercy wiped her fingers on a napkin, then swallowed. "So we look for a bigger place."

She didn't dare tell them. She couldn't stand the sympathy—or Mercy's unspoken *I told you so.* Cass looked from one to the other, snagging the first thought that scrambled past. "You two are trying to kill me, aren't you? As if I don't have enough stress in my life right now, you think we should *move?*"

Her partners exchanged something resembling guilty glances, and Cass felt a few muscles relax.

"Sorry, honey." Mercy clasped Cass's wrist. With slightly sticky fingers. "I don't know what we were thinking. Of course we could manage for another few months here. Right, Dana?"

"Like my mama says," Dana concurred, "you can always pack one more thing into the suitcase. Besides, I think sometimes the customers find the clutter kind of…amusing."

"Oh, that makes me feel *much* better," Cass said.

Dana checked her watch. "Showtime," she announced, then bounced up off her seat. "C'mon, Mercy—gotta open the doors before the crowds break 'em down."

"If you two don't mind," Cass said, "I think I'll stay back here for awhile and continue sorting through these things."

Both ladies tripped all over themselves to tell Cass it was okay, they could manage, to be sure to lie down on the futon against one wall if she needed to, to take it easy….

"Go *away,* the pair of you!"

They went.

Sorting through the sacks of clothes Mrs.—she checked the name pinned to the bag—Henley had brought in was about all Cass was up to, she had to admit. Her back ached, the Braxton-Hicks wouldn't leave her alone, and she basically felt like crud. Between Blake and selling the house and the mess that Alan had left and Blake and Shaun and Blake…

Her head hurt. She pushed herself up out of the chair behind the desk and tried to stretch out the kinks, especially from her lower back, walking over to the doorway that separated the office from the jumbled sales floor. Both Mercy and Dana had customers—a very pregnant young woman with her slightly dazed husband in tow, and an even more dazed-looking mother with snoozing triplets, whose tandem stroller took up most of the available floor space while she frantically pawed through racks of toddler clothing before, Cass assumed with a smile, the babies woke up.

Who would have thought three such totally disparate personality types could turn a marketing-class assignment into a flourishing business? That they could not only stay in business past the crucial two-year mark but make money? To lose what she'd worked so hard for…

Damn you, Alan, she thought without the least twinge of guilt. *Damn you for dying, for lying, for not being the man I thought you were.*

Damn you, Blake, for tempting me to believe you're the man I so desperately wanted you to be.

And damn herself for being so tempted to fall off the wagon…again.

Cass slowly pivoted and swayed back inside the office, dropping heavily into her desk chair once again. Yeah, the business was going well. Yeah, they were three smart cookies, her partners and she. When it came to men, however, they were three of the sorriest women ever to walk the face of the earth.

With a weighty sigh, she yanked over another bag of baby clothes and dumped them out on her desk.

Bed was the only thing on her mind by the time she got home. Tugging off her maternity pantsuit, she flung it in the general direction of the chaise. It missed. She didn't bother picking it up. Couldn't have, even if she wanted to, having reached that point where whatever fell on the floor could jolly well stay there until after the baby came. She pulled on an oversize T-shirt and climbed into bed, only to be immediately joined by both kittens and the puppy—dubbed Dude by her son—who quickly divvied up assorted spots in and around her knees and thighs.

Alan would choke, she thought with gleeful perverseness. She flopped both hands by her hips with a sigh loud enough to make Dude lift perplexed eyes to hers, before settling his snout back across her shins. Lucille had lobbed messages at her between the front door and the bedroom—the real estate agent wanted to do an open house on Sunday, the accountant wanted to see her tomorrow, Blake would be here not this weekend but the next, although he wouldn't stay at the house this time.

At least that, she thought, shutting her eyes. A sharp rap on her door popped them open again.

"Come in?"

"Lucille said I wasn't to come back unless this was empty." Shaun settled a bed tray with a bowl of homemade vegetable soup over her knees. "So please eat, Mom, or I may never finish high school."

With a smile, Cass shoved away assorted curious bewhiskered faces. "I think I can get this down," she said, picking up a spoon. When Shaun didn't immediately leave, she lowered the spoon again, her brow knit. "What is it?"

"I need to talk to you."

Instantly, shards of worry pierced her already-overloaded brain. "Is something wrong—"

"Cripes, Mom, get a grip. Nothing's wrong. I just…" He dropped onto the edge of the chaise. The hole in his jeans over his left knee was larger than she remembered. Several strands of his wheat-colored hair had escaped the rubber band holding it back and now tangled with his eyelashes. Skateboarding again, probably. She vaguely wondered if he was getting his schoolwork done, decided she was too tired to ask.

"I overreacted again, huh?" she asked, which got a smirk. "Don't take it personally. It doesn't take much to get me going these days."

"I know. That's why I…" He stopped, rubbing the back of his neck.

"Shaun…would you like to spit it out before the baby comes?"

A slanted smile far too much like his father's hitched up one side of his mouth. "Sorry. It's just, well, I've been thinking about…stuff, since Dad left." He glanced at her, as if expecting her to help him.

"And…?"

"And…I was wondering how you'd feel if…if I went up to Colorado for a while."

"Over spring break, you mean?"

He took too long to respond, and her breathing went shallow.

"No," he said at last. "To live."

Her gaze fell to the soup she knew she'd never eat now. "I see," she said quietly, then looked up. "Is this your father's idea?"

"Sorta. I mean, he said it might be one solution."

"One solution?"

"To our seeing more of each other."

Cass told herself to stay cool, not to go bonkers. Not to think ill of Blake or be angry with Shaun.

Or blame herself for screwing things up so badly.

"I know what you're thinking, Mom," Shaun said, interrupting her thoughts. "That I'm just reacting to everything that went down this past year. I swear, it has nothing to do with that. Really."

"But…it would mean leaving all your friends," she said over her trembling insides.

"Yeah, I thought of that."

Having seen the chink, she decided to probe a little more. "You never said you wanted to live with your father before this. Why now?"

The boy rose from the chaise and walked over to a chest of drawers where she kept some photos, including one of herself and Shaun when he was a baby. He picked up the photo, fingering the frame. "Dad finally said he'd like me to, for one thing," he admitted, then turned to her. "And you're going to be tied up with the new baby. I figured maybe it was just better…if you didn't have to worry about me, too."

For a couple of seconds she couldn't catch her breath. When she did, she flapped her hands at the bowl. "Shaun, take this tray away. Put the bowl down on the bathroom floor, let the animals fight it out. Then come sit."

He did as she'd asked, then perched on the edge of her bed, his expression reminiscent of someone who's just been told an enema is in his immediate future.

"Now you listen to me, young man," she said quietly. "I'm going to say my piece all at once, then you can think about it. First off, if you want to go live with your father, I'm not going to try to talk you out of it, even though everything in me is screaming to do just that. But you do it because you want to be with him, not because of some idiotic notion that this baby is going to somehow take your place in my heart, or that you would be in the way. If you leave, it would leave a hole in my life so big it would never fill up. And I'm not saying that to make you feel guilty, but only to make you understand how much you mean to me have always meant to me, and always will. So don't you ever think, not for one single second, that I don't want you around. You got that?"

Poor baby. He nodded, but she could see how hard he was fighting tears. Being a teenage boy was such a pain.

"So," she ventured. "You still want to go?"

After a long moment he nodded again, and her heart cracked a little. But she didn't let on. She'd had him for fifteen years, almost entirely to herself. She'd tried to find him a substitute father, and that had failed miserably. Now his own father wanted to make up for lost time, and she couldn't find it in herself to play the bitch and not let him. Not after all this.

"But I have to tell you," he said, "going with Dad isn't my first choice."

She frowned, puzzled. "It's not? Then what is?"

The brown eyes bounced off hers, then skittered away. "It's like you kept telling me, when it was just the two of us and I'd complain about not getting to do all the stuff all the other kids got to do. We can't always have what we want."

Before she could ask him what he meant, he pushed himself off the bed and went into the bathroom, then came back with the bowl, set it on the tray and carried it out of her bedroom, softly closing the door behind him.

"Did you hear what I said?"

Slowly Blake let his partner's face come back into focus, backdropped by the hunter-green walls of his office. He noticed the blond stubble blurring Troy's jaw, surmised the twins had once again thwarted his attempts to shave.

"Sorry," Blake said on a heavy sigh, sagging back into his leather swivel chair. Six stories below, a wet, nasty, spring snow snarled traffic and tempers, while on the other side of his office door faxes spewed, keyboards clattered, phones trilled, the mechanical medley occasionally relieved by a human cough or laugh. Blake found the constant buzz of activity a welcome respite from the relentless silence in his condo.

He swung one booted foot up onto the edge of the mammoth mahogany desk he'd found in a secondhand store last year. "Guess my mind wandered."

Troy grunted. "Your mind," he said, "has yet to roost inside this office for more than ten minutes straight since you got back. Now, I know we've always said our personal lives were personal, that they didn't belong in the office, but if you give me a clue as to why you've been on another planet this past week, I might be less predisposed to kick your butt."

That got a smile. For one thing, agreement or no, Blake and Troy were more than acquainted with each other's personal lives. In fact, Troy Lindquist had scraped Blake off a Colorado Springs bar stool ten years ago, which ignoble position Blake had assumed as a consequence of his first and final foray into drunken oblivion—an appropriate way, or so it had seemed at the time, to mark the second anniversary of his divorce. Apparently, he'd mumbled something to lead the quiet, introverted giant who'd offered to drive him home to believe that when Blake wasn't stewed, he knew something about running a business. So, instead of depositing Blake in a heap on his doorstep, Troy had dragged him to a Denny's and forced a dozen cups of black coffee down his gullet. An hour later— before Blake had totally sobered up—the smooth-talking son-of-a-gun had somehow convinced him to trade his nice, reliable track coaching job at a nearby community college for the thrill of running a defunct ice cream parlor Troy had inherited from some uncle or other.

A week of cleaning up about a million years' worth of mouse poops had thoroughly persuaded Blake of the evils of making decisions with more Jack Daniels than blood in your veins. Until he found, in the bottom drawer of an old desk in the back of the parlor, a crackly, yellowing journal with what appeared to be ice cream recipes. And with that came the sweet—literally—memories of hand-cranked ice cream on his grandmother's back porch.

And thus was Ain't It Sweet born.

Blake had never asked, and Troy had never divulged, why he happened to be in that bar that night. Just one of those things, was all. But the partnership had proved to be a strong one, both professionally and personally—even to Blake's sharing his friend's anguish when Troy's wife had died from a rare, and completely unforeseen, complication resulting from the births of their twin sons, three years before.

Still, it was a very "male" friendship, Blake supposed— lean on words, long on grunts of understanding. But they'd always demanded honesty from each other…which was exactly what the pair of incisive, blond-lashed hazel eyes boring into him from across his desk now demanded.

"I don't really want to be here," Blake admitted.

"Tell me something I don't know." Then Troy narrowed his eyes. "This have something to do with your ex?"

"Partly." He wasn't about to be that honest, to reveal he was still in love with a woman who hadn't been a part of his life in any meaningful way since their son was a toddler. "But it's not just that." He scrubbed his jaw with the heel of his hand. "It's Shaun. It hit me, hard, how I've only got a few years before he's gone, out on his own. That I've as good as missed seeing my own kid grow up." He frowned. "And if I let things go on the way they have been, that's not going to change."

After all this time, he and Troy were able to intuit each other's moves like long-term football teammates. Now Blake saw recognition flash across Troy's features as he tilted the sturdy wooden armchair onto its back legs, his massive forearms crossed over an equally massive chest. "Meaning?"

"Meaning…what do you think of relocating headquarters to Albuquerque?"

As expected, the pale-blond brows shot up a good inch. "Thanks for letting me in on your plans, pal."

"I haven't made any plans, for God's sake. And I won't do this unless we can somehow work this out. But…why are you laughing?"

"'I won't do anything unless we can work this out…*but*.'" Troy jabbed an index finger across the desk. "It's that *but* that gets mine into trouble, every time." Still chuckling, he folded his hands across his University of Minnesota sweatshirt—no dress code in this office. "So spill it. Every detail. If I hate it, you'll be the first to know."

So Blake pointed out how tired they'd both become of the Denver winters—even Troy, who'd grown up in a small town on the Canadian border. How strong Albuquerque's economy was. How Albuquerque would be the perfect place to open the frozen desserts plant they'd been talking about for the past year.

"I'd have to think about this," Troy said at last, his brows tightly drawn together.

Blake got up, walked over to the window. Rivulets of melted snow streaked down the glass, blurring the view. Inside his head, however, everything was clear. Clearer than it had been in years, in fact. "I have to go back," he said quietly, then turned to his partner. "With or without the company."

Still tilted back in the chair, Troy angled his head at Blake. "You really think you have a shot?" he asked in that gentle, right-to-the-heart-of-the-matter way he had.

"You mean, working things out with Shaun?"

"No, I don't mean Shaun at all. Oh, I'm sure you meant what you said about wanting to get to know your kid. But you could do that without uprooting yourself and the whole damn company to do it. I'm no fool, Blake. So why don't you just admit it, real slow, so you don't get the bends. You've still got feelings for your ex-wife, and you want to see if you can get back together."

Blake felt his lips tilt. "You're a pain in the can, Lindquist."

"So you've said. So? You gonna be honest or you gonna continue to play these little mind games with yourself?"

"I'm not playing any games, if that makes you feel better," Blake assured him. "In fact, it's not how I feel that's the problem. It's figuring out what to do about it." He paused. "She's not exactly interested."

Behind him he heard Troy's chair legs thud to the floor as he righted himself. Seconds later his partner joined him at the window. "Then you get her interested."

"She also just buried her second husband," Blake pointed out.

"I would think that would kind of make things easier. Extra husbands scattered about can be a real nuisance."

Blake winced, but he couldn't help the smile. "Just trying to be realistic, here."

"Screw *realistic*. Hell, Blake…if we'd been thinking *realistic* ten years ago, we wouldn't be here now, having this conversation. You gotta dream, man. Otherwise, you're doing nothing except looking down at your feet, instead of reaching for something in front of you. You think you've got a shot?"

Blake was silent for several seconds. "You don't think I'm an idiot, then?"

"Didn't say that."

He chuckled then sighed. "Right now, frankly, it's not looking good." He shrugged. "I only know I'll never be able to live with myself if I don't try."

Troy nodded, then knotted his arms across his chest again, staring out at the snow. After several seconds he said, "You're right. These winters really suck. I mean, I spend a half hour getting the boys into their snowsuits to spend about five minutes outside before they freeze their little tails off." Another chin scrape. "I'd miss the skiing, though."

"Now, see," Blake said around the smile he couldn't completely hide, "the great thing about Albuquerque is that winter stays mostly in the mountains. So you can go skiing without having to drive through snow to get to the skiing."

"Yeah?"

"Yep."

"Huh." Now Troy's hands slid down to his hips, which was his seriously considering-his-options stance. "What would I do about day care, though?"

"Rumor has it they have day care there. Most of the places even have running water and electricity."

Troy smacked Blake lightly on the back of the head before pivoting to pace to the other side of the room. At which point he pivoted again to pace back. "What about severance for anybody who doesn't want to go?"

"We could do six months, easy. Maybe even more. I checked with Alice already." Then he waited.

Troy stopped dead. "You checked with Alice? Guess-what-I-found-out-today Alice? And just when did you check with Alice?"

"Three days ago."

On a muttered cussword, Troy slid down into the chair in front of the desk, his head in his hands. "So they all know, right?"

"They all know."

Green eyes met his. "And...how many said they would go?"

A slow smile spread across Blake's lips. "All of them."

Troy swore again. "When were you planning on telling me? When I got to the office one day and no one else was here?"

"Nah. I figured I'd give you a couple of days' notice, at least." He met his friend's grimace with a grin. "It didn't hurt that this has been the worst winter in Denver's history. By the time I'd finished extolling the virtues of Albuquerque's weather, half of them had already called moving companies."

A stream of air hissed from between Troy's teeth. "Man, you're

good." He leaned back with his hands behind his head, his long legs stretched out in front of him. "So what's the plan?"

"I go back as soon as possible, scout out possible factory sites. Depending on how long it would take to set up the plant, we could be ready to go in as little as six months."

"Before next winter."

"Before next winter. Why are you looking at me like that?"

"Let me guess. You've left your ex out of this little loop of yours, too, haven't you?"

Blake rubbed his thumb and forefinger along the sides of his mouth, then clamped his arms together. "I might have."

"How about your kid?"

"He thinks I want him to move up here."

Troy squinted at Blake. "Which would not make Cass very happy, would it?"

"That's what I'm betting on."

"Thereby giving her a choice between having you around or not having her child. Man—" a half laugh "—you are the most devious human being I think I've ever met."

"This from the man who talked me into going into business with him when I didn't have full possession of my faculties."

"What can I tell you? I was desperate."

"Yeah, well, so am I, buddy." He frowned at the snow, at the city he couldn't wait to leave. "So am I."

Chapter Seven

Her sweatshirt hiked up underneath her breasts, Cass stared at her profile in the mirror, then faced front again. Honestly. From this angle, she didn't even look all that pregnant. Sideways, she stuck out clear to Santa Fe. No wonder her back hurt all the time. Perhaps it was just as well there was no man in her life at the moment. Who would want her like this?

A blush crept up her neck when she remembered her last few months with Shaun. Blake seemed to think the extra acres of skin simply meant someone had increased the size of his playground.

Muttering something very unladylike under her breath, Cass yanked down the sweatshirt over the acreage, then made her way to the kitchen. Surrounded by every bowl and mixing apparatus they owned, Towanda was putting the finishing touches on some chocolate concoction that in Cass's nonpregnant state would have turned her into a drooling fool.

Eyes the color of coffee grounds gave her the once-over. "You get any rest?"

"Some." She grabbed a glass out of the dishwasher and lumbered over to the stainless steel refrigerator for some milk, which she then forced to her lips. "The baby didn't stop moving the whole time. Were there any calls?"

"Meaning, did the store burn down without you being there? No, missy, there were no calls. So I assume it's still standing."

Cass humphed, then found herself mesmerized by this cake or whatever it was. "You're a mean, mean woman," she said, heaving herself up onto a bar stool. "You know I can't eat that."

"Who said this was for you?"

"Well, Lucille sure as hell won't touch it."

"I ain't talking about Miss Lucille, either."

"Oh," Cass said. Much to her surprise, Blake had actually kept his promise to come down for the weekend. And Lucille, bless her little heart, had insisted he have dinner with them tonight. "It's for my darling ex-husband?"

"Always said you were smart. Hey!" she erupted when Cass swiped a fingerful of frosting from the bottom of the cake. "Thought you said you couldn't eat this stuff?"

"That doesn't mean I can't fantasize." A blush threatened. She'd been doing far too much of that lately. Especially when she was asleep and helpless to prevent it. She savored the chocolate, letting it ooze off her finger and dissolve onto her tongue. "Oh, Lord, this is good. Mmm," she said, closing her eyes. "Sinful, even." Reluctantly she opened her eyes again. Yep, her life was still there, in all its muddled glory. "This one of your grandmother's recipes?"

"Uh-huh. I told Mr. Blake about it, last time he was here. Said he couldn't wait to try it."

Cass sucked on her finger for another couple of seconds, waiting until the wave of melancholia passed. They happened with such regularity these days, she paid them little mind. She removed the finger with a soft pop. "And you couldn't wait to let him, huh?"

"What can I tell you? I have a soft spot for any man who likes my cooking."

"Anybody ever tell you you're easy?"

"Not in a long, *long* time, baby," the housekeeper said on an exhaled breath. "Oh…listen. That must be them."

It was. Cass tried not to react, either to the effect Blake's low, sensuous laugh had always had on her or to Shaun's sudden and wholehearted grafting onto his father. She shouldn't resent their getting along so well, after all these years of a half-baked relationship. Not after all the grief she'd given Blake about not being more a part of his son's life. So she'd gotten her wish. So she should be happy about it. Relieved. Instead, she could only equate their new camaraderie with the fact that Shaun wouldn't have any qualms about leaving her. *That* she hadn't figured on.

But then, neither had she figured on this inexplicable re-surgence of desire for Shaun's father.

Damn hormones. Or whatever.

"I want to tell her," she heard Shaun say, right outside the kitchen door.

"Uh…I think maybe I'd better do this—" Talking on top of each other, father and son burst into the kitchen, stopping dead—and silent—when they saw Cass. Dude scrambled to his feet and bounced over to Shaun, who squatted down to fuss over him.

She fixed a neutral, hormone-free expression to her face. Never mind that her nipples lurched toward Blake like damned divining rods. "Tell me what?" she said mildly, tak-ing a sip of her milk.

Scratching the dog's exposed belly, Shaun grinned up at her. "We just came from looking at apartments."

"Apartments? For whom?"

Blake braced his hands on the other side of the island, smiling into her eyes. She glanced away, but not before she noticed the play of bunched, taut muscles underneath his T-shirt, the corded veins on his hands that seemed to positively scream, "You wanna come out and play?" to her nipples.

"For me," he said.

Well, that dried the errant thoughts right up, boy.

"Why on earth do you need an apartment, Blake?" she asked, shifting uncomfortably on the stool. She wished he'd stop looking at her that way, but then realized he was just looking at her. The "that way" part wasn't something he could help. Concentrating on the glass of milk, she slowly circled the rim with her index finger. "Even if you come down two weekends a month, wouldn't it just be cheaper to stay in a motel?"

"Dad's moving back!"

She looked at her son, then Blake, then Towanda, who seemed to be taking this all in with irritating calmness, then finally back at Blake. She felt a little dizzy. "You're *what?*"

Blake, however, had discovered the chocolate temptation on the end of island. "Is this the cake you were telling me about?" he asked, ignoring Cass.

"Sure is, baby—"

"What do you mean, you're moving *back?*"

Blake scooped up a dollop of frosting. Cass didn't miss that Towanda didn't give *him* grief. "Troy and I have decided to move Ain't It Sweet's headquarters here. Man, this is good," he said to the housekeeper. "What's that flavor?"

"Rum," she said. "In the frosting. Not flavoring. The real stuff."

Cass turned on Towanda, momentarily derailed. "You let me ingest rum in my condition?"

"I didn't *let* you do anything. You sorta helped yourself, if memory serves. Besides, there's not enough booze in the whole cake to light up a bug. Just enough to give it some pizzazz."

"Your grandmother have any more recipes?"

"Forget the damn cake!" Cass said, smacking the counter. "And no, Shaun," she said over the kid's chuckle, "just because you heard me swear doesn't mean you can." She turned her gaze to Blake's, ignoring her son's mirth. "What do you mean, you're moving headquarters here? Isn't that going to put a lot of people out of work in Denver?"

Blake took another swipe of frosting, which at last earned him a smack with a dish towel. "Oh, we'll still keep a factory there, but most of the office staff is only too happy to relocate. In any case, it was the only way I could figure to be closer to Shaun, other than having him come live with me for a while." She saw his downcast face when Towanda preempted his next swipe by removing the cake to the far counter and plunking a cover over it. The cow eyes drifted—reluctantly, she thought—back to hers. "I didn't think you'd like that very much, though."

She met his gaze as steadily as he met hers, her heartbeat anything but steady. "No. No, I wouldn't have."

"Well, I weighed all my options, discussed it with Troy and finally realized this is where I need to be."

"You're willing to disrupt your life, just to be with Shaun?"

She couldn't read the expression in his eyes, but figured she'd gotten out of practice. "Doing what's right isn't a disruption, Cass."

It was stupid, this odd thud of disappointment in her chest that he'd moved back only for Shaun's sake. Especially considering how hard she'd worked at becoming impervious to thuds of disappointment, odd or otherwise. And anyway, she reminded herself, she and Blake were completely incompatible. Well, except for the sex thing. And even though the sex thing had been pretty damn good, that wasn't enough to risk another mangled heart, she reminded herself. She'd had enough of those for one lifetime, she *really* reminded herself.

Men simply didn't need women the way women have been led to believe they need men, a basic fact that had taken an extraordinarily long time to penetrate her thick skull. You let yourself fall in love, begin to think you can depend on a man, only to discover he's never around when you really need him. Not in the way that really counts. So what's the point?

As one, all her hormones raised their hands.

Ginger bounced into the kitchen, sliding across the tile floor. Cass gathered the furball onto her lap and began scratching her behind her ears. the kitten immediately settled in, her tiny motor going a mile a minute; she smelled like Blake, dammit. The urge to cry, Cass told herself, was nothing more than a combination of stress, exhaustion, and those stinkin', rotten hormones.

Although Blake's relentless scrutiny wasn't helping matters any.

"So," she said at last, daring to look up at him. "You're back."

"It looks that way," he said, giving her one of those smiles that made her want to scream and run as far as she could in the opposite direction. Which, in her present ungainly condition, would be about two blocks. Maybe three if she didn't get winded.

Things were not getting better.

Lucille stood in the middle of Blake's soon-to-be living room, one hand on her hip.

"So," she said, "you really want to live here?"

"What's wrong with it?"

"What's wrong with what?"

"The apartment."

"Did I say anything was wrong with the apartment?"

"Isn't…that what we're talking about?"

"Hell, no. Like I could care about this apartment."

Blake was lost. But he figured Lucille would eventually reach out with those claws of hers and yank him back into whatever conversation she was having, so he decided to wait it out.

The weather had warmed sufficiently for her to exchange her baggy sweaters for baggy knit tops, though skintight tights or leggings or whatever they called them these days were still part of the charming ensemble. Today's were purple, with little sparkly threads woven in. Although a silver-and-turquoise squash-blossom necklace that weighed more than she did plastered her black top to her chest, the neckline was too wide to stay up on both skinny shoulders at once, which meant one skinny shoulder was hanging out for God and everybody to see. Blake decided he'd rather not know what sort, if any, undergarments she wore underneath.

In wooden platform sandals that looked too heavy for her feet to lift ("Would you believe it," she'd said when he'd commented on them earlier, "I bought these in 1976, and here they are, right back in style! Isn't that something?") Lucille clumped into the blandest kitchen in decorating history and began inspecting cabinets. "My comment," she now directed into the depths of the refrigerator, "has to do with you." She twisted around, wrinkling her nose. "What's that smell?"

"What smell?"

"That smell…you can't smell it? It's terrible, that smell. Like something upchucked behind your stove. Or died, maybe." She stretched as far as she could go, but was still too short to see behind the appliance.

To humor her, Blake walked over, took a peek. "There's nothing there. And I still don't smell anything."

Suddenly she turned around and glared up at him. "So. What are you going to do about it?"

Blake frowned. "I told you, I can't smell anything—"

"Oh, for Pete's sake—who's talking about a smell? Cass, I'm talking about. Since you're moving down here, I assume you have some sort of plan?"

He wasn't ready to talk about this with anyone. Anyone other than Troy, at least. If things didn't go the way he hoped, he preferred to come off looking like an idiot to as few people as possible. So, for now, it was best to play it cool. "I'm moving back because of my son."

The way Lucille narrowed her eyes shot the playing-it-cool idea to hell and back. Several times. "Please," she puffed out between shimmering lips. "Do I look like I was born yesterday?"

He swallowed a smile. Decided to give dissemblance one more try. "It's true. Cass wants nothing to do with me, except where Shaun is concerned. Why would you assume I have some sort of plan?"

Out of nowhere, a lethally sharp fingernail jabbed into his chest. Repeatedly. "Because—" jab "—I'm not blind. Because—" jab, jab "—I know you're still in love with her. Because—"

He sidestepped the next jab. It was like being interrogated by a woodpecker.

"And here I thought you just wanted to see my new apartment." Somehow, he managed not to rub at his chest, where he could feel a veritable mountain range of tiny, crescent-shaped welts already rising.

"Right. Like I've never seen cheap light fixtures before." She heaved out a sigh which smelled faintly of peppermint TicTacs, then slanted him a heavy-lidded glance. "So?"

He tried to stare her down for several seconds, then finally yielded to a resigned chuckle.

That was all she needed.

"Yee-ha!" she exploded, slapping her thigh. "Now we're getting somewhere." Her motion had made the neckline shift to expose the other shoulder. She yanked it up, only to ignore it when it slipped again. Spying a window seat in the breakfast nook, she clomped over to it, then sat. "So get over here, hot stuff, and tell me what you're thinking. Then *I'll* tell you what I'm thinking, and we'll see what we got."

He angled his head at her. "Are you saying...you want me to get together with your son's wife?"

"Preferably before the baby comes," she said, then patted the window seat. "So sit, and we'll talk. What could it hurt?"

Rubbing his chest, Blake quickly realized he had little choice but to play along. The woman wasn't any bigger than a minute, but those nails of hers were deadly.

The following Monday the house sold. Cass was stunned. And extremely relieved, since that had been the only offer. The buyer, C.J. said, hadn't haggled over the price, and said he'd be interested in taking whatever furnishings off her hands she didn't want, since he was moving in without a lot of his own stuff.

"Who on earth—"

C.J. shrugged as he pushed a sheaf of papers across the dining table toward her, allowing a good-natured grin for Fred's attempts at ambushing them as they made their short trip. "I don't actually know," he said, scooping the kitten into his arms and scratching him behind the ears. "A company bought it.

The man who made the offer was only acting as a representative." At her raised eyebrows, he explained, "Tax write-off, I imagine."

She nodded, then glanced at the top of the contract. LC Enterprises, she read. "Oh, well. What do I care, right? Money's money." She spent another few minutes skimming the document, then signed.

"Now for the bad news."

She met the gentle blue eyes, thinking idly they seemed awfully flat for someone seemingly so on top of his game. "Bad news?"

"The buyer wants to take possession in three weeks."

"Three weeks?" Her eyebrows shot up. "Good Lord—I haven't even started looking for a place yet. And all this packing…"

C.J. took the papers from her, gave her a smile. "I suggest you hire someone to do the packing for you." His eyes dropped to her middle, then returned to her face. "You shouldn't be doing that now, anyway."

The thought of how expensive that would be made her slightly ill. "Nonsense. We moved twice when I was carrying Shaun. If I did it then, I can do it now. I'm much more concerned about finding someplace to put all our things *in* once they're packed."

"Don't be. It's a buyers' market. We'll find something, don't you worry."

Cass sighed, realizing it was time to come clean. Clean*er*, anyway. The second mortgage had seriously eroded the house's equity. What was left would provide a decent down payment, if she could secure a mortgage. But with her other bills, even her otherwise adequate income from the shop wasn't going to be enough…

"Cass?"

She scraped up the nerve to meet C.J.'s concerned gaze.

"Look," he said, "someone at Security Mortgage owes me a favor. I'll have a courier run the paperwork over today. I'll get you the forms to fill out, and we'll get the ball rolling. In the meantime, I'll line up several properties to show you—"

Her slightly panicked laugh stopped him in his tracks.

"Oh, C.J.," she said, shaking her head. "I'm afraid I haven't been totally honest with you, I guess because I kept hoping for some sort of miracle. The truth is, only a fool would lend me the money to buy another house right now. It's not even worth putting through my application."

"Now, you never know until you try. And I'm a great string puller…."

"I'm afraid it would have to be one helluva tough string." She struggled to her feet; the agent followed suit. "But you can tell the buyer he can have the house in three weeks if he wants. We'll be out of here."

Her gaze swept the room. Except for her clothes, her books and her son, there was nothing of hers, of *her,* in this house, anywhere. She wouldn't miss it. And, frankly, she couldn't wait to get her own things out of storage. Neither could Lucille, she suspected. She extended her hand, meeting the agent's warm handshake firmly, confidently.

"Thank you for everything. You have no idea what a relief this is."

"She didn't suspect?"

"I doubt it," C.J. replied on the other end of the line. "Although, I think closing in three weeks threw her for a minute."

Blake hooked his hand on his hip, staring out his window at the early rush hour traffic whizzing past on I-40. He had to get out of this apartment soon, before the carbon monoxide did him in, if for no other reason. "I figured it was better for her to make the move now, before she hit her last month."

"What do you want to do with the house?"

"Sit on it for a bit. If it goes back on the market too soon, it'll look suspicious."

"Good point. But I wouldn't wait too long, if I were you. A month, tops. My indicators tell me we're in for a market downturn." C.J. paused. "And you paid top dollar for this baby."

Blake smiled into the phone. "I know that. It's not a problem. If I sell at a loss, I can always take it off my taxes."

There was a deep chuckle on the other end of the line. "I sure hope she's worth it."

"You and me both," Blake said on a sigh, which got another laugh. "So, when are you showing her other houses?"

After a too-long pause, C.J. said, "I'm not. She's looking for an apartment."

"An apartment?" Blake switched the phone to his other ear. "With three other people?"

"My guess is," the agent said carefully, "she's in hotter water than she's letting on."

"In other words, there won't be anything left over after the sale."

"I...really couldn't say."

Blake knew C.J. was already straining client confidentiality to the limit, so didn't push it. "Hell. She'll never find anything large enough." He thought for a moment, then released his breath on a whoosh. "You free tomorrow morning?"

"Let me check...yeah, after eleven. What do you have in mind?"

"Oh, something with four or five bedrooms, a mother-in-law quarters, a large yard..."

"Mister," the agent said around a deep chuckle, "I like the way you do business."

Blake grunted out a sigh. "Let's just hope somebody else feels the same way, or my butt's going to be in one hot sling."

"At least you'll have your choice of slings to put it into," C.J. pointed out.

A thought from which Blake took little comfort.

Cass let out a startled yip when she swung open the front door to find Blake standing with his finger extended to poke the doorbell.

"Now *there's* a great way to bring on early labor," she managed over her thudding heart. "What are you doing here, anyway? Aren't you supposed to be working or something?"

He shrugged. "Thanks to the miracles of modern communication technology, I'm done for the morning." With an insouciant, lazy smile, he leaned against her doorjamb, his arms casually tucked across an array of well-worn denim. In his boots and jeans, he looked far more like an out-of-place cowboy than an ice cream tycoon. An out-of-place cowboy with mischief blazing in those warm brown eyes. "Heard tell you were fixin' to go lookin' for apartments, ma'am," he drawled. "Figured maybe I'd tag along, if that's all right."

He looked too good. Sounded too good, dumb western accent and all. Smelled way too good. She backed up a step, not even bothering to ask where he got his information. This one had *Lucille* written all over it.

"I'm perfectly capable of apartment hunting on my own, thank you. Besides, this is completely unnecessary. I know we agreed to mind our manners around Shaun, but Shaun isn't here." She hitched her shoulder bag into place. "Let's not push this friendship business, okay?"

"You know, sunshine, if I didn't know better, I'd think you were afraid to be alone with me."

"Don't be ridiculous. Of course I'm not afraid to be with you—"

"Good. Because I'm not letting you traipse all over town in this heat, that pregnant, on your own."

"Excuse me? You're not going to *let* me?"

"Hey, I've watched you go through this before," he replied without a trace of repentance. "When it comes to taking care of yourself, you've got less sense than a mule. I don't know where you got this notion that you're somehow invincible, but you're not. Especially not now."

"Blake, I'm perfectly okay. And I've still got nearly eight weeks yet, for goodness' sake." She tried storming past him, only to yelp when Blake swung her back around. "You know, for somebody who says he's so worried about my condition, you're not exactly helping things, here—"

"You can sit in the car while I scout out places. If I think something's a possibility, I can call you."

"If *you* think something's a possibility…? What are you, my father?"

The words were no sooner out of her mouth than she reached behind her to steady herself on the door frame. When the brief wave of dizziness passed, she blinked to see Blake glowering at her.

"What was your blood pressure reading the last time you went in for a checkup?"

"What's that got to do with anything?"

"A lot. I know it ran high with Shaun, and you're much more stressed this time. What was it?"

It had been borderline, true. The midwife had sternly told her to not overdo it, or it might get worse. But damned if she was going to tell Nurse Nancy that. "It was fine. Now, if you don't mind, I've got ten apartments to see before Shaun gets home—"

"Not without me, you don't," Blake said, ushering her out

the door. She dug in her heels so hard Blake's choice was to drag her down the stairs or stop. He stopped. *"What?"*

To her immense satisfaction, she detected actual irritation in his voice. "Why do you give a damn about how I am? Our lives took separate paths years ago. Why now, do you care?"

"I told you. I never stopped caring. I'm not one of those people who can share what we shared, then simply pretend it never happened."

She barked out a laugh. "Aren't you? Isn't that exactly what you did?"

"No," he said with enough oomph to actually make her back up a little. "I was never even tempted to pretend it—us—never happened. Not even at the beginning. Okay, yeah, I botched things up, big-time," he said when she let out an exasperated breath. "I admit that. And, yeah, I suppose you could say I've got a real long learning curve, so it's not as if I can blame you for being skeptical about my intentions now. If it were me, I'd feel the same way."

And if she wasn't careful, he was going to slip past her defenses. Just as he always could. "So I repeat, why the change of heart now? I mean, if you're going to drive me nuts, I'd at least like to understand the motivation behind it."

He looked at her long and hard. Then, on a rush of breath, he said, "Because your husband's death jolted me into realizing how suddenly life and opportunities can be ripped away. Because I realized I'd spent twelve years staying out of your way, instead of figuring out how to at least make up for the fact that our marriage didn't work. For Shaun's sake, especially."

"That's all well and good," she said. "But the fact remains—"

"That you don't want anyone to help you. Yeah, I got it. Hell, in my lucid moments, I can even understand why. But you gotta admit, you could use a leg up right now. And if you're too stubborn to accept help for your own sake, then, dammit, accept it for Shaun's. And for that baby inside you. Pride's all well and good, and no one's more impressed with how well you've done without me—" his mouth tilted into a rueful smile "—than I am. But stressing yourself out isn't going to do your children any good, now, is it? So, forgive me, but no way am I going to stand around and watch you run yourself into the ground, just because you hate my guts, when one of those children happens to be mine."

"I don't—" She caught herself, realized she wasn't breathing, she was so angry. Angry at his impudence, yes. But angrier that he was right. She *had* let her pride cloud her reason, convinced that letting her guard down for a single second would mean giving up her hard-won ability—tenuous though it might be—to function completely on her own. Because he was dead wrong about one thing—there was no way he could understand why it was so dangerous to let herself depend on him, or anybody else. Not now, not ever again. Oh, *God*—she just wished he would *go away,* already.

Mainly because she didn't want him to go away at all.

Brother. This modern-woman stuff was a real pain in the patoot.

She realized Blake was watching her. Waiting for a reaction. She filled her lungs with air, then slowly released it. "Okay, fine. I suppose I have been a bit stubborn."

"Just a tad."

"And you're right—"

"Was that a wince I saw when you said that?"

She swung her purse at him, but he dodged it.

"You're right," she continued, glaring at him. "I really haven't been thinking about the kids. I mean, I have, but…"

"It's okay, sunshine, I understand. All those hormones have short-circuited your brain."

Cass swung her purse at him again, this time inflicting a glancing blow to his upper arm. The bum laughed, then slipped one hand in the crook of her elbow to begin leading her slowly down the stairs. The heat from his touch, his scent, did nothing to help her blood pressure. "You sit. I'll drive. I'll look. You say yes or no."

She grunted. As if the man would understand "no" if it broadsided him with a two-by-four.

That was close. And, if he did say so himself, that last bit—making her feel guilty about the potential harmful effects her actions might have on her children—was a stroke of genius. Since it was completely true, however, Blake didn't feel even a single twinge of guilt himself. Even if his skin was still clammy from the sweat he'd broken out into while pulling off this little coup.

He should have known she wasn't going to simply let him whisk her away. Cass didn't let anyone simply do anything. Especially whisking. But he hadn't expected to be put on the spot about his motives. Which, at this point, were beginning to get a little…complicated.

For centuries it had been an accepted fact that men's brains primarily resided in an area of their anatomy far south of their skulls. He didn't doubt that most women didn't much cotton to this setup, but the vast majority of them probably accepted it, and, with their superior feminine brains, lodged as they were quite snugly where they were supposed to be, simply learned to work with what they were given. So women coped and men did what came naturally, and all was cool.

Then someone decided men needed to evolve, and life as most men knew it was doomed. No longer could a man declare his love for a woman simply because hormones surged hither and yon in her presence. There had to be more. Love, men were told, was an emotional reaction, not a physical one, which left many men standing around scratching their... heads, wondering what the hell all these People Who Knew were talking about.

Blake, however, had always taken pride in his ability, from the time he was fifteen, to distinguish between lust and love. Not that he hadn't taken advantage of whatever came his way from time to time. But he'd always known the difference. Always.

Until now.

Okay, so it had been a while. A long while. Still, he couldn't remember the last time a woman's scent, for God's sake, was enough to make his eyes glass over.

Yes, he could. Only one woman had ever affected him like that. And the woman—not to mention her blasted scent—sat barely two feet away from him.

He wriggled carefully behind the wheel, trying to somehow adjust the front seam of his jeans without being noticed.

"You okay?" Cass asked.

So much for that.

"It's the heat." Well, it *was* warm. At least seventy-something. And seventy-something inside a car, especially in Albuquerque, translates to hot. "Everything seems...tight."

"Yeah, I'm a little warm, too. Maybe you should turn on the air-conditioning?"

"Oh. Yeah. Right." He punched it on, directing one vent to his face, the other to his crotch. "That too much air on you?"

"No," she said toward the windshield. "It's fine."

He let his eyes wander to her middle, cursing under his breath at his reaction. Pregnant women were the sexiest things on earth. Cass was the sexiest thing on earth. Put 'em together...

His hand tightened around the steering wheel as he bumped up the air-conditioning a notch.

Chapter Eight

Ten apartments, every one either too small, too expensive, too inconvenient or just plain butt ugly. Hot and disgusted, Cass awkwardly climbed back into the car—Blake had to give her a boost, no less, which really fried her clams—crossing her arms over her undulating midsection. Her T-shirt and undies had fused to her damp skin, her ankles looked inflated, and she felt as if the baby was going to momentarily erupt from her navel like one of the creatures in *Alien*.

And Blake had been so patient for the past three hours she was ready to deck him one.

Speaking of whom, he climbed into the car beside her, twisted the key in the ignition and said, "Are you as miserable as you look?"

"For crying out loud, Blake! Would you stop being so damn *kind!*"

He calmly plucked a tissue out of a mangled box he'd scavenged from underneath the front seat and handed it to her. She eyed it warily for a moment, shook out the dust, then wiped her eyes and blew her nose. "Can we go home now?" she asked.

"Yes, ma'am."

Something about that "yes, ma'am" put her on immediate alert.

Twenty minutes later they pulled into a cottonwood-shaded driveway in an older part of town, splinters of sunlight dancing like fireflies on the iron-gated adobe wall enclosing the front yard. Edging the wall, hundreds of white tulips shuddered in the breeze, sunk in a sea of deep purple grape hyacinths. A wisteria in heavy, clove-scented bloom dripped over the wall from the other side, tangling with a rambling rose just beginning to leaf out.

Without even seeing the house on the other side of the wall, Cass knew how much it would be like the one they used to talk about having someday, when they were first married and living in that godawful studio apartment.

"What's this?" Cass asked, hardly daring to breathe.

"A house?"

"Funny. I mean, why did you bring me here?"

"To torment you."

That got a raised eyebrow. It also got her out of the car. But then, she could no more have resisted looking inside than she could have resisted giving birth to this baby when the time came. She briefly wondered how Blake came to have the key, decided she didn't care.

She was in love before she even set foot inside the tiled entryway. And every step further into the house she took only made things worse. Wood floors, mullioned windows that probably leaked like sieves, troweled plaster walls, a claw-foot tub in one of the three Mexican-tiled baths. A mother-in-law quarters for Lucille; a kitchen to die for; a beamed family room with a stone fireplace; and a walled, shaded yard perfect for puppies with basketball-player sized feet. And a baby who'd love the swing set she'd put right over there....

"Why did you bring me here?" she asked through a clogged throat.

"I said, to torment you."

"Well, it's working. I can't afford this, Blake."

"You don't even know what the price is."

"It doesn't matter. I'll never get a mortgage. I already checked. Why do you think I've been looking at apartments? Hell, I can't even afford to *rent* a house, let alone buy one."

In the dining room, Blake walked over to the oversize patio door, sliding it open. Birdsong filled the room. "Did you see the mother-in-law quarters for Lucille?"

"Of course I saw them—"

"And I thought that end room would be perfect for Shaun."

"Oh, he'd love it, but—"

"And the dog would go nuts in this yard, wouldn't he?"

"He'd think he'd died and gone to doggy heaven. Blake, you're not listening. I can't buy this house. No matter how perfect it is."

Then the tears came, and with them, the anger she'd been trying to keep at bay for three weeks. At Alan, at Blake, at life, at herself. She was doing her best, but her best wasn't cutting it. And she wasn't feeling well, and she didn't know how she was going to muddle through, and *damn* but it would be easy to simply give up and let someone else take care of her.

To let Blake take care of her.

When he gathered her into his arms, she didn't resist. She was tired and unhappy and—if she admitted it, which she was—frightened, and, just for a minute, it felt good to let someone else be the strong one. Just for a minute...

She was ten feet deep into the kiss before she even knew what she was doing. What he was doing.

What *they* were doing.

Twelve years vanished—poof!—just like that. Her arms entwined around his neck, even though she had to sort of shift sideways to get close to him, and she heard herself sigh as he worked a magic with his mouth she'd thought she'd forgotten and instantly realized she'd never forgotten at all. And, oh, how wonderful it felt, to be kissed, to be held.

To be cared about, on whatever level.

To be wanted. Oh, yes, she had no doubt he wanted her, although she was still a little shaky on the *why.* He might even believe he loved her, but she wasn't that far gone as to believe it, too. Nor, she thought as he came up for air only to possess her mouth again, was she going to let things go that far. Still, just for the moment it was nice…

"Say the word, and the house is yours," he murmured into her hair.

She froze. Then pulled back. Well, as far back as her extended figure would let her. Her lips were stinging, and she realized to her utter amazement how aroused she was. Which might have had something to do with the fact that, somehow, he'd managed to get his thigh between her legs. No mean feat considering she was wearing a midcalf-length jumper. "And, um, what word is that?"

"Yes."

It took a good five seconds for her fogged brain to process what he was talking about. The instant it did, though, fury boiled up from somewhere underneath the baby she carried, blasting the arousal to kingdom come. A screeched *"What?"* erupted from her throat as she rammed both fists into his chest with enough force to send him careening backward into the island.

"Good Lord, woman! You been working out or something?"

"You're asking me to *marry* you?"

He was massaging his hip where it had made contact with the counter. "Seemed to make as much sense as anything else I could come up with, seeing as I didn't think you'd be amenable to my just *buying* the house for you."

"You got *that* right—"

"And, anyway, it seems kinda dumb for us to keep up two households in the same town."

A headache tried to surface, right behind her eyes. "Blake, forgive me if I got this wrong…but didn't we get divorced because we *couldn't* live together?"

"Nah," he said, plowing over her objection. "The way I see it, we split up because we were young and stupid. We're older now. More able to work around little problems like incompatibility."

All she could do was stare at him. "Let me get this straight," she said, her words ringing in the empty room. "You want to set up housekeeping with a teenager, your extremely pregnant ex-wife, and an eighty-year-old woman, who, as it happens, is the mother of your ex-wife's second husband?"

"Yep."

She rolled her eyes, then winced as her back protested standing for so long. "I gotta sit down. Somewhere." Her head spinning and aching and buzzing, she made her way toward the family room and the hearth in front of the fireplace, only to realize she'd break her neck—if not her can—if she tried to sit down. Blake read her mind, grabbing her elbows in order to lower her gently into place. Unfortunately, he sat beside her, which was when she realized she was now his captive audience. Since, now that she was down, no way was she getting up. Not on her own steam, anyway.

"I've been mulling this over since…for a while," he was saying, and she realized she might as well listen. "Think about it. Shaun's only going to be around for a few more years, right?"

She nodded, studying her swollen ankles.

"I think he should have as much of both of us as he can, don't you?"

"But that doesn't mean—"

"Besides, you could use a father for little snicklefritz there."

Her head swung around. "You're not serious?"

"Somehow, that's what I thought you'd say."

"With good reason! Like you did such a bang-up job with your own son, you think you're the perfect candidate to raise someone else's?"

Her low blow apparently bounced right off. She must be losing her touch.

"You know it's a boy?" Blake said gently.

"Yes." She sniffed. "His name's Jason."

"Good name."

"You're trying to distract me."

"Is it working?" he asked with a slight grin.

"Oh, Lord." The sound that finally worked its way out of her mouth was half laugh, half sigh. "You're absolutely nuts, you know that?"

"Maybe. But I'd also like to think I'm a helluva lot smarter than I was at twenty-five." He licked his lower lip, then peered out from beneath his lashes at her. "That I'd make a much better daddy than I did then, too."

"For God's sake, Blake…he's not yours. Why would you—"

"Care? Maybe for the same reason you so obviously care about Lucille. Or Wanda, for that matter. Because that's what life handed you, and because sometimes you don't need a reason to love somebody. Just their being part of your life is enough."

"Isn't that a trifle simplistic?"

"And maybe the world would be a little less screwed up if more folks stopped trying to complicate things so much."

Too worn-out to argue, she went silent. Bad move, but whatcha gonna do?

"Think about it," he persisted. "About what it's going to be like in a few weeks, once the baby gets here."

"You're not going to give up, are you?"

"Nope." He paused. "I don't do that anymore."

A tiny, vulnerable part of her ached to believe him. The bigger, hardened part of her, however, knew better. "I'm not going to be alone, you know."

"Lucille's not going to get up at three in the morning, Cass. Neither is Shaun. Wanda's only going to be around during the day, right?"

"Well, that's all true, I suppose, but—"

"So I could help."

Her buns were going numb on the bricks. She tried to shift, but it didn't do any good. "I can't marry you, Blake."

"Why not?"

She gawked at him. "I can't believe you're asking that. For one thing, we tried that already. And I, for one, am not overly fond of déjà vu situations. For another thing, how am I going to explain to the mother of my second husband—who hasn't been dead a month—that I'm remarrying my first husband? For another thing, what makes you think I'd be even remotely interested in sharing my life, let alone my bed, with you again?"

He had the nerve to grin at her. "For one thing," he said, counting on his fingers, "I'm a firm believer in the if-at-first-you-don't-succeed philosophy of life. Second, Lucille thinks this is a great idea—close your mouth, you'll catch flies."

She clamped shut her mouth.

"And third, you didn't seem any too repulsed by that kiss a few minutes ago."

The blush shot clear up from her toes.

"Yeah," he said. "That's what I thought."

"Fine. So I got turned on. It happens. I still can't marry you."

"Oh, yeah?" He leaned back on his elbow, flicking dust off his knee. Pinned her with a cocky glance. "And where are you going to live? You know you'll never find an apartment large enough." One hand swept out toward the empty room. "But here's this house…"

"You're trying to *blackmail* me?"

"I prefer to think of it as trying to save your tuchus, as Lucille would say."

She rammed her arms together over her middle, opened her mouth—

"Uh, uh, uh…" she heard behind her. "There you go again."

"There I go again, what? I haven't said anything."

"Darlin', I'm the world's expert on body language." He skimmed two fingers down her arm; to her annoyance, she shivered. "Especially *your* body language, which is as eloquent as it gets." Suddenly she didn't know what to do with her arms. Blake chuckled, then said, "You really have to do something about this pride of yours, you know? Now come on, honey—you really think Lucille and Shaun are going to be happy crammed into a tiny apartment? And where are you going to put the baby?"

"The baby can sleep with me."

"You went nuts when Shaun was in the room with us. Every time he moved, you were wide awake."

This was true. But it was also true that marrying Blake—again—wasn't the right solution to her dilemma. The easiest solution, maybe, on the surface. But not the right one. And the longer she stayed in this house, the harder it was going to be to convince herself she was making a decision based on prudence rather than desperation.

Her face stinging, she struggled to her feet and out to the kitchen, Blake close on her heels. She snatched her purse off the kitchen counter and headed for the front door, but Blake grabbed her, easily, before she'd gotten five feet. "You haven't given me an answer," he said, his breath caressing her cheek.

"Then, since you obviously haven't been listening too carefully, let me spell it out for you. *N-o.* No way, uh-uh, over my dead body, no. Is that clear enough for you?"

"Not even for this house?"

"Not even for Kensington Palace, a live-in masseur and a lifetime supply of chocolate mousse cheesecake."

How had his hand landed on the small of her back? Damn him. He knew good and well she had this major erogenous zone right there, and...oh! Oh...hell...

She shifted, trying to get away from his touch, but he'd wedged her between a low wall in the entry, the door and his body.

"Not even for this?" he whispered, and she realized his pupils were too dark for the amount of light coming into the house.

"How can you want me?" she asked, bracing her hands against those rock-hard shoulders. Frankly, she was more amazed than provoked, which was going some, considering how ticked off she was. "I'm fat, waterlogged, a poor risk, and I'm not sure that I don't hate your guts."

"Guess I've always been a sucker for waterlogged, gut-hating women." Her hands on his shoulders notwithstanding, his lips found their way to the side of her neck. So, since he didn't get the message the first time, she hauled off and slugged him in the arm.

"Ow," Blake said, rubbing his arm. But grinning. "You know, I never realized you had this violent streak."

"You bring out the best in me," she retorted, then took a deep breath and let 'er rip. "I'm not marrying you, I'm not taking your money or your house or your sympathy. You had your opportunity once, and you blew it. I'm not putting myself in that position again. Is that clear?"

Finally he backed away. "Perfectly." But she did not like the look in his eyes. At all. Damn. If that look had been there twelve years ago—

But it hadn't. And she had no way of knowing how long it would stay, even now. Well, honey, it had only taken a lifetime, but she'd finally learned her lesson.

"Please take me home, before..." She caught herself.

"Before...?" A hopeful grin curved his lips.

"Before Shaun gets there," she finished.

But once in the car, Blake seemed to be in no hurry to get going. Instead, he shifted to look at her, one arm propped on the steering wheel. "Okay, so maybe the marriage proposal was a little extreme. Hell, if I were you, I sure wouldn't be swooning at my feet, either. But I'm buying the house, anyway."

She nearly laughed. "Blake, for heaven's sake...what on earth are you going to do with a place this big?"

On an exhaled breath, his gaze drifted back out the windshield, where it remained fixed on the house for several seconds before he said softly, "You're real good at keeping your thoughts to yourself, but your face betrays you, every time. So I knew exactly how you felt about this place from the moment we walked inside." His eyes veered back to hers. "I felt the same way. God, Cass..." He leaned forward, crossing both arms over the steering wheel, every muscle in his face taut. "I don't think I even realized how sick to death I was of living in apartments and condos until I walked out into that backyard and caught myself getting excited at the idea of messing around in the dirt and planting stuff."

She had to laugh. "You? Planting stuff?"

For the first time since she could remember, his grin wasn't cocky. "Lightning might not strike often, but it does strike. And, anyway, I need someplace big enough for Shaun to bring over his friends, if he wants to. And the dog, since I doubt you'd be real happy about looking after the mutt when Shaun's with me."

"Wow." Cass turned away, as if that would somehow allay the weird ache in her chest. "You've really thought of everything."

"Hell, no, not by a long shot." After a long moment he added, "But I'm just saying, if the apartment thing doesn't work out, for whatever reason..." He twisted the key in the ignition, looked over at her. "There's still a place here for you. For all of you."

"What am I going to do with you?" she said on an exhaled breath.

"Nothing, apparently," he said, then put the car in Reverse.

As they pulled out of the drive, she noticed a bank of budded-out irises along the side of the garage. She wondered what color they were.

"What are you, *crazy?*"

Both kittens jumped, Dude growled, and Cass shaved another few months off her rapidly dwindling lifespan as Lucille swept into her bedroom in a flash of vibrantly flowered nylon. The room instantly reeked of permanent solution and about a quart of moisturizer.

"Cripes, Cille—ever hear of knocking?"

Her mother-in-law batted the air with one hand, shuffling across the floor in gold leather ballerina flats. With a huff, she planted herself on the edge of Cass's bed, gathering a wriggling Fred onto her lap. "Give me one good reason why you turned down Blake's proposal."

Cass slammed shut the book she was reading. The kittens jumped again.

"And you know about this how?"

"I asked, he told. Well?"

Honestly. "Give *me* one good reason why I shouldn't have."

"Mother-in-law quarters."

"I'm not going to marry a man because of a house, for God's sake."

"There could be worse reasons."

"Fine. Then *you* marry him."

"Believe me, if he were Jewish…" She sighed. "And there was something else. Oh, right—he didn't ask me. He asked *you.* He said he even offered the house by itself, no strings— or rings—attached."

"And you believed him?"

The old woman's mouth flatlined. "I'm guessing you didn't."

Cass released a long, guilt-ridden breath. "You really don't want to move into an apartment, do you?"

"With three other people, two cats and a dog? What do you think?"

"I thought we agreed—"

"To make the best of things. I know, I know." Then her eyes slitted. "But the best of things just got better, if I'm not mistaken, except Miss High-and-Mighty, here, is refusing to take the hand that somebody's trying to deal her!"

Cass opened her mouth, only to close it again, propping her book on top of her belly in what she knew would be a futile attempt to cut off any further conversation.

And sure enough, a red claw hooked the top of the book and yanked it down. "Cassie. Blake's a good man. A kind man. And he obviously wants to do the right thing. So what was so wrong with him, you couldn't work it out before?"

Back up went the book. "And since this is personal business between Blake and me," Cass said, calmly turning a page she hadn't yet read, "why do you care?"

This time Lucille wrenched the book out of Cass's hands and tossed it over her shoulder, where it bounced off the carpet. "Since your accepting his offer or not means the difference between cramming all my stuff into a twelve-foot-square room and having my own quarters, trust me, I care. But, trust me again—even if we were staying here, or about to move into a mansion, for God's sake, I'll still be asking you this question." She leaned forward. "You were in love with him once, right?"

"Yes, but that—"

"And you're still in love with him, aren't you?"

"I loved your son, Cille—"

A single, choice epithet shot out from candy-apple-red lips. "Please. I don't sleep well at night. I wander around a lot. How many nights, in my meanderings, did I find one or the other of you up all hours, fiddling at your computers? This is a couple in love, who never sleep together? I'm beginning to wonder if this is the postman's baby."

"Lucille!"

"Okay, so not really. But once the baby was conceived, the sex stopped, didn't it?"

Cass flushed up to her roots, stroking the purring Ginger for several seconds before her voice was steady enough to speak. "It was a dry spell, Lucille, that's all. All marriages go through that from time to time."

"Sure they do. But not when you've only been married a few months. Alan's father and I, we couldn't keep our hands off each other. *We* were in love," she added, wagging a finger before reaching over to take Cass's hand in hers. "I had such high hopes, when I first saw the two of you together. That, somehow, you'd bring my son back to me." She pressed a hand to her chest, her mouth flattened. "The son who'd once made me so proud. So it broke my heart, seeing the way he treated you, those last few months. You wouldn't believe the fights we had about you...."

"Fights?"

Lucille nodded, the rollers bobbing. "When you weren't around. Ignoring me was one thing, but ignoring you...no."

"It wasn't as if he was mean to me—"

"No, he simply wasn't *anything* to you, was he?"

After a long pause Cass shook her head. Lucille checked her watch. "I've got five minutes, tops, before I have to neutralize, but..." She reached out and wrapped her bony arms around Cass's shoulders; on a sigh, Cass gave up. "Oh, sweetheart," the old woman said, "you deserved so much more than that son of mine was willing to give." She leaned back, her head tilted. "And unless I'm very mistaken, I see what you deserve in Blake's eyes, every time he looks at you."

She didn't need to hear this. She didn't *want* to hear this. But if she didn't give the old girl at least some sort of explanation, she'd never let up. So she twisted the truth into a slightly different shape in order to slip past it.

"Cille, look...Blake and I got married before either of us was ready, before either of us had a clue that it was about more than...how much fun we could have with each other. If you get my drift."

"Yeah, yeah, I got it. Go on."

"Anyway, Shaun was a surprise. And things were hard for us financially, to say the least. My parents were both gone by then, and Blake's were in no position to help out, even though I know they wanted to. Even so, things were okay until after the baby came. Between Blake and me, I mean. At least, I thought so, but what did I know? I was barely twenty years old."

"That's not so young, really."

"Oh, looking back, it was incredibly young. I had no idea what I was doing with Shaun—neither of us did, frankly—and he was a colicky baby, we weren't getting a lot of sleep, and Blake started working longer and longer hours, which in turn put more of a strain on me. At first I thought, well, yeah, we needed the money. Of course he had to work so much. But gradually I began to realize that wasn't it, that he was avoiding us."

Lucille reached over, touched her hand. "Most new parents feel overwhelmed at first, sweetheart. Especially when money's tight."

"I know that," she said, and suddenly she wasn't being so careful. "I even knew it at the time, that we were both exhausted and over our heads, that we didn't have any real sort of support system, but still. But then he finally landed a job that paid well enough that he could cut back his hours, and I thought, okay, maybe this will give us another chance. And Blake promised, too, to be home more, to take care of the baby more so I could get out, maybe go back to school. To take us away for the weekend, maybe even on a real vacation for the first time since we got married."

She felt a rusty laugh scrape from her throat. "Only, you know what? He didn't cut back. If anything, he worked even longer hours, to impress his new boss, to get ahead…"

One after the other, the memories resurfaced, faster than she could keep up with them. "Promise after promise after promise," poured from her lips on a serrated breath. "Big ones, little ones, ones that shouldn't even have been any big deal…all broken, to the point where I just never believed anything he said anymore. Oh, he'd apologize up one side and down the other, about how he'd make it up to us, that he wouldn't let it happen again, that things would get better…only to turn right around and do the same damn thing. And whatever had been holding us together before the baby simply disintegrated."

And I was too blind to see it coming.

"Then Shaun got sick," she said quickly, barreling over the thought. "Nothing serious, just enough to keep me up for three nights straight, with virtually no help from Blake. When I finally lost it and screamed at Blake that if he wasn't going to be around anyway, he might as well leave…"

Cass hadn't realized the tears were there until one plopped on her hand. "He wasn't supposed to take me seriously, Cille," she said in a small voice as the truth trampled her resolve to remain dispassionate. "He was supposed to stay and comfort me and tell me we'd get through it. But I'd offered him an opening, and by gum, he took it."

And there it was, wasn't it? The hurt, stinging every bit as much now as it had then. But a hundred, a thousand times worse was the vulnerability fostering the pain, suckling it on demand. A vulnerability that a dozen years of concerted effort hadn't been able to eradicate…as evidenced by her most recent trip down the same primrose path.

Lucille sat quietly for several seconds, stroking Cass's hand, before she said at last, "And the two of you never tried to patch it up?"

Somehow, Cass met her mother-in-law's concerned green gaze. "Oh, we met a few times afterward, but…but how can you patch up something that shouldn't have happened to begin with?" She took a deep breath and said, "As hard as it was to raise Shaun on my own, it was way better than having to see the fear in Blake's eyes every day. And to know that Shaun and I had put it there."

And that part was true enough—as a father, Blake had been completely out of his depth. What had derailed Cass, however, wasn't nearly as easy to define.

Or, apparently, overcome.

"It was a long time ago, sweetheart," Lucille said. "And I sure as hell don't see fear in his eyes now."

Unfortunately, Cass couldn't disagree. But even as she heard herself say, "Fear, no. Regret and guilt, yes," her own fears—now swollen to something approaching terror—danced grotesquely inside her head, taunting, heckling, luring her into the same trap that had so badly mangled her heart before.

Her mother-in-law smiled. "Hey, whatever works, right? So maybe you should give the man the benefit of the doubt."

"Oh, yeah?" Irritation surged through her as she remembered her place in her own script. "And why, exactly, would I do that? Because heaven knows things didn't get better after the divorce. For years, Blake has substituted money and gifts for spending time with his child. Shaun used to plead with Blake to come down for the weekend, to see him play a soccer game or just hang out. Blake was always, *always* too busy. Apologetic but busy. Or if he did say he'd come down, he'd break his promise at the last minute, leaving Shaun devastated. At least, with Alan, I knew what I was—or wasn't—getting. But with Blake…"

She shook her head. "There was a time when I loved that man with everything I had in me. But he broke my heart, just as he's broken his son's, over and over. If he really wants to make it up to Shaun, I'm not going to stand in his way. But I'd be a fool to let him get close enough to screw me over again."

Lucille was scrutinizing her far too intently for her comfort. "And it's too late, isn't it? He's already gotten too close."

"No," she said with a lot more conviction than she felt.

"You should be ashamed," she said gently, "lying to an old woman."

Somehow Cass managed not to flinch. "Truth, lies…what does it matter, as long as you survive?"

"Yeah, but where's the magic in that?"

She pushed out a dry laugh. "Oh, Cille…magic's an illusion. Nothing but a bunch of tricks. I gave up believing in that a long time ago."

"Well then," the old woman quietly said, stiffly getting to her feet, "it's a damn good thing some of us haven't." She leaned over to plant a kiss in Cass's hair, then shuffled out the door, tossing "Try and get some sleep" over her shoulder as she went.

Yeah, like that was going to happen.

Blake's phone rang just as the Channel 4 weather guy was about to start his schpiel. He punched the mute button on the remote and snatched the portable off the end table by the hideous sofa, barely getting out his "Hello?" before Lucilie hit him with, "Okay, I heard her side of the story, so now it's your turn. And you better make it good."

So much for the rest of the news. "Somehow, I never figured you for one of those old ladies who got her kicks from interfering in other people's lives."

"Well, you figured wrong…oh, I get it. Sarcasm." He heard a huff on the other end of the line. "So? What happened between the two of you? How come you broke up?"

"I was young and stupid and I panicked?"

"Huh. That's pretty much what she said, too. Along with some stuff about you breaking a lot of promises."

Blake winced. "Yeah. That, too."

"And that she got upset one night and asked you to leave, and you actually did?"

"That was the panic part."

"Boy, you really were stupid."

"We've already established that, Cille."

"And then, after the divorce? The business with the boy...?"

Blake leaned forward, holding his now-throbbing head in his hands. "Yes, your honor, I've been a lousy father. And no, I have no excuses for it."

"No excuses, maybe. But there must have been a reason."

"A lame one."

Another huff. "I'm not getting any younger, here. Spit it out, for God's sake."

"I was ashamed, okay? And the longer I stayed away, the worse I felt. Then once I got the business up and running, I really was busy. But by that time..."

"You'd figured it was too late."

"Something like that, yeah."

"Huh. No wonder she's afraid to let you get near her again. I wouldn't trust you, either, if I were her."

"Thanks."

"Don't mention it. So. Answer me one thing."

"What?"

"Have you really cleaned up your act? I mean, if by some miracle she did take you back, if things get tough, you're not going to run away again, are you?"

Blake chuckled softly. "I'm here, aren't I?"

"Good point. But you do realize you've got some serious sucking up in your future, don't you?"

"It hadn't escaped my attention." He paused. "I'm not going anywhere, Cille. And for sure I'm not going to break Cass's heart again, not if I can help it."

"You swear?"

"I swear." When she didn't say anything, he ventured, "Is this where you offer me your sage advice?"

"Hell, no." she said. "I was just checking to make sure your stories gibed. Except…"

"What?"

"I have no idea," she said after far too long a pause. "I'm telling you, this getting-old business is for the birds—you go to say something, poof! It's gone. Pain in the butt. Although I do want to leave you with one thought."

He almost smiled. "And what's that?"

"Mother-in-law quarters," she said, then hung up.

Chapter Nine

The man, Cass decided over the next several days, was taking sucking up to new heights.

First there were the flowers. Not ostentatious bunches of roses, but sweet little bouquets of jonquils and lilacs, sometimes left on her doorstep with funny little notes attached, sometimes delivered in person when he showed up to take Shaun to the movies or just hang out and watch TV with him.

Which was the second thing: his going out of his way to pay more attention to their son. Granted, it could have been all for show, nothing more than a tactic to get in both their good graces. For absolution, if nothing else. Except now, as standing at the door of the family room, she caught the look on Blake's face as he listened to Shaun recount the events of his day, a mixture of awe and amusement, overlaid with absolute, unconditional love, and she thought, *Oh, hell. This is for real*. And it caught her up short, threatening to unravel every thread of her resolve, this dead-serious side to her ex-husband she'd never seen before.

She waddled back to the kitchen for some juice, the plan being to grab a bottle and return to her bedroom to do some more packing. They had to be out in a week; she still couldn't figure out how so little could take up so many boxes. However, as with most of her plans these days, this one, too, went belly up when Blake ambled into the kitchen behind her.

"Popcorn?" he asked.

"By the microwave. I buy it by the case."

"I can understand why." Blake ripped the cellophane off the package, set it in the microwave. "Bottomless pit just finished up two peanut butter sandwiches a half hour ago."

"Never mind that all through elementary school he ate so little I was half afraid he'd starve to death."

The hum of the microwave did little to soften the immediate silence that grated between them.

"I'm sorry," Cass said. "I really didn't mean to—"

"It's okay, don't worry about it."

The popcorn started to ping inside its bag. Cass grabbed her juice and tried to scurry past Blake and out the door, but he put out a hand, gently wrapping it around her arm. "You know," he said softly, his thumb massaging her elbow through her sweatshirt, "I'm doing my damnedest here to prove to you I'm not running anymore. The least you could do is return the favor." He had her there. Except then a grin—The Grin—spread across his face. "Unless you're afraid you'll fall under my irresistible spell?"

Afraid? Honey, this was serious *Fear Factor* material here. "It's nothing personal, believe me. I just haven't finished packing yet."

Blake let go of her arm to retrieve the popcorn. Unconsciously, she rubbed the warm spot where his hand had been. "Shaun said you were done."

"*Shaun's* finished. Yes, I know, could've knocked me over with a feather, too. I'm not. Wanda's going to do the kitchen tomorrow, but I've still got all my books and stuff on the shelves in my bedroom…what are you doing?"

He'd yelled for Shaun to come get the popcorn, it was on the counter, then tugged her down the hall toward the stairs. "You are not lifting books in your condition."

Cass opened her mouth to protest, then thought, *This is stupid. The man wants to pack, let him pack.* She wasn't sure if that was a step in the right direction, or a major regression, but not even she was dumb enough to turn down free labor. This sucking-up business had definite advantages, she thought as she crawled onto her bed to relieve her screaming back.

"Man, you have a lot of books," Blake said, surveying the hundreds of tomes stacked every which way on the shelves of the floor-to-ceiling built-ins.

"One of the curses of being literate," she said, and he chuckled.

"So…any particular way you want these?"

"In the boxes," she said, curling up on her side with her feather pillow squooshed up underneath her cheek. "Other than that—" she yawned "—I do not…care…"

She woke up sometime later to find the light dimmed, both kittens curled up against her legs, several towers of taped boxes in front of the now-empty shelves, and a note on the bed in front of her. Groggily, she sat up, shoving her hair out of her face as she tried to focus on Blake's scrawl. Finally she made out:

Dog's in, cat pan's changed, Shaun's in his room studying (supposedly), house is locked up. Lucille said to tell you there's mail on the kitchen counter for you, she accidentally picked it up with hers. Oh, and this is the first time I can remember our being in the same room for two hours and not getting into a fight. Of course, you were comatose the entire time, but still…

Against her better judgment, she smiled, only to let out a sigh. This, she missed. But…

But as long as there were "buts," there would never be anything else.

"Too little, too late, Blake," she whispered to the note, then crumpled it up and tossed it into the trash, wishing she could toss at least some of those "buts" in there with it.

She pushed herself off the bed to go pee and put on the tent that passed for her nightgown, only then remembering about the mail in the kitchen. The last thing she wanted to do was haul her carcass back downstairs, but since she knew she'd only lie awake, anyway, consumed with curiosity, she figured she might as well get it over with.

The kitties played tag with the hem of her nightgown trailing down the stairs behind her, impeding her already snail-like progress. She finally made it to the kitchen. Yawning again as she flipped the switch to the lights over the island, she instantly spotted the seemingly innocuous white envelope…and just as instantly, dread knotted in her stomach.

Another bank card statement, one she hadn't known about. With iced fingers, she ripped open the envelope, scanned the list of cash advances.

"*Damn* you, Alan!" came out on a strangled cry as she slammed the paper down onto the granite surface. "Damn you, damn you, *damn you!*"

Panic choked her, heating her face, as she scrubbed her belly with short, agitated strokes. She had sold everything she had to sell, except her rings, which she didn't think she could do and not insult Lucille. She'd scrimped and fudged and crunched more numbers than there were grains of sand. There was nothing left, except to sell her share of the business.

Or…

Or.

For several minutes she stood with her hands braced against the edge of the counter, listening to her heart slam against her ribs, avoiding the inevitable.

Avoiding, she thought as she finally forced herself to leave the kitchen, what was beginning to seem like some bizarre date with destiny.

The house's customary silence seemed to part for her as she crossed the great room, then began the arduous climb back up the stairs. She didn't stop at the master suite, though, instead continuing on to Shaun's room. It was past eleven. Unable to quite tell whether his light was still on, she knocked softly, then realized she could hear his CD player. He mumbled something she took to mean she could come in, but out of habit she still opened the door cautiously. Boxes lined the starkly furnished room, crammed with more stuff than Cass wanted to know about. But the bare, white walls had nothing to do with their impending move. Even after more than a year, Sean had never bothered to paint the room or even stick up a few posters. Like her, he had never made the house *his*.

He'd been lying on his bed. Now he sprang to a sitting position, apprehension flickering in his eyes. "You okay?"

"Yes, yes," she reassured him, wishing she could reassure him about other things as well. "But something's…come up." At the guilty look she decided teenagers kept "on call" that flashed across his features, she added, "Or maybe there's something you need to tell me first?"

He laughed—nervously—then shook his head.

Dude had followed her into the room, promptly lugging

himself up onto Shaun's rumpled bed. Cass sat on the mattress's edge, knotting her hands in her lap.

And came clean about their situation.

Shaun sat quietly for several minutes after she finished, absently rubbing the dog's belly. His shoulders had gone rock hard, his brows vee'd over his nose. Naturally, Cass worried about dumping so much on a fifteen-year-old. And she feared she expected too much, even though she had no idea what, exactly, that was. Understanding, she supposed.

"We're really that stuck?" he finally asked.

She nodded. The baby thumped her in the groin, making her wince. This time, her first son didn't notice. "If it makes you feel any better, I'm not exactly overjoyed with the options, either."

"But you're willing to share a house with Dad?"

He'd never know what this decision had cost her. Then again, judging from his querulous expression, maybe he did.

"I'm willing to accept what I have to do," she said carefully. "For all of your sakes."

Trenchant brown eyes bore into hers. "You really hate Dad that much?"

"Oh, Shaun…" How could she admit to her son what she hadn't ever been able to figure out herself? "Honey, I don't hate your father at all. I never have. I hated that he left us, and the way he neglected you, but never him."

"That doesn't make any sense."

"No. I don't suppose it does."

She half expected him to take her to task for her ambivalence, but instead something like relief flickered in his eyes. Although she couldn't tell—and he wasn't divulging—the source of that relief. Instead, he got to his feet and began wandering around his room, the dog attacking his shoelace as he walked. The kittens, having worn themselves out with the nightgown hem battle, had curled up together in a pile of dirty clothes on the floor at the foot of the bed. "I don't have to change schools again?"

"Not unless you want to."

"And Cille goes with us?"

Cass smiled. The unlikely pair had been thick as thieves from the moment they'd met. "Absolutely." She managed a tight smile. "Just your average American family, that's us."

He didn't comment. Instead he paced some more, his ragged-nailed fingers hooked onto his hips. "And what if it doesn't work out?" he asked after a moment. "What happens then?"

"I don't know," she admitted. Rubbing the flat of her hand against her thigh, she added, "I'm not going to lie to you or give you any guarantees. But in any case, your Dad and I...wouldn't be living together for romantic reasons, only practical ones. None of that messy emotional business to complicate things."

The kid's intense scrutiny unnerved her. "Is this supposed to make me feel better?"

"What do you mean?"

His hand streaked through his hair; it flopped back into his face. "I'm not sure. I mean—" He collapsed across the bed on his stomach, propping his head in one hand. "You told me you were marrying Alan for 'practical' reasons, giving me this cr— uh, garbage about how much better it would be that way."

A shard of guilt—albeit a very tiny one—pricked Cass, that she'd deliberately misrepresented her relationship with Alan to Blake. Not the genuine respect she'd felt for him, at least at the beginning, or the loneliness that had left her vulnerable to his charm. But while she'd certainly felt an affection for her husband, her feelings had never blossomed beyond that point.

She lifted her eyes to find Shaun glaring at her. "I don't

know why," he said, " grown-ups think kids can't tell when things get screwed up, you know? You and Alan barely even talked to each other, those last few months. You and Dad can't be in the same room for ten minutes, hardly, without getting into it. So why would you do this to yourself?" His mouth flattened. "To all of us."

Rather than even attempt to explain something she didn't fully understand herself, she paid homage to the time-honored tradition of steering the conversation in another direction. "And here I thought teenagers were supposed to be self-centered."

"Huh?"

"Well, for one thing, I can't believe you actually *wanted* to move into an apartment. And for another…" She glanced down, then back into those skeptical brown eyes. "You can't tell me you haven't been hoping all along that your dad and I got back together. So why the objections?"

Shaun locked his gaze with hers for a long second, before rolling off the bed and crossing the room to stare out into the darkness. Finally he said, not looking at her, "Moving into Dad's house because we're flat broke and you're freaking up against the wall isn't exactly what I had in mind, okay? I've already done the pretending-to-be-one-big-happy-family thing." He turned around, and Cass's breath caught at the anguish in his eyes. "I'm really not hot to do it again."

His words vibrated painfully in the space between them, as Dude belly-crawled over to Cass's feet, whimpering softly. She bent over as far as she could to let the pup lick her fingers. "And for your sake, sweetie, I wish I could say what you want to hear. But I can't." When he didn't comment, she said, "Besides, so maybe on the surface my marrying Alan didn't exactly work out—" she grimaced at Shaun's concurrent snort "—but even that had its up side. The baby, and Lucille, and you made some new friends, right? Right?"

After a moment his body twitched in combination shrug and nod, then he fixed her with that disconcerting gaze of his. "And this time?"

"How should I know?" she let out. "I'm not a fortune teller. You think we'd be in this fix now if I could have predicted any of this?"

"So, what you're saying is, we really don't have any choice."

"Other than homelessness?" she said bitterly. "Or my having to sell my share of the business? No. We really don't. Frankly, if this solution hadn't presented itself…well. As much as it pains me to say this, I have to be grateful for your father's generosity. He could just as easily offered to take you and leave the rest of us to fend for ourselves."

"But Dad's not like that."

Cass's throat worked for a second or two before she could speak. "No. He's not."

Shaun dropped into the steno chair at his desk, twisting it back and forth as he talked. "You remember how, when I was a kid, I kept trying one thing after another, then giving up right away? Like soccer and karate and stuff? And how you got really fed up with my quitting something every time it got a little hard? So when I wanted to play the trombone in midschool, you said if I did—remember?—I had to commit to at least three years, because it would take me that long to get good enough to really know if I liked it?"

"Where is this going, honey?"

He lifted his eyebrows.

"Oh. I see." She gave a sharp sigh. "I'm sorry, Shaun. This isn't about your dad and me, it's about his offering us a home, and about my not being in the position to turn down him down. I'm not going to give you assurances I can't make." She followed his eyes, riveted to her stomach. "What is it?"

"Is that the baby doing that?"

She smiled. "Is it ever. Do you…do you want to feel?"

Tentatively the boy got out of the chair and crossed to her, getting on his knees so he could place his large, still-slender-fingered hand on the spot with the most activity. The baby kicked his palm, making him giggle like the kid he'd been only fifteen minutes ago, it seemed. "Now *this* is the soccer player," he said, then removed his hand, a little quickly. When he looked back up at her, his expression had sobered. "Okay. If you really think this is what you have to do, go for it. I just hope this turns out better than the trombone experience."

Vivid memories of three years of ear-shattering torture blared through her thought. "Yeah, honey. So do I."

"Cass! What on earth are you doing here—?"

It was well after midnight, but there she stood in the door-way, a Pendleton blanket poncho wrapped around her night-gown. "Got any crow, Blake? Broiled, if possible. Fried stuff gives me heartburn."

"Pardon?"

"You win," she said simply. "If your offer still stands, I'm accepting."

"You'll marry me?"

That got an in-your-dreams-buddy eye roll, followed by, "Not that offer, the house offer."

She was dry-eyed, but even in the weak landing light, he could see the strain in the crease between her brows, the set to her mouth. As much as he wanted her back in his life, this wasn't how he'd wanted it to happen.

As much as he wanted to pull her into his arms, he folded them instead. Not wishing to die young and all that. "What happened to 'over my dead body'?"

"*My* body, I don't care about. However, as you pointed out, I have three other bodies I'm responsible for. And I don't relish the idea of those bodies living under the I-25 overpass. And I'm freezing to death, thanks for asking."

"Oh, hell, I'm sorry…get in here."

She was actually shivering by the time he got her inside. He made her a cup of decaffeinated tea, noticing her acerbic perusal of the meagerly furnished room as he handed it to her. "Charming."

"Stop-gap," he corrected, then asked, quietly, "What happened?"

She told him, and revulsion set his stomach to churning. "You think there are any more charge cards?"

Her fingers worried the fringe on her poncho as it lay puddled in her lap, her wedding rings glittering like ice in the light from the end-table lamp. "God, I hope not. But it's been nearly a month. I imagine I've gotten all the statements I'm going to." She stared into her tea for a moment, then asked in a low voice, "So. Do we have a deal?"

He forced the muscles in his face to relax. "Yes. We have a deal."

"Good." Her shoulders sagged with relief; however, the line etched between her brows grew even deeper.

Slowly he crossed the room to squat in front of her, taking her free hand in his. "This is really eating you up, isn't it?"

Now he saw the tears, poised several inches over a chin as stubborn as ever. "Now you get this straight, Carter," she said, the wobble barely noticeable. "I'm up the creek, yeah, but the only reason I'm agreeing to this is because of my children and Lucille. And only temporarily."

He frowned. "Temporarily?"

"Blake, get real." She slipped her hand out of his. "Whatever caused us to split up to begin with hasn't simply faded away because some time has passed." She set the mug on the end table, tapping her finger on the handle for a moment, then added, "I thought about it on the way over here, and the way I see it, by the time Shaun's gone, I should be back on my feet. By then, there really wouldn't be any reason to continue living with you." Her mouth thinned. "I raised one child on my own, I imagine I can do it again."

Blake shut his eyes against the stab of pain, even though he knew better than to argue. The Good Lord Himself couldn't convince Cass she was mistaken once she'd set her mind to something. Except, as he stood, it occurred to him that if she still didn't have feelings for him, she wouldn't be raising such a stink. Point for the home team, hurrah. And once she was in his house—

"And no sex," she said.

He almost lost his balance. "What?"

"You heard me." Her voice had steadied, but she'd gripped her hands so tightly in her lap her knuckles looked like marble. "I need a home. You need to be with your son more. That's all there is to this. We're sharing a house, not shacking up."

He almost laughed. And then—because it was late and he was too tired to censor his mouth—he challenged her with, "And now it's time for *you* to get real. You really think we can ignore all this…stuff that's crackling between us?"

"We're not twenty-somethings anymore, Blake. I think we can manage."

"I don't get it." And God help him, he really didn't. "I mean, if we're living in the same house, and we both enjoy it…" He frowned at her. "You do still enjoy it, don't you?"

Her mouth might have twitched. "That's not the point, Blake."

"Then what is?"

"Look," she began with an impatient edge to her voice, "the one area in our marriage we didn't have a problem with was sex, right?"

He grinned. This he understood. "Right."

"And our marriage still tanked. Right?"

He frowned. He understood that, too. "Right."

"So…?"'

"So…" He looked to her for a clue. "So…we can't have sex because…"

"Because," she supplied when he fizzled out, "it only clouds the issues."

The light dawned. Dimly, granted, but he did see a glimmer of reason in what she said. "Oh. Yeah. I knew that."

"And you don't have to get up with the baby. He's not yours, after all—"

Blake rested one hand on her stomach; to his shock, she shut up. "A baby's a baby, sweetheart. None of this has anything to do with him."

Her eyes lowered to his hand on her belly. A small sigh preceded, "You think Alan's a snake, don't you?"

"Let's just say…yeah, that about sums it up."

Several beats passed before she said, "Welcome to the club. Well. I guess that's settled." She stood, worry once again skittering across her features. "I have to be out of the old house in a week. Do you think you can close on the other one in time?"

"Trust me. It won't be a problem." She'd barely gotten all the way across the room when he thought of something. A tactic, of sorts. "Cass?"

She turned, a little awkwardly, one eyebrow cocked.

"If it helps, think of this as…" He halted, searching for the right words. "Well…as if you stumbled, and I held out my hand to steady you so you wouldn't fall. That's all."

In the shadowed light her eyes had darkened to a luscious teal. A hundred emotions swirled in their depths, not the least of which was apprehension. On one level he understood her fears, understood that despite her strengths and abilities, she was still a very pregnant, recently widowed woman with enough on her plate for a half-dozen people. On another level, it seared right through to his gut that she clearly didn't trust him, no matter what he said. Or at least—he thought of Lucille's conveniently "forgetting" what she was about to say on the phone a few days before—that she sure as hell didn't trust *something*.

However, she allowed a nod and a small, tired smile, and said, simply, "Thank you."

She left, gently closing the door behind her. The breeze that shunted through the living room afterward raised goose bumps on his arms.

He picked up her still-half-full mug off the end table and carried it over to the sink, dumping out the cold tea. Sharing living space full-time with a woman who regarded him as she might her hangman was not a pleasant prospect, he had to admit. But then, whose fault was it that she regarded him that way?

There'd been a time when he'd felt reasonably justified in taking at least some credit for turning a timid, insecure eighteen-year-old girl into the exuberant, trusting young woman he'd married. Years later, it wasn't nearly so easy to accept that he might now be equally responsible for her metamorphosis into this frightened, cynical creature. He had no problem, however, with accepting not only the challenge to reverse the damage, but the golden opportunity to do just that. Once she was under his roof again, he vowed, he would show her, every day, how much he cherished her and their son. He would simply make life so good for her, she'd never even think about leaving….

Hell. He'd have better luck predicting who'd win the Indy 500 three years from now.

Chapter Ten

The midwife pumped the blood pressure sleeve until Cass thought her eyes would cross, then released the valve, her brows dipping further with each hitch the needle made in the gauge. Even worse, Angie's mouth had twisted that way that always made Cass feel she should apologize. The woman— a vanilla version of Towanda, complete with the same "take no prisoners" demeanor—lowered her chin to her formidable bosom and glared at Cass. "One-forty over ninety. Again. What does this tell us?"

"That someone needs to stay off her feet," she heard Blake say. He was leaning back in the second chair beside Angie's desk, booted feet crossed at the ankles, arms laconically crossed over his chest, piling on the charm so thick it was hard to breathe. There he went, giving Angie that canted smile, the one that always liquefied assorted parts of Cass's anatomy. Judging from Angie's decidedly softer features once Blake had wormed his way into the conversation, Cass surmised the midwife's molecular structure had undergone a few changes, as well.

He'd insisted on coming, insisted on accompanying Cass into the examining room. Honestly, she'd been half surprised he hadn't followed her into the bathroom while she peed on the glucose/protein stick. Which perhaps might have been preferable, considering how cozy he and Angie had become by the time she'd come out.

"So Blake tells me you're moving in with him?" Angie asked, entering information onto Cass's chart.

Cass's "You will die" look in Blake's direction glanced off his grin—a grin which crumbled into a frown when Angie then went on to say, "Although you should probably forgo sex as long as Cass is still having such strong Braxton-Hicks activity." She peered through her glasses at Blake while Cass fought to catch her breath. "After all, we don't want this little guy to make his appearance before he's fully cooked, right?"

"Oh, but we're not—" Cass started to say.

Angie kept going with "Although once she hits thirty-seven weeks, which should be—" she checked the chart "—about two weeks from now, whatever she feels like doing, go for it."

"No, Angie, you don't underst—"

"Yes, ma'am," Blake drawled as his full-of-the-devil gaze moseyed over in Cass's direction, raking her body from head to toe, leaving behind the faint aroma of scorched cotton.

Thus turning her into the only woman on the planet *wishing* for Braxton-Hicks. Still, she snagged the midwife's wrist and said, "Uh, hello? *Moot point?*"

Angie frowned. "But I thought…"

Cass shook her head. "No."

Angie glanced over Cass's shoulder at Blake, then leaned

over to pat Cass on the knee. "Yeah, let me know how that works out, okay?"

Great.

What made things even stickier, though, was that if Blake's expression had been one of lust only, Cass could have dismissed it without a single thought. But it never had been that with Blake. It had always been deeper, meatier, a look of connection, and yes, possession, which try as she might, always, always turned her inside out.

There'd been a reason why the sex had been so good. And back then it sure as heck hadn't been because of any technical expertise on either of their parts. And if she had a snowball's chance of saving what little sanity she had left, she'd do well not to think too hard about the good old days.

Some liberated woman she was. One "you my woman" glance and her hormones snapped to attention, as eager to please as a bunch of trained seals. Not for the first time, she wondered how on earth she thought she was going to go through with this, how she was going to keep their arrangement a matter of convenience, since it was patently clear that sharing a house with Blake was going to be anything but. Cripes, her breasts tingled just from breathing in his scent. If he actually made contact...

"You okay?" Blake asked, touching her wrist, which made her jump, knocking her purse to the floor. "You seem flushed."

"Pregnant women do get overly warm sometimes," the midwife calmly replied.

Cass mumbled something vaguely resembling an agreement, snatched her retrieved purse out of Blake's hand and made for the office door.

They walked—well, Blake walked while she trudged—to the car in silence, Blake's hand insinuating itself in the small of her back, right in the spot screaming for a massage. Her breasts ached, her belly felt leaden, and if there was some phantom comfortable position she could get into, she sure as hell hadn't found it yet. Day after tomorrow, they were closing on both houses; the following day, she was moving.

Stay off her feet? Hah!

Once in the car, she sank so deeply in thought she didn't realize they'd pulled into a parking lot until Blake opened her car door and held out his hand, clearly expecting her to take it. Jerked back to reality, she glanced out the windshield at the familiar restaurant, its whimsical conglomeration of turrets and Spanish roof tiles a cheerful contrast to the murky, tumbling clouds suddenly threatening the distant valley. She slipped her sunglasses down and squinted up at him over the tops. "What are you doing, Carter?"

"Buying you lunch. So get the lead out, lady. It's hotter 'n blazes out here."

So much for charming.

Blake more or less pried her out of the car, then guided her inside. A dozen people hopped out of her way at her approach—she'd reached that point in the pregnancy where people eyed her the way they might a suspiciously ticking package left on their doorstep.

"I haven't been to Garduño's in ages." The first stirrings of something close to hunger rolled around in what was left of her stomach. "Alan hated Mexican food," she said as she collapsed onto a banco inside the lobby to wait for a table, since they'd hit the place right at the peak of lunch hour. Blake wove his fingers with hers; she surprised herself by letting him.

The last time she'd been here, he'd done the same thing. Near the end of their marriage, she realized. Her feelings had been pretty much the same then, too—a mixture of anxiety and melancholy. But there was something different about now, she had to admit. Maybe it was because she had nothing to lose. After all, she'd gone into both of her marriages full of hope and confidence, only to watch them both crash and burn. This time there were no delusions about happily ever after, no pretense that this was either a permanent or love-inspired relationship. No burden of commitment, hovering like a ton of bricks over her head.

For the first time in longer than she cared to remember, she felt at peace. Maybe it was false, and maybe it was only momentary, but she could practically feel her blood pressure lowering as she sank against the back of the banco and shut her eyes.

And felt Blake's fingers soothingly caress hers. Because fighting something as innocuous as having her hand held, she decided, was simply not worth it. Even if she knew how insidiously dangerous letting down her guard even that much could be.

But hey—we were talking hands, here. Not breasts. As long as he didn't touch her breasts, she was fine. In the middle of a crowded Mexican restaurant, she felt fairly certain this would not be a problem.

"Hungry?" he asked a few minutes later, after they'd been seated.

She scanned the huge menu, torn between beef fajitas, the Mexican shrimp salad and green-chili chicken enchiladas. With extra sour cream. "I actually think I am."

The rumble and laughter of the other patrons, the spicy scent hanging in the air, Blake's puckered brow as he tried to decide what he wanted, all settled in her psyche, further lulling her into a haze of contentment. Even the baby seemed to be snoozing, floating away in his warm, safe sac, oblivious to everything.

A waitress brought chips and salsa, then left. "I remembered," Blake said, dipping a chip into the salsa between them, "we always could talk here, for some reason."

She took a sip of her water, fighting to hang on to the mellow feeling now in imminent danger of being shattered. "Is this why you brought me?"

He leaned back in his chair, flicking nonexistent crumbs from his fingers. "We haven't discussed…arrangements," he said with a half smile. "As in, who sleeps where after tomorrow."

Her brow knotted. "There are four bedrooms, besides Lucille's quarters. I assumed we'd have separate bedrooms."

"Ah. Unfortunately…until I can add on an extra room, I need the fourth bedroom as an office. Since I plan on being home more. Anyway, my bed's a king size, so there should be plenty of space." A grin tugging at his mouth, his eyes lowered to her middle. "Even for all three of us. Or, if you insist, we could do the twin-beds routine. Like Rob and Laura in the Dick Van Dyke Show."

Her eyes once again lowered to the menu. "Or," she said calmly, "I could sleep in the nursery until the addition's complete." She looked up at him. "Right?"

On a heartfelt sigh, Blake mumbled something about a guy having to try, and she humphed. A second later the menu toppled over like a felled tree as her eyes boinged back up to his.

"What do you mean, you plan on being home more?"

He casually dunked another chip. "I thought we might both work part-time after the baby came, so one of us would almost always be around. Troy and your partners all agreed with me—"

"Whoa, Nellie—you talked it over with my *partners?*"

After several seconds he leaned forward and said, very quietly, "I'm not the enemy, honey. So why don't you listen to what I'm saying, instead of whatever it is you're so afraid to hear? Now…" He returned to studying the menu, his face expressionless, while she sat there feeling as though she'd just been blasted by a hose turned on full force. "Have you decided what you're going to order?"

Her heartbeat thunking unpleasantly in her ears, she clapped the menu closed. "I'm not hung—"

One dark eyebrow lifted.

She opened the menu again. "You do realize you're making this very difficult."

Those deep-brown eyes threatened to pull her right into the undertow. "It's like having a splinter taken out," he said. "The more you struggle, the more it hurts."

Her peace of moments before now completely shattered, she gave her order, then relinquished the menu as, outside, the first fat drops of rain began their lazy assault on the landscape.

The rain beat relentlessly on the flat roof overhead as, from her command post on her slightly worn English chintz-covered sofa in the middle of her new living room, Cass—having effectively blocked out the scurrying to and fro of a half-dozen people distributing boxes and lamps and furniture and what-all—glowered down the hall. Toward the bedrooms. Specifically, toward the bedrooms in which nobody would be sleeping, or doing much of anything else, thanks to an undetected leak the previous owners had seen fit to camouflage with a couple coats of new white paint.

A leak that, having clearly been neglected over the course of God knows how many years, had not only rotted out most of the plasterboard along the outside wall, but had finally settled into a trio of lovely lakes over much of the now-ruined carpet in all three rooms. A leak that might have gone undetected for God knows how many more years if it hadn't been for a record-setting, two-day-straight deluge, the likes of which Albuquerque—with its eleven-inch annual rainfall—hadn't seen since sometime in the fifties.

Their homebuyer's protection plan would take care of the damage, of course. Eventually. Unfortunately, however, not within the next—she checked her watch—six hours. Oh, there were still alternatives, she supposed—sharing Lucille's space, staying in a motel, camping out with Shaun in the family room—none of which were workable for at least the two weeks it would take to get the rooms back in order.

Cass looked up at the ceiling. *Okay, God, I know You work in mysterious ways and all, but this takes the cake.*

Blake had been *so* understanding and apologetic when it became apparent they'd have to share a bed, assuring her he'd be the perfect gentleman, that she didn't have to worry for a second about his trying anything.

Uh-huh. The man had done everything but shout "Yes!" when they walked into the dripping nursery.

The thing was, words were cheap. And not, unfortunately, only *his* words. It was one thing to calmly and rationally spell out the ground rules while fully clothed and upright and surrounded by a small herd of friends and family, quite another to adhere to those rules while sharing, despite its being a California King, a still remarkably narrow bed. Especially when her brain and her body seemed to having a helluva time coming to any sort of an agreement, here.

From a practical, logical standpoint, Cass knew giving in to her body's whining was a disaster waiting to happen. From a practical, logical standpoint, she didn't even *want* to fool around with Blake. Physically was something else entirely. Physically, she wanted Blake so badly her tonsils hurt. And you know you're in deep trouble when your tonsils morph into an erogenous zone.

"Honey? Where do you want to set up the bookshelves? Family room or in here?"

Cass swiveled her head—and her glower—from the hall

to her new roomie. Her slightly sweaty roomie, his navy T-shirt molded to his torso, his hair damp and waving over his ears, at the back of his neck. And her mouth watered.

Yeah, well, no sense drooling over a scrumptious-looking dish when you're allergic to one of the main ingredients.

"You mean, you're actually *asking* me?"

"I'm in a generous mood."

Gee. I wonder why.

"Family room," she pronounced, and off he went.

On a soft groan, Cass slumped down deeper into the sofa cushions, staring up at the ceiling. On the surface she might look relaxed, but she was anything but. Maybe she'd accepted that Blake and she would be sharing a bed, and that his talking with her partners about her working part-time after the baby had only stemmed from a desire to make things easier for her. Maybe she'd even begun to accept—even if she didn't fully understand it—Blake's willingness to take such an big part in Jason's care.

What she couldn't accept—didn't dare let herself accept—was that any of this was permanent. He'd given lip service to atonement before and had failed miserably, every time. If he ran true to form, she'd no sooner get used to having him around than the novelty would wear off and he'd start spending more and more time away, leaving her right where she started.

And right where they'd ended up before.

The irony was, she really didn't feel like making decisions. In fact, at the moment, it felt kinda nice having the Big Strong Man around, taking charge and spoiling her rotten. She didn't like how much she liked it, but she couldn't seem to help it. There was a lot to be said for being able to sleep better, and even eat better, knowing she wasn't going to have to bed the baby in a stack of cardboard boxes. Of course, they'd gotten into a tussle over utility bills, which he refused to let her help pay. But she'd put her foot down about the charge cards, when he tried to strong-arm her into letting him pay them off. Exasperated nearly to tears, she'd finally told him exactly how much it would take to do that. She'd expected him to blanch. Gasp. Drop his jaw. Something. Instead, he'd just shrugged.

After she picked her teeth back up off the floor, she once again insisted this was her problem. Not his. Which had prompted Lucille to call her something in Yiddish that Cass strongly suspected meant *idiot*.

Her brain hurt from all this thinking. On a groan, she let her head loll against the back of the sofa. Less than five weeks to go until the baby came, but she already knew these were going to be the slowest five weeks in history. Especially if she spent them plastered to this sofa.

Clamping both hands on the arm, she heaved herself up and slowly made her way back to her bedroom, Dude at her heels. She half expected to see their old brass bed, even though she'd sold it years ago. Instead, they were using Blake's, the headboard actually a pair of richly stained, hand-carved Mexican twin bed headboards bolted together, the craftsmanship conjuring up images of romantic haciendas and Antonio Banderas and sinuous guitar music floating over heady, bougainvillea-scented night breezes. With a sigh, she sank onto the bare mattress.

"I sure have a knack for getting myself in deep, don't I, boy?" she asked the dog, whose only reply was a shlurp across her knuckles.

Wearily, she stood, rummaging through a few boxes until she came to the one with her sweaters in it, which she then began to stack in the closet. Blake had somehow already put his clothes inside; she remembered with a breath-sucking pang the first time she'd opened their closet after he'd moved out, the gaping emptiness he'd left behind….

"Hey—let me get those for you."

She jumped at the sound of his voice. Damn the man for having the gentlest voice in the world.

"It's okay," she answered, more sharply than she intended. "I'm not lifting anything heavy—"

But he clamped his hands around her arms, moving her to one side, then lifted the remaining sweaters up onto the shelf.

"You're making me feel like a slug."

Shoving the last pile into place, he glanced at her enormous middle. "Enjoy it," he quipped. "The minute this kid is born, I expect you back on that tractor plowing up the back forty."

And being able to make her laugh was definitely not fair. They'd laughed a lot, in the beginning. Blake said it was because they both had perverse senses of humor.

"When did you last eat?" he asked, pulling a set of sheets from another box. He shook out the bottom one, began making up the bed.

Their bed.

He caught her expression, smiled. "It's okay, I'm bunking with Shaun in the family room."

Her eyes filled. *Damn* it. But all she said was, "Thanks."

"You're welcome. After all—" He yanked the last corner of the bottom sheet around the mattress. "Making you nervous isn't going to do your blood pressure any good, is it?"

Cass shook her head, then watched half dreamily, half apprehensively, as he went about his task with an easy, masculine grace that made her blood sing. Meanwhile the dog leaned against her shin, following Blake's every move as though making a bed was the most astounding thing in the world. "An hour ago," she finally said. "I ate an hour ago, when you forced that hamburger down my throat."

He stuffed a down pillow into its case, tossing it against the headboard as he tossed her a grin. "Admit it. You enjoyed every bite."

She had, but she wasn't going to let him know that. "I admit nothing. And stop hovering. It makes me crazy."

"Then take better care of yourself and we won't have to." With that, he pointed to the expanse of cool, pale blue percale, the fluffed-up pillows. "Off your feet, woman. For thirty minutes, minimum."

She opened her mouth—

"Or I'll tell Angie."

With a sigh, she kicked off her shoes and collapsed on her side, heaving a loud sigh. Never, in the history of mattresses, had one felt this good. She grimaced at his chuckle.

"Well, Wonder Woman," he whispered, bending over to stroke her arm. "We wouldn't be a little tired, would we?"

She scrunched the pillow underneath her cheek. Yawned. "You're a creep, you know that?"

"Flatterer."

She grunted.

"How about Chinese food later?" he asked.

It was stupid, but even that provoked tears. God, who *was* this basket case who'd taken over her body? "Hot and sour soup?" she asked. "And shrimp in garlic sauce?" The bed creaked softly as she twisted to look up at him. "Extra spicy?"

With a laugh he said, "This kid's gonna come out breathing fire."

Suddenly, the haze of self-pity cleared enough for her to realize the position he'd put himself in, temporary or not. She still didn't completely understand why, and the whole thing still scared the bejesus out of her, but she was damned if he was going to think her ungrateful. He was halfway to the door when she called him back.

"This means a lot to me," she said in answer to his raised eyebrows. "For Shaun's and Lucille's sakes, especially."

Their eyes met for several seconds. After a moment he simply nodded, calling the dog out of the room before he left.

* * *

I need you.

Not that he deserved it, God knew, not after everything that had—or hadn't—gone down between them. And yet that's all he wanted to hear her say. *I love you* was meaningless, in their situation; *I want you,* while he wouldn't dismiss the sentiment out of hand, wasn't enough. Crazy as it was, he wanted to break down those defenses, to earn her trust enough that she could feel comfortable admitting what he suspected was true. She was like an abused puppy, obviously craving love and affection, yet petrified to accept it.

And he could hardly blame her, could he?

"Who *are* you?" she'd asked as he divvied up all the Chinese food amongst the hungry hordes he now lived with.

And he'd looked her straight in the eye and said, "Just a poor slob who finally woke up."

An answer which, much to his annoyance, instead of erasing the worry in her eyes, only seemed to add to it.

Still, after the extra, nonfamily bodies had taken leave, after she'd dispatched an entire pint of garlic shrimp by herself, after Lucille and Shaun had gone to bed, they'd sat outside on the patio until well past midnight, listening to crickets. And talking. Like they used to when they'd first met. She kept her distance, and there was plenty of caution in her voice, but for the first time, she asked him about Ain't It Sweet, listened to his plans for expansion. Even admitted she regularly indulged in their low-carb, low-fat products, which she pronounced "far superior" to anybody else's out there. "I mean, they actually taste enough like the real thing that I still feel guilty afterward," she'd said, and he'd laughed. He didn't want to pin too many hopes on one conversation, but it sure seemed like a major step in the right direction to him.

She hadn't even argued when he suggested she not go into work today.

Which obviously meant, he now mused as he watched her haul herself into the kitchen, dressed for exactly that, that she'd simply decided not to argue and just do what she damn well pleased, anyway.

So there she stood, lavender circles hammocked underneath eyes shooting "not one word" daggers at him, her face pinched with exhaustion and stress, but by golly, she was determined to bring home her part of the bacon. He let the morning pleasantries between Lucille and Cass pass without comment for a minute or two, then rattled his newspaper in a time-honored *Father Knows Best* gesture.

"And just where do you think you're going, young lady?"

"To work," she said with a hard smile.

"You're not going anywhere," he said quietly, catching Lucille's raised eyebrows out of the corner of his eye. "Remember?"

"Oh, yeah?" Cass opened the refrigerator, grabbed a jar of olives, yanked off the top and popped one into her mouth. "Says you and whose army?"

He lowered the paper. "You want me to call Angie?"

Another olive disappeared into her mouth. "You heard her," she said, chewing. "She said I could work up until the end—" she swallowed "—as long as I felt okay."

He glanced down, but she was wearing long floppy pants so he couldn't see her ankles. The outfit was mostly black with a white front. He thought better of telling her she looked like a penguin. When he lifted his eyes back to her face, he almost laughed at her smug grin. "So no contractions?"

"Nary a one," she returned, only to snap shut her mouth as a flush rocketed up her neck.

And Blake smiled. *Gotcha.*

"I need to work." She capped the jar and replaced it in the fridge. "Nesting isn't my style."

"If it's the money—"

"It's my *business,* Blake," she said. "I'd think you, of all people, would understand that. It's not fair dumping everything in Mercy's and Dana's laps."

"I'm sure they'd understand."

"I'm sure they would. That's not the point." She grabbed a piece of toast from his plate and gave him a little wave. "I'll see you at dinner." With that, she came as close to flouncing out of the room as her unwieldy form would let her.

When he turned to Lucille, she was giving him The Eye.

"What?"

"This is no good."

"What isn't?"

"This pretending business."

He went back to his paper. "Nobody's *pretending* anything. In fact—" he turned the page "—this is a lot more honest than some marriage of convenience—hey!" he said when a cream-cheesed English muffin flew over the top of the paper, landing glop side down in his lap.

"Hey, yourself!" came the indignant reply. "I don't care what you call this, if you think I'm going to share quarters with another half-assed arrangement, you've got another think coming. She deserves more than that. *You* deserve more than that. And God knows, your *son* deserves more than that!"

With a heavy sigh, he folded up the smeared paper, then grabbed a napkin to wipe the cream cheese off his jeans. "And what, exactly, do you expect me to do?"

"Does the word *seduction* ring a distant bell?"

He nearly choked on his laugh. "Oh, right. I'm supposed to seduce a woman who's a hundred months pregnant. Who told me, point-blank, there would be no sex."

"You can't be serious!" boomed the deep voice from the back door as Towanda came in, fending off kittens and the dog as she hung up her purse. Back to blond today, Blake noted. "She actually said that?"

"Those very words."

"Huh. Now I *know* the child isn't eating well enough."

Blake looked from one to the other. "There's no way I can gracefully back out of this conversation, is there?"

"Nope," they both said at once, and he sighed.

"The object here is to get the woman to trust me. Not beat me off with a stick. So why would I even consider coercing her into doing something she doesn't want to do?"

Both women howled with laughter; Wanda yanked back a chair and plonked down on it. "Before, when she was pregnant with Shaun…was she interested?"

Blake scrubbed a hand over his face to cover the blush. "Uh, yeah. You could say that."

The two ladies exchanged glances, then Lucille leaned forward as if about to impart a major secret. "She's older now. If she felt amorous then, I can guarantee you she's probably to wall-climbing stage right now—"

"You better believe it, honey," Wanda chimed in.

"When I was carrying Alan, I could hardly think about anything else—"

"Mmm-hmm, ain't that the truth," Wanda concurred, then laid a hand on his wrist. "Honey, let me tell you something. When you're feeling fat and ugly, the one thing you most need is for your man to make you feel loved and beautiful. Desired, you know what I mean?"

"Except you're missing one important fact, here. I'm not 'her man'. And if she even *thought* we were having this conversation we'd be dead."

"You see anybody else who's gonna qualify?" Wanda said,

undeterred. "And let me tell you something else—in case you didn't know it, everything's more…sensitive when a woman's pregnant."

Catching Lucille's enthusiastic nod of agreement out of the corner of his eye, Blake wasn't sure whether to be amused or embarrassed. "Yeah, well, I remember all the words to 'Annabelle Lee,' too, but I don't see anybody exactly clamoring for a demonstration of that, either."

"Child, you got a serious apples and oranges problem," Wanda said, then turned to Lucille. "You know, Miss Lucille—I think it's high time you came and spent the night with me. Have ourselves a good old-fashioned hen party."

"I don't think—"

Lucille brightened like a sunlamp. "I think that's a terrific idea." Then she frowned. "But what about Shaun?"

"Now hold on, you two—"

"That's his department," the housekeeper said, then turned her "And no lip from you" glare on Blake. "And I've yet to meet a man who couldn't figure out how to arrange to be alone with a woman if he really wanted to be."

Criminy. He felt like the newly married groom in the Middle-Ages who had to produce the bloodied sheet to prove the marriage had been consummated. And he wasn't even married, for God's sake, an oversight that didn't seem to deter either of these two—who clearly weren't taking Cass's no for an answer—in the least. "I'll, uh, see what I can do."

"You do that, honey," Wanda said. "Because I am really tired of seeing that poor woman so miserable all the time."

To which Lucille added a heartfelt nod.

Chapter Eleven

"What the hell are you doing here, girl?" Curls and breasts aflutter, Mercy stomped across the sales floor, sidestepping two rockers, an antique crib and three cradles. "No pregnant woman who just moved into a new house should be anywhere near this store today. Unless, of course, she's a customer."

From the frying pan into the hotter'n red chili fire.

"So sell me something," Cass said.

Mercy huffed, then twisted her arms over her bust. "So? How are you?"

"Is that a new high chair? I don't remember seeing it before—"

"You're ignoring me."

She met the chocolate eyes with a smile. "I'm ignoring you."

Clearly misinterpreting her reticence, Mercy said around a sly grin, "Just answer me one thing—does the jewelry fit as well as it did the first time around?"

To avoid the inevitable barrage of whys, Cass had been at least reasonably truthful with her partners about why she'd moved in with Blake: because Alan had left her in debt— vague though she'd been on the details—and because Blake had offered to take them all in. Not that she was at all enamored of playing the poor-relation role in a Dickens novel, but better that than Mercy's inference.

"Hello?" Cass said, rearranging a rack of toddler dresses. "I'm just sharing a house with the man. So, you know, *nothing happened?* And anyway, what gives with the interrogation? How would you like it if I did that to you?"

"Honey, if I moved in with a hunk like that, you better believe that A, *something* would happen and B, you wouldn't have to interrogate me. I'd be broadcasting the details on Channel 4 News." She spread her hands, as if imagining the headline. "Hard-up old maid finally gets l—"

"Excuse me?" asked a rosy-cheeked young woman, her posture the protective-hand-on-the-tummy stance of all pregnant women. "Can you show me where you keep the newborn layettes?" Cass somehow knew *her* cheeks were anything but rosy. The glowing theory didn't apply to pregnant women who felt more like seventy-five than thirty-five.

"Sure, honey…right over here. Let me guess," Mercy asked, leading her quarry away, her tight little fanny switching in her tighter skirt. "This is your first, right?"

Cass turtled back to the office and sank heavily behind the desk.

Leaving Blake by himself on the patio last night had taken more willpower than she'd even know she'd had. It had been like old times, sitting in the evening cool, watching the stars and talking, letting his voice wash over her, soothing her. Back then, they would have gone to bed—if they made it that far—and made love. To say that it hadn't been tempting, for

a moment—okay, for a lot longer than that—to throw her resolve out the window, to take advantage of his unspoken in-
vitation to let him soothe her need as well as her nerves, was
an understatement. Especially knowing that he would have
loved her slowly, sweetly, making her blood hum, making her
feel again like a woman in the most basic, wonderful, heady
sense. And she would have enjoyed the hell out of it.

Then morning would have come and she would have realized what she'd let happen and she'd've been even more depressed.

Strike that. She yanked a tissue from the box on the corner of her desk and blew her nose. Maybe *as* depressed, but
she doubted she could become any *more* depressed.

Nope. Alan's leaving with more debts than a fair-size third-
world country paled in comparison to the specter of terminal
horniness. But since she wasn't into sex without commitment, and commitment came at too high a price…

Well, there ya go. One chocolate-covered dead end with a
cherry on top.

Dana swished into the office and plopped down behind her
desk, dumping a pile of price tags in front of her.

"Wow," Cass said, trying not to wince. "That just from Saturday?"

"We're talking wall-to-wall preggos and strollers. I think
I know why last fall was so warm," Dana said evenly as she
began to sort the tags. "All that baby making was heating up
the atmosphere."

Surgery the year before had destroyed Dana's chances of
having her own children; yet, if she harbored any bitterness
about her fate, she didn't let on. When Cass had announced
her own pregnancy, in fact, Dana had nearly knocked her
over with hugs.

Humbled, Cass decided to count her blessings and ignore

the constant ache in her crotch. She'd told Blake no sex, and she'd told him why. If he seemed willing enough to go along with it, she was going to look pretty danged stupid changing the rules, now, wasn't she?

It wasn't until Dana looked up, frowning, that Cass realized she'd groaned out loud.

Before Wanda whisked Lucille away for the night, Blake begged her to leave them food, preferably something already cooked that he couldn't screw up in a low oven. As it happened, Shaun asked to spend the night at a friend's up by school with whom he was working on a project due in a couple of days, anyway. Blake had thought it might make more sense to take Cass away somewhere, but Wanda and Lucille had both been adamant they needed to, as Lucille so succinctly put it, "break in" their new house.

Not that she was putting pressure on him or anything.

By six-thirty, Blake was thoroughly convinced he was the biggest fool on earth. Cass had said "no sex." With the sort of fierce look in her eye that made men protectively cover themselves. She was pregnant and stressed and vulnerable.

And, if his memory could be trusted, probably ready to climb the walls.

He wouldn't push. If things happened, they happened. If they didn't…that was okay, he'd live. A few things might explode, but he'd live.

When he heard her car pull up in the drive, he lit the candles, flicked on the stereo. Classical guitar. Good, good…she loved classical guitar. The front door opened, making his heart jolt the same way it had the first time he attempted this, nearly seventeen years ago.

He stood by the table, waiting, his heart going thumpathumpthumpa in his chest, out of sync with the music. She came to the dining room door, Ginger tucked against her breast.

"Where is everyone—?" Her eyes lit on the table, set with Lucille's good china. The garlic and oregano scent of eggplant parmigiana wafted from the kitchen; nonalcoholic wine sparkled in crystal goblets. The music purred between them like a cat in heat.

She lifted her gaze to his, her face expressionless. "Why, Blake Carter…are you trying to seduce me?"

"No…of course not," he stammered. "I just thought…we could use a nice dinner…what are you doing?"

"Damn you," she said, crossing the room in a blur, the kitten abandoned somewhere along the way. Before he could get her in focus, her mouth was on his, her hands unbuttoning his shirt, her blouse, raking through his hair and down his back then back to working on his shirt. It took a second—barely—before he caught on and began reciprocating, between kisses that made his ears burn.

"I thought you didn't want—"

"I don't. So I suggest," she hissed into his mouth, yanking his shirt out of his pants, "you shut up while you're ahead." Clothes flew like popcorn from a popper with the lid left off.

"The eggplant—"

"Can wait. I can't."

He'd never been so thrilled, turned on and eyeball-popping terrified in his entire life. "No Braxton-Hicks?"

They were halfway back to the bedroom and he'd just unsnapped her bra. How he managed to keep his eyes on her face, he had no idea. Especially when she leaned against the wall and lifted one hand to sweep her hair out of her face, bringing one rosy, taut nipple *really* close to his mouth. Although it was a blur—he had excellent peripheral vision— what with her breathing so heavily and all.

"See," she said, her pupils roughly the size of his fist, "this is where I should lie and tell you, yeah, I've been having them, so I shouldn't be doing this."

He braced his hands on the wall on either side of her head. "But that would be dishonest."

"It would. And if you don't touch my breasts, I'm going to die."

"You and me both, honey," he said, palming the one that had been taunting him the most. She wasn't exactly huge in that department, but the pregnancy had made them firm and full and smooth as silk, and Blake thought heaven couldn't get any better than this. Well, actually, it could, but this would do until then.

He idly thought about moving to the bed, but figured they'd get around to it soon enough. In the meantime, since things were going so well right here…

He gently twisted her nipple between his fingers; she let out a small, wavery, high-pitched cry, and his heart nearly cracked in two. He wasn't a kid anymore, he knew sex wasn't the be-all and end-all of existence, but he also knew that at that moment, nothing mattered more to him than hearing her cries of pleasure. Not that he didn't want to hear his own, as well, but he could wait for that. After all, he'd held off this long, what was another half hour or so?

Or—he swallowed—longer.

But if this was all she would let him give her right now, then by golly, no man would be more generous. Hell, he'd make Santa Claus look like a piker by comparison.

Twirling her nipple with his fingertip, he caught her hissed breath in his mouth as he kissed her again, and again…slow kisses, sweet kisses, steaming-hot-off-the-fire kisses.

"I don't want to take advantage of you," he whispered, and she grabbed his shoulders and cried, "*Take,* for the love of

Pete! *TAKE!*" So he shoved his thigh between her legs, feeling a rush of satisfaction when she pushed herself against him. Even at the beginning, she'd never been shy about sex, as eager to explore and experiment as he, completely trusting that he would never hurt her, never ask her to do anything she didn't want to do.

Breathing hard, he pulled back for a moment to gently trace her eyebrows, her cheeks, her slack mouth with his fingers, loving her so much it hurt, wishing, *willing* her to trust him again the way she once did. Her eyes were closed, her face flushed as his fingers continued their journey, down her neck, over her collarbone, as he whispered his intentions in her ear, told her over and over how beautiful she was, how perfect. She grabbed his head, planting kisses across his forehead, his cheeks, their mouths finally meeting in a frantic, almost clumsy kiss, propelling long-buried memories to the surface. But the past had to damn sight remain buried, if not forgotten: nothing mattered except what was happening *right now*.

And right now was pretty damn good. Emotion tumbled over desire in Blake's gut when Cass opened her mouth on a gasp that was half plea, half welcome, as both simply savored the sweetness of tongues becoming reacquainted with each other. It was the slow dance of kisses, the kind where time stood still and nobody else existed except the two people involved, the kind that made no bones about what it was substituting for, the kind that was downright embarrassing to watch anybody else do.

The kind of kiss a man would remember, with an inscrutable smile, to the day he died. Which, considering how hard Blake was getting, might be a lot sooner than he'd counted on.

Cass did that little moaning thing that said she was having an equally good time, so Blake pinned one hand against the wall over her head, letting the other mold once again to her breast, hot and heavy, the nipple leaking a bit when he squeezed.

Her gasp this time brought his eyes to hers. "You okay?"

"Oh, you have no idea," she whispered. "Do that again."

"What?" He gave it another little tweak. "This?"

She sucked in a breath, nodding. And pushed up more insistently against his leg.

"Let me guess," he breathed close to her ear, placing a kiss on her neck while he was there. "You're close?"

Her response was something between a growl and a groan, but Blake took that as a yes. And so, since his mama had always told him it was rude to keep a lady waiting, he performed that most unselfish of all male acts:

He made her scream.

Cass knew she was in trouble when, even before the waves subsided from that first orgasm, she was immediately looking forward to round two. A state of mind that apparently Blake picked up on, since he then dragged her to the bedroom—already softly lit with the sheets turned down— more or less demolished what was left of their clothes and picked up where they'd left off. Eventually the fog would burn off and reason would return—that was the plan, anyway—but for now...

For now life didn't get much better than this.

Still, her conscience nagged at her enough that she took Blake's face in her hands as they lay there—he, solid as marble, she, walrusesque—and said, "I honestly don't know why I'm doing this," and he kissed her and said, "Are you having fun?", and she said, on a slightly hysterical laugh, "You can't tell?", and he said, "Then that's all that matters." Then his mouth closed over her nipple, and he started to do this thing with his tongue that made her brain short out for a couple of seconds, and she got all heavy and liquid and hot all over again, and somehow, all her objections went *poof.*

She reached down, closing her fingers around that which felt as familiar to her as her own body, even after all this time, letting them do what they still remembered on their own how to do, even after all this time. She knew better than to read too much into his having held off in order to send her to the moon first—he'd always been good at that, if memory served—but still, that she *wanted* to read more into it said something. Something she wasn't entirely sure she wanted to explore too deeply, but there it was.

At moments like this, she thought as he gently turned her on her side to spoon up against her back, it was almost preposterously easy to forget who they were, to believe in magic and promises and happily ever after. But then, it had been easy to believe in all of it at the beginning, too.

Especially when his hands were doing what they were doing, and his mouth was doing what it was doing, and…and…

He shifted them both to gently slide into her from behind; she gasped, tears springing to her eyes.

"Oh, hell…I'm hurting you…"

"No! No—"

More than you'll ever know.

"I'm fine, it's just…"

I had no idea how empty I'd felt until now.

"…it's just I'd forgotten how habit forming this could be."

Blake chuckled softly into her neck. "That's the idea," he said, placing a kiss on her shoulder, moving inside her, each thrust careful and determined and so mind-blowingly tender she had to bite her lip to keep from crying out. Another climax rippled through her, glittering, joyous, like a flock of white butterflies in the sun; Blake followed, only waiting a second after he finished to protectively wrap himself around her.

And she thought, *Oh, hell.*

He'd done it. Broken through her defenses, rickety though they may have been. Love—glorious, painful, pointless—for this crazy, impossible man rushed through her as everything she'd fought so hard against went flying out the window.

Leaving her every bit as depressed as she thought she'd be.

Blake could almost pinpoint the exact second when reality knocked Cass upside the head. He could also play the dumb guy and do his damnedest to ignore it for as long as possible.

"The dog wants in," he mumbled against her neck, stroking her thigh. They'd closed the door at her insistence, teenage boys being an unpredictable lot, given to showing up at odd or—in their case—inopportune moments. Still snuggled up to her back, his skin sighing against hers, he could feel her heart jackhammering inside her chest, although whether from physical exertion or anxiety he had no idea. Both, would be his guess.

"Tough," she said. "He can go find someone else to play with." She reached down for the sheet, covering herself. Blake slipped his hand underneath her arm so that her breast just happened to land in his palm, figuring he might as well work with the tools the Good Lord had given him, right?

"Chilly?" he asked, her scent doing a Dance of the Seven Veils number in his nostrils. She nodded. Taking the easy way out. But he wasn't going to let her do that. Even if it killed him.

"Talk," he softly demanded.

Not surprisingly, she didn't answer right away. Instead, she wriggled his hand out from its nice, warm spot and entwined their fingers, then said, "I'd forgotten how good this felt. With you, I mean."

Okay. That didn't sound too bad.

Then she rolled onto her back and looked at him with

huge, conflicted eyes, and he thought, *Damn.* "You make me feel wanted," she said. "Maybe even…needed."

He stroked her hair away from her forehead as his own heart started up some pretty fierce jackhammering of its own. "And this is a problem why?"

"Because…because it's an illusion. You want to be with your son, and you want sex, and I'm a convenient route to both."

Blake propped himself up on one elbow, his head in his hand, knowing he had to tread verrrrry carefully. "I don't suppose you'd believe me if I said that's not true. That I want a helluva lot more than that."

"I think *you* believe it. That doesn't mean I can."

He looked up, letting out a long stream of air. "Fine," he said, lowering his eyes again. "Then let's take this at face value. First off, there's *nothing* convenient about you. And second, you want to be with Shaun, too. And as for the sex, Miss *Do That Again*—" at least she had the good sense to blush "—I'm not sure I see what the issue is here. Why can't we just enjoy each other?"

"If only it were that easy," she said with a smile that was heartbreakingly sad. "But this has nothing to do with wanting you. Or enjoying it, obviously." When he made a face, she palmed his cheek, locking their gazes. "I probably shouldn't say this, but I don't know how else to make you understand what I feel…" A tiny crease marred her brow. "Believe me, this wasn't about getting something out of my system. If anything, giving in has only made things ten times worse, because—dumb me—I've just freshened up the memories." She removed her hand, tucking it underneath her cheek. "But having sex with you…it's like scarfing down a dish with an ingredient that makes me sick. It might feel good at the time, but, oh, there's hell to pay afterward. Especially since I need a friend right now. Not a lover."

Ice-pick-to-the-chest time. But Blake managed to look her straight in the eye and say, "And why can't I be both?" His jaw hardened. "I was once."

"Once, yes. But things are different now." Another regretful smile. "*I'm* different. And I can't go back to the way things were. I don't dare."

He searched her eyes for several seconds before he swung his legs out of the bed and yanked on his jeans, then stalked out to the living room and the rest of his clothes. By the time Cass appeared, her robe tied up underneath her breasts, he was nearly dressed. He felt his jaw tighten as he jerked on his boots.

"You can yell at me, if you want," she said, shoving her hands into the robe's deep pockets. "I'd completely understand. I shouldn't have let things get out of hand." A pause. "That wasn't fair to you. At all."

Seated on the couch, Blake stilled for a moment, his hands braced on his thighs. Then he lifted his eyes to hers. "I was the one who set the stage, Cass," he said quietly. "I've got no right to be pissed off with anybody but myself. And in any case, nobody forced anybody else to get naked, right?"

Her mouth twitched. "Right." But the pain and confusion in her eyes squeezed his heart. Well, hell. How was he supposed to keep the flame of hope alive when she kept taking a damn hose to it?

"Maybe I should leave for a while," he said, only to see her eyes darken. "For a *while,* Cass. An hour or two, that's all. To clear my head."

"But you went to all this trouble with dinner…"

"I'm not hungry," he said, his voice rough, then grabbed his jacket and car keys and stalked out the front door.

"It's not going the way you planned, is it?"

His business partner's words barely penetrated as, leaning

back in the old-fashioned wooden swivel chair in his make-shift office in the family room, Blake watched Shaun trying to teach the pup how to catch a Frisbee out in the backyard. Thumping and hammering and scraping from assorted contractors filtered through his miasma as, finally, he clicked in enough to respond.

"Why do you say that? I just told you, the office space is secured and ready to set up—"

"I'm not talking about the business, jackass. I'm talking about your new living arrangements. In case you didn't realize it, you sound like hell."

Irritated that his personal problems were apparently readily discernible to anyone he came in contact with—Lucille and Wanda had been merciless over the past several days—Blake strangled the pencil in his hand, neatly snapping it in two.

"I take it from the ominous silence," Troy calmly observed, "that I hit the nail on the head?"

"So give me the sales figures from the northeast," Blake said, ignoring him.

"Those, I can fax to you."

"So fax them, dammit."

After a long second, Troy said, "Give it time, buddy. You knew going in it wasn't going to be easy, right? *Right?*"

"Yeah, yeah, okay, I get the point."

"Maybe she's just gotta get used to the idea, you know? Or maybe you need to figure out another angle. What was it you said a few weeks ago? Something about keeping her off balance?"

Blake leaned forward, tossing the pencil pieces one after the other into the brass trash can on the side of his desk, where they each landed with a satisfying clang. "So now you're some relationship guru?" he said, parodying Lucille.

"Wash your mouth out. But all I'm saying is, it sounds as if she's had it rough these last few months. And she's pregnant, to boot. As scary as women's brains are when they're not pregnant, that's nothing compared with when they *are*. So what did you expect? Miracles? Listen, Alice is bugging me, so I've gotta run. I'll fax all those figures to you ASAP. Catch ya later."

Maybe he had expected a miracle, Blake thought as he hung up the phone. What he'd forgotten, though, was that miracles— most of them, anyway—take time. Patience. And a lot of work.

And it might help if he stopped thinking with his hoohah.

Except…except there'd been something in her eyes that night a week ago, both when they'd made love and after, something that lurked barely underneath the surface of that lame it-was-lovely-see-ya speech, he couldn't slough off. Oh, she was genuinely tormented, that was obvious, genuinely believed there was no point in even trying to resuscitate their relationship. It was the why behind that torment that eluded him…and made him more determined than ever regain her trust. The question was…how?

He pushed himself away from the desk and out of the office, finding himself in front of the room they planned on using as the nursery, the walls freshly replasterboarded, the wooden floor stripped of its mildewed carpet. Hard to believe there'd be a baby in here in a few weeks, he thought, strolling into the cheerful room, even as a splinter of apprehension tried to work underneath his skin. They were miracles, too— messy, noisy and expensive though they might be—and look how much time, patience and work they took.

None of which he'd demonstrated to any great degree when Shaun had been little, had he?

Ladies and gentlemen, the light dawns.

Splotches of buttery sunlight winked on the worn, nearly dry oak floor and across the primed wall, playing peek-a-boo with the shadows cast by the lush mulberry tree in the back-yard. Dana and Mercy had brought over a crib, a chest of drawers and a changing table from the shop—all of which were stashed in the garage until the repairs were completed—but the room hadn't been "done" yet.

Blake felt his lips curve into a smile. Where there's life, there's hope. Or something.

Chuckling to himself, he strode back to the office, grabbed his car keys and called out the window to Shaun.

Chapter Twelve

Cass heard the throbbing beat, like a Poevian heart, emanating from the house the minute she opened her car door. At first she assumed it came from one of the workers' radios, until she realized they'd all be gone at this hour. Cautiously she went inside, following the hip-hop down the hall, to the nursery.

Her hand went to her mouth, trapping the sudden laughter in her throat.

A pair of sweaty, bare-chested males strutted more or less—but more *less* than *more*—in time to the pounding tattoo while they rolled tangerine-hued paint on the walls of Jason's room. Shaun's beanpole frame, jutting up from saggy jeans shorts bordered at the waist by four inches of plaid boxers, contrasted with his father's solid, muscular back and shoulders, narrow waist, firm butt in faded jeans. She swallowed back a brief but remarkably detailed sense memory involving that butt before taking in the Burger King paraphernalia scattered about the room, the flimsy plastic drop cloths over the floor, the stack of wallpaper books on a chair in one corner. Then her gaze, totally of its own accord, swung back to Blake's cute little tush, swishin' away in time to the music.

Said gaze was firmly attached to said tush when the rest of the man turned around and saw her. A thousand-watt grin split his face.

"Hey, sunshine!" He waved the roller toward the wall. Myriad tiny dots of tangerine paint, like fluorescent measles, flecked his forehead, nose, cheeks. "Whaddya think?"

She was beginning to wonder if she'd imagined their tryst, and its angst-laden aftermath, what with Blake's standing there beaming at her and all. Someone watching them might even have thought theirs the perfect family, the man of the house, the older brother doing up the new baby's room. And right now did seem perfect—the glow of the paint, the cool breeze swirling around the room, Blake's silly grin.

The problem with *now,* though, was that it never lasts.

"Lucille and Shaun picked the color," Blake said in a rush, clearly assuming her hesitation was due to the room's, um, vibrancy. "They said you'd said you wanted something bright."

The laugh finally popped out. Light yellow was more what she'd had in mind. "This definitely qualifies," she said, glancing around the room. But with lots of white trim, the color worked beautifully. She'd never have considered it on her own, either. She offered him a smile. "It's terrific," she said, and meant it.

"Yeah?" he breathed, clearly relieved.

"Yeah. You done good."

His smile this time—of understanding and forgiveness far greater than she deserved—nearly broke her heart. Because whether they had sex or not made absolutely not a shred of difference in how she felt about this man. Her heart belonged to him, just as it always had.

Which meant it was his to break, just as it had always been.

Averting her eyes, she ambled over to one of the Burger King bags, nearly doing herself in to pick it up off the floor. "Any fries left?" she asked as she poked inside it, in a voice that sounded hollow and almost shrill in the carpetless room.

A dry, too-warm April settled into a wet, chilly May, for which one immensely pregnant woman was immensely grateful. In two weeks—God willing—this interminable pregnancy would be over.

Dressed to kill in an old olive cardigan over the only nightgown that still fit, her knees splayed, Cass balanced on the end of the Windsor chair at the small rolltop desk in the master bedroom, sifting through the latest crop of bills, which, unfortunately, would *not* be done with in two weeks.

Nor would, she supposed, the ambiguous nature of her relationship with Blake.

On the surface, everything seemed almost oddly normal. But despite the good feelings generated by Blake's doing up the nursery, unresolved issues still crackled between them like loose wires. Even though, in the light of Cass's early dilation and a renewed onslaught of preliminary contractions, Angie had suggested a period of abstinence—a period that had officially ended last week—it was hardly a secret that Blake hoped for a relapse. That she wouldn't exactly be averse to the idea was a secret she guarded with everything she had in her.

Ah, the things we do in the name of self-preservation.

Cass signed yet another check, grimacing at its piddling amount compared with the balance due, thinking for the thousandth time that had it not been for her current predicament, she wouldn't be dealing with quivery stomachs and hammering hearts and a libido whose idle was set far too high for her own good.

Thank you, Alan.

Rotating her shoulders, she picked up the next envelope— What was this?

Her brows drew together as she noted the return address of yet another bank. But surely she'd gotten all the charge card bills she was going to?

She slipped the tip of her index finger underneath the flap and popped it open, the frown deepening at the safe-deposit box bill enclosed. Not at the bill itself—compared with the vast sums she owed everybody else, this was paltry by comparison. No, it was the safe deposit box's existence that befuddled her. Alan had never mentioned it.

Yeah, well, Alan had never mentioned a lot of things.

Carefully, as if the paper were fragile, she laid the bill on the blotter, tapping one finger on it. When she heard Blake's knock on the door frame, though, she hastily folded it up again, slipping it underneath the stack of bills she'd already attended to.

"Hey, you—it's past eleven. What are you still doing up?"

Her head began humming slightly the way it did every time he came close. She whisked her tongue over an envelope flap, grinding the side of her fist against it to seal the envelope. "I need to be sure these are all taken care of, in case this little guy decides to jump the gun on me. And this was first chance I got, since Shaun was particularly chatty this evening."

Blake came all the way into the room, cautiously, she thought, lowering himself onto the edge of the bed he never slept in, having moved officially into his office the instant the repairs were finished. "Oh? What about?"

"Not a whole lot, actually. School stuff, mostly. Except…"

She glanced back at the door, making sure Shaun wasn't about to walk in on them, then whispered, "Between you and me, I think someone has his first real crush."

Blake's eyebrows went up. "Really?"

"Mmm-hmm." *Look at us,* she thought. *Just your average parents of a teenage son, having your average discussion about his goings-on. Perfectly normal, perfectly civilized, perfectly perfect.* "I've seen her, too. That cute little brunette who lives down the street." She grinned, even getting up the nerve to meet Blake's gaze. "Suddenly he's ready to switch schools."

"You mean, the younger version of Mercy with the green fingernails?"

"I think they were red, white and blue today, but yep. That's the one."

Blake groaned, then chuckled. "Considering my son wears more jewelry than Lucille, I guess I can't say too much, huh?"

"Considering what you looked like when I met you, you can't say anything at all."

The skin around his eyes crinkled as he laughed, and she laughed with him, savoring the moment of…affection, she supposed it was. Right now, like this, it seemed so easy. So natural.

Even, she supposed, so *right*.

The laughter died as she forced her eyes away from Blake's soft hair. Then his hands. That left his mouth, which was no help whatsoever. Her skin tingled briefly from a faint but unmistakable shudder.

He looked at her for a moment, and the relaxed moment evaporated like smoke. The box springs protested softly as he stood, then came to stand behind her. "Put your head down," he gently commanded.

Uh, boy. If she admitted how dangerous it was to have him touch her, she'd be playing right into his hands. So, like a fool, she obeyed, playing right into his hands—literally—anyway. The groan slipped out before she even thought about it as his incredible fingers began sweetly torturing her shoulder and neck muscles. Distant erogenous zones sent out hopeful signals; she silently ordered them to shut up.

They didn't listen.

So much for grossly pregnant women not being in the mood.

"How's that?" he asked.

"Mmm" was all she could manage, which got a low, syrupy chuckle in return. She shifted her head to lay one cheek on her forearms, her legs spread far apart in order to accommodate her heavy belly, the bottom of which actually rested on the chair between her knees, rather than her lap.

"Did Towanda tell you her news?"

Instantly on alert, both of Cass's eyes popped open. "News?"

"Dammit, Cass—you just undid five minutes of hard work. Now relax."

She tried, but no dice. "Here's a thought—why don't you just tell me whatever you're going to tell me, and let me be the judge of whether I can relax or not?"

"And when are you going to get it through your head," he said, removing his hands from her shoulders, "that you're not responsible for everything and everyone in the entire known universe?"

He'd moved to perch on the top of the desk beside her. Wriggling her shoulders in slow motion, she pulled herself upright, her mouth set. "Well, smack my wrist for trying to survive."

She flinched when he lifted her hand, kissed her wrist instead. The underside, where her pulse beat. The very point he damn well knew was particularly sensitive. "And then there's the way you get defensive every five minutes," he murmured, brushing his lips across the top of her palm.

She snatched back her hand. "Who says I get defensive?"

"Anybody who's every spent more than thirty seconds in your charming company," Blake said mildly. "Now, darlin', if I reassure you that what I'm about to say neither threatens the status quo nor your own independence, may I continue?"

Cass huffed a sigh, then nodded, deciding to be grateful his lips and her skin were no longer communicating with each other, since her skin and her *brain* obviously weren't.

"You know all those old recipes Towanda's been doing up for me?"

She nodded again, a little fuzzily.

"I've hired her as a consultant for the new baked goods operation. We're going to modify her recipes for mass production, start out with maybe a half-dozen items or so, see how it goes…what?"

"Ohmigod. You've turned into a corporate raider."

He laughed. "Not hardly." Then his hand cupped her cheek before she even saw him move. "Honey, Wanda's like a boomerang—I couldn't pry her away from you guys if I tried. The position's only part-time, but you should see how excited she is. She'll get a share of the profits, too…."

But he'd hooked her with his eyes, and she no longer heard what he was saying. Not with his lips, anyway. A breeze rattled the miniblinds as she realized his thumb was drawing lazy loops across her jaw. Loneliness and need swirled up from the pit of her stomach, tempting, tempting…

"You're not supposed to do this," she whispered, her eyes filling with tears.

"I know," he said, then lowered his mouth to hers.

The sweetest kisses were the most dangerous, she decided as his lips made contact, the deliberate chasteness of the embrace clearly designed to tease. To hint. To drive her slowly mad.

Of course, as hard up as she was, he could have blown a

kiss across the room to her and she'd been ready to rumble. Actual lip-to-lip contact was tantamount to brushing against a hair-trigger bomb.

Only two weeks to go. Angie had said she could do anything she wanted, since going into labor at any time wouldn't be a problem. And her hormones were chanting like rubber-neckers underneath a person standing on the ledge—"Jump…jump…jump!"

Only they weren't saying "jump."

"I can't," she said, jerking away.

Frustration glinted in Blake's eyes, but not anger. Something else, though, burned there. Something she refused to name, because naming it would mean having to deal with this on another level she simply wasn't prepared to handle. Not now.

Not ever.

Heartsick, Blake searched Cass's face for something, anything, that would explain her distress. For more than a month he'd played by her rules. For more than a month he'd swallowed down his irritation every time he'd see the sparkle of humor in her eyes fade into a sadness he didn't understand. Like now.

"Cass…" Blake drew a thumb across her bottom lip, then lifted it to catch the tear as it trickled down her cheek. And decided he had nothing more to lose. "I love you, honey. I swear to you, I'm not about to do anything to screw this up."

He saw her shoulders stiffen, undoing the massage. Again. "No, Blake, you're confusing love with…with responsibility, or, or guilt or something…"

For some reason he laughed. Not what she was expecting, apparently, judging from the "Huh?" look on her face. "Let's see, I'm voluntarily living with a fifteen-year-old boy, an eighty-year-old Jewish Chihuahua, and the world's most pregnant women…yep, I'm pretty sure this is love." He slipped from the desk, crouching beside her. Taking both her hands in his, he recaptured her eyes, that sea of sad, sweet blue. "Cass…I may be sticking my neck in a noose here, but my guess is, if you didn't still have feelings for me, too, you wouldn't be fighting this so hard."

She looked away, but not before he saw his answer in her eyes.

Not that this made things any easier. But at least he now knew what he was dealing with. And as long as there was hope, he could deal with Cass's stubbornness. He was pretty sure he could, anyway.

The baby kicked; Blake saw, then rested his hand on her stomach. "Hey there, slugger, kick Daddy's hand again—"

"Don't *say* that!"

The panic in her voice made him jerk up his head. "Cass…?"

She stood so quickly the chair nearly tipped over. "Jason can't think of you as his father, Blake. It wouldn't be fair. Especially since this is a short-term arrangement."

"Says who?"

He could see her pulse throbbing frantically at the base of her throat. "Says us. Or at least, that's what we agreed to. Isn't it?"

"Well, honey," he said as he drew himself upright, "now I'm saying I don't agree to the terms of our original agreement. I'm saying I want this to be permanent and forever after, and that no man shall put asunder, the way it should have been the first time. The way it should have been *this* time, not this cockamamie living-together business. I'm saying…"

Then it occurred to him to stop yapping and pick up where he'd left off a minute before, more urgently this time, melting his lips into hers as he gently imprisoned her flummoxed face in his hands. Twice, at least, during the not-in-any-hurry kiss, he sensed she was about to pull away. Twice, at least, he recaptured her mouth before she could. When he finally did, she was blinking up at him as if she'd just emerged from a cool, darkened theater onto a blisteringly hot, bright sidewalk. And a faint, triumphant bell went off in his brain. She was even swaying a little, literally as well as figuratively off balance.

"I'm saying," he finished, backing away, smugly noticing her brow crinkling with confusion, "that maybe, just maybe, what's sizzling between us is about more than sex. That it always was. That, yeah, we've already established that I was an ass, but that maybe instead of stewing about the past, we should figure out what's good about the present so we could maybe look forward to the future. And that maybe you should think about that for a minute or two and see what you come up with."

Then, without further comment, he left her to do exactly that.

Blake was barely out of the room before Cass sank onto the bed so hard the baby whonked her a good one. Yeah, well, Blake, she thought, her eyes burning, thinking about *now* was exactly what got her into trouble before. And what was that line about those who didn't pay attention to history were doomed to repeat it?

Lucille, Wanda, Shaun, her partners—none of them were making any bones about how much of an idiot they thought Cass was being. And who could blame them? Especially since she was more than a little inclined to agree. For heaven's sake, the poor guy was turning himself inside out in order to make things up to her. And doing a bang-up job of it, she had to admit. But while his kindness and generosity were a bandage for her trampled, wounded soul, it was one that would hurt like hell when it got ripped off. Oh, God—what she wouldn't give to be able to simply give up and give in, to let Blake be what he was trying so hard to be.

To confess that, for all the noise she'd made about not trusting him, it had never really been about *him* at all.

Rubbing her belly, Cass's eyes drifted back to the desk. Back to the pile of bills and the mystery safety-deposit-box bill underneath them.

A box procured by the baby's real father for God knows what reason.

Jason's *real* father? Now, there was a joke, she thought with a sharp little laugh. Blake had already shown more interest in this baby who wasn't even his than Alan had in all the months leading up to his death.

She fell over onto her side on the mattress, leaking hot, silent tears. *No, Blake,* she thought. *You're not the ass.*

I am.

Blake stalked down the hall and into the kitchen, his lips tingling, his fists balled hard enough to cramp his fingers. His bravado of only seconds before quickly fading, he yanked open the refrigerator, saw nothing he wanted, slammed it shut again.

"What the *hell* are you so afraid of, Cassandra?" he muttered, sick to death of this refrain but unable to get it out of his head. "Is it me? Does it have something to do with that slimeball second husband of yours? *What?*"

He had a hundred times more to offer her now than he had the first time around. Yet the more he gave—or tried to give—the more sensitive and understanding he tried to be, the more she gave him that rabbit-with-a-shotgun-pointed-at-its-head look.

With a groan, he fell back against the refrigerator, his noggin thunking on the enameled door, jarring loose the one possibility he hadn't considered. Had refused, in his myopic determination to get what he wanted, to consider.

That, his delusional hope notwithstanding, she simply *didn't* love him anymore. And wasn't going to. Was that was she was afraid to tell him? That, as far as she was concerned, this really was only about keeping a roof over everyone's head?

Was he really that dense?

"Dad? You okay?"

Blake slanted his head forward to see Shaun standing in the kitchen doorway, barefoot and disheveled, a two-sizes-too-large T-shirt skimming his lanky frame over a pair of Taz-embellished boxers. And in the half-light, he saw the boy's eyes littered with questions that Blake knew—hoped—he wouldn't ask, and with emotions he probably didn't even understand, and couldn't articulate even if he did. Questions and emotions Blake knew damn well neither of them could avoid facing forever.

"What are you doing up?" Blake asked, madly straightening out his cluttered brain.

"Working on an English project," the kid cagily replied. Blake stepped aside as he ambled over to the refrigerator.

"Due tomorrow?"

Shaun flicked Blake a furtive glance, then nodded. He pulled out a carton of milk and popped it open, barely stopping himself from taking a swig right from the carton. Blake reached behind him and pulled a glass out of the drainer, handing it to his son. "And when did you start?"

"Tuesday," Shaun mumbled around the rim of the glass as he lifted it to his lips.

This was Thursday. "And…how long have you known about it?"

"Man, you are one nosy dude, you know that?" the boy said, sidestepping the question, his hair swishing over shoulders that stretched out the cotton jersey surprisingly well.

Blake laughed, but it faded as he thought how accustomed

he'd already become to being around his son again. To being around Cass, who could be quite pleasant—and a hoot—when she wasn't running scared. For more than a decade, he'd denied an essential part of his makeup, which was that he needed family. He actually did like being a father. That he'd missed so much…well, that was no one's fault but his.

The realization that this might not work out after all ripped through his gut like a dulled knife. As if reading Blake's mind, Shaun said, "So. You really think you'll stick around this time?"

And there was at least one of those unasked questions, laid at Blake's feet like a cat's half-devoured mouse. If there was any bitterness underlying the words, though, the kid was doing a damn good job of squelching it, as if there was little point in letting the subject get to him anymore.

"For you, absolutely," Blake said, meeting his son's gaze. He saw Shaun's throat work. "And for Mom?"

"I suppose that's up to her."

"But I thought you guys were getting along okay."

Folding his arms over his chest, Blake said, "Guess that depends on how you define 'getting along.' But after everything that happened between us…she's still really gun-shy, Shaun. I'm sorry."

"Then you just have to change her mind, dude. Win her over, y'know?"

Blake looked down at his feet, shaking his head and laughing softly, before again lifting his eyes to his son. "*Dude*— I'm doing my best, here. But I can't exactly force her to fall back in love with me, can I? And you know your mother." He cleared his throat. "Probably a lot better than I do, actually."

The kid took a long sip of milk, then let out a ragged breath. "Yeah. I do. Man, I would not want to be in your shoes, that's for sure. Even though…"

"What?"

Uncertainty flared in eyes eerily like Blake's before the boy shook his head. "Forget it, it's nothing."

"Shaun, I'm finally here, you might as well milk it for all it's worth."

After a moment his son let out another huge sigh, this time apparently reluctant to look directly at Blake. "Yeah, well, that's kinda the problem. That you're here."

"I don't understand."

Shaun backed his spare frame up onto a bar stool, his face a study in confusion. "Don't get me wrong, I'm really glad you're back. That you want to work things out with Mom and everything. But sometimes…" Another puffed breath. "Sometimes I get really mad, thinking you'll be around for Jason when you never were with me. Well, not *never,* but you know what I mean. It just seems so damn unfair, you know?"

"Yeah," Blake said softly, as the knife made an encore appearance, gouging even more deeply this time. "I do. And you're right, it is unfair. One of the many things about this whole mess that will haunt me for the rest of my life." He leaned back against the counter himself, bracing his hands on either side of his hips. "But how come you didn't say anything about this before?"

Bony shoulders hitched underneath the T-shirt. "Dunno. 'Cause it sounded dumb and selfish, I s'pose."

Blake shook his head. "No, Shaun. Not dumb. Or selfish. And you have no idea how much I wish I had some magic words to make it all go away. To somehow change the past. And now…" He let out a harsh sigh of his own. "Now I see that maybe it's not even possible to make it up to you, or your mother, no matter how much I want to. Just…just don't take it out on your brother, okay?"

Shaggy brows shot up. "Dad, geez, give me *some* credit. It's not Jason's fault, he's just a baby. Besides, the way Alan was acting? I'd kinda already figured I'd have to show the little dude the ropes, anyway, 'cause trust me—that guy didn't have a *clue*. This way, with you around…well, I guess it's all working out okay, anyway. Weird, yeah, but okay."

"You're sure?"

Shaun seemed to think it over for a second or two, then shook his head. "Mostly, yeah. I'm glad…" His shoulders hunched again. "I'm glad I said something, though. Instead of keeping it in and stuff."

"Yeah. Me, too."

With a nod, the boy slid off the stool and set his empty glass on the counter, then turned to leave. A grunt from Blake, however, drew him back.

"Dishwasher, bud."

Shaun shot Blake a look as he opened the dishwasher, set the glass on the top rack. "Man, you sound like Wanda."

"Being male is no excuse for being a slob. Or inconsiderate."

A grin slanted across the boy's narrow face. "Now you sound like Mom."

"That good or bad?"

"I haven't figured that out yet."

Unwilling to let the boy go just yet, Blake said, "Speaking of whom…she says you have a new…friend."

The seemingly nonchalant shrug said it all. "Just Martina from down the street. Her folks own a restaurant out on Rio Grande, so we go there sometimes, after school, you know?" Another grin lit up his face, both shy and devilish. "Free food is free food."

"Ah." Blake rubbed his jaw, deliberately not looking at his son. "What's she look like?"

Another shrug. "Dunno. Average, I s'pose. Big brown eyes, dark, really shiny hair. But she doesn't giggle and act all dumb like the other girls. She plays in the school orchestra. Violin. She's really good, too—"

Blake suppressed a chuckle as the gate to his son's innermost workings slammed shut.

"Well." Shaun tucked a hank of stringy hair behind a very red-rimmed ear. "I, uh, better get back to that project."

"Yeah. Time's awastin'."

"Yeah." Shaun, too, seemed hesitant to leave, tapping his fingers against the counter, and Blake glimpsed the little boy whose life he'd more or less missed. Ignoring the warning that said he might be rebuffed for the second time this evening, Blake crossed the few feet between them and engulfed the kid in a swift hug, which, to his immense relief, was returned. Then, with an embarrassed grin, Shaun turned and strolled out of the kitchen.

His throat knotted, Blake wandered around the house for several minutes after that, checking doors and windows, making sure all the lights were out. It was hell, this dual frustration and peace that warred continually in his gut. Even though he knew Cass had only accepted his offer because it was the only decent solution to a monumental problem, Blake had found the home he'd been missing for more than a third of his life. The thought of giving it up, of giving up the relationship he was finally beginning to forge with his son, made him sick to his stomach.

But not nearly as much as the thought of making Cass unhappy.

Chapter Thirteen

The next morning, before Cass was due to go into work, Wanda and Cille said they wanted to check out the new domestics outlet that had recently opened near the mall. Since the bank was nearby, Cass decided to see what, if anything, was in that safe deposit box before curiosity pickled her brain any more than it already was.

The bank officer listened to Cass's request, nodded, then asked to see the requisite proof of her identity. Five minutes later she sat with the box in front of her, drumming her fingers on the top for several seconds before she finally sucked in a breath, inserted the key into the lock and swung back the top, jerking back a little as if expecting bats to fly up out of it.

No bats. Instead, at least a dozen folded paper packets lay inside, unmarked and unremarkable. Almost without curiosity, she lifted one out of the box, unfolded one flap and tilted it upside down.

Glittering like laughter, a half dozen somethings that looked suspiciously like diamonds tumbled out into her palm. Cass blinked, sure that any moment the *Candid Camera* people were going to pop up out of nowhere. If not the Feds.

Her first coherent thought—and it took a while for one to make its way through—was that they couldn't possibly be real. Her second coherent thought was, why would anyone put a bunch of fake gemstones in a safe deposit box?

Holding her breath, she carefully checked each one of the packets, her heart rate increasing with each one. Some of them contained rubies and emeralds, one sapphires. She had no earthly idea how much the stones might be worth in the current market, or even the quality, but she suspected she held a small fortune in the palm of her hand.

Then she noticed some papers at the bottom of the box…which turned out to be bills of sale. Bills of sale that gave her a damn good idea how much they were worth.

"Oh my God," she breathed. "Oh. My. *God.*"

They were indeed real. And they were hers. Alan had left a simple but quite legal will, assigning his entire estate to her. Up until this moment, his generosity had seemed little more than a cruel joke.

Her brain swam with a million thoughts as she pressed one packet to her chest. Why hadn't Alan mentioned the jewels? Why hadn't he sold them, instead of hocking everything else? What had he been thinking?

She would never know, she supposed. And none of it mattered now.

Still not quite believing these were hers to do with as she pleased, Cass slipped one of the packets into her purse. Fear dampened her hands as she stood, locking the box and slipping it back into its slot. She always felt this way when she had to take the day's cash to the bank, too, as if she were wearing a flashing sign announcing how much money she was carrying. Brother. Good thing she hadn't gone in for a life of crime—she'd've been caught her first time out.

She picked up the ladies at the store; they'd all barely settled into their seats before she said in a breathless rush, "The first one to spill a word of this to Blake is dead meat. Got it?"

Both women nodded their puzzled assent as Cass rooted in her purse for the packet, momentarily freaking when she couldn't find it for the wad of tissues that had exploded in the bottom of the bag. Finally her fingers closed around the smooth paper; she drew it out and handed it to Lucille, who was sitting beside her. Towanda had skootched forward, her face poked between the headrests of the bucket seats.

"What is it?"

But Lucille, like Cass had done before her, had gone mute, red lips flapping up and down in speechless astonishment.

"What *is* it?" Towanda repeated with some exasperation, leading Cass to snatch the packet out of Lucille's claws and practically thrust it at the housekeeper, as if it were hot. She opened two of the flaps, then hissed a slow, pungent swearword. "I don't suppose I'm looking at cubic zirconia, am I?"

Cass finally started the car. "Uh-uh." She returned her gaze to Lucille. "Alan ever say anything about buying jewels?"

The poor woman stared straight ahead, her hand at her throat. "I'd forgotten. Once, years ago, he said he was thinking about buying up some diamonds. But he only mentioned it in passing, and I didn't think anything more about it. You know, since he had his fingers into so many pies. I had no idea he'd buy so *many.*"

Cass let out a sharp laugh. "You should see what I left in the safe deposit box."

Lucille swore this time, which got an "Amen, sister" from Towanda.

"So," Cass continued, wriggling the car through midtown traffic, "anybody have a clue where's the nearest place to unload these puppies? I got me some bills to pay."

Lucille insisted on going into the exchange with Cass, so here they were—the world's most pregnant woman and her Tammy Faye sidekick, wheeling and dealing over a small handful of diamonds which turned out to be worth more than Cass had even thought. If she was getting ripped off, she didn't know and she didn't care, although, considering the reputation of the company, she didn't think that was likely. Immediately after making the offer on the loose stones, the salesman commented on her solitaire and wedding ring, asking her if she'd had them appraised recently.

She looked down at the rings as if she'd quite forgotten they were there, imbedded in her finger because of all the water she was retaining. Lucille's fingers feathered against her wrist.

"I know what you're thinking," she said quietly. "Sell 'em, if he'll buy."

Cass started, then peered down into that overly made-up face that had become so dear to her. "You wouldn't mind?"

Lucille titched, shook her head. "There's no sentiment attached, I don't imagine. Am I right?"

A little sadly, Cass shook her head in agreement, then said, "But I'd thought of keeping them for the baby. Maybe, when he grows up—"

But Lucille interrupted her again. "If it's not love that makes them sparkle, they're just glass. Not the legacy I want my only grandson to pass to his future bride." She angled her head. "You won't hurt my feelings, sweetheart, if that's what's worrying you."

Cass looked up at the guy standing behind the counter, a

patient, enigmatic smile tugging at his lips. She waggled her fingers at him. "Would you be interested in buying these?"

He held out his hand. "May I?"

Cass placed hers in his palm, whereupon he bent over the rings, inspecting them through his loupe. After several seconds he straightened up, smiled. "Very interested. I could sell the stones in a heartbeat, no sweat."

"Fine," she said, then crooked her mouth. "If you can get them off my finger, they're yours."

She drove the ladies back home, then on to the store, where she found Dana and Mercy an inch away from coming to blows over the disposition of a six-foot-square display area. Cass planted her big belly between them, effectively cutting off any opportunity the two much shorter women had to do each other in.

"What?" Cass demanded.

Spanish-tinged accent vied with Southern as each vehemently tried to convince Cass that her items needed the space more. Dana, Cass finally deciphered, wanted to put lamps and accessories on the shelves, while Mercy insisted the recent shipment of newborn toys were more important.

With one sharp downward motion of her hands, Cass shushed them both, then scanned the crowded shop, desperately hunting for a nook or even half a cranny so both women would be happy. Seeing none, she finally suggested intermixing the toys around the lamps and accessories, replacing the stock as the items sold. Both brunettes muttered, "Yeah, okay, guess that'd work," and peace was restored. For the moment.

Customers came in, further distracting her two partners, freeing Cass to retreat to the office and the nearest chair. She thought of the check she had in her handbag, of the cache of stones still in that safe deposit box. Of the possibilities that total financial freedom would give her. She should be feeling relieved, if not ecstatic.

What she was feeling was slightly unhinged. And anxious. Keeping her discovery from Blake wasn't a possibility, she knew. Maybe this wasn't a real relationship—whatever the hell that meant—but she couldn't very well not tell him that she was no longer destitute. That she no longer needed him. Or at least needed his money. Which is where the unhinged part of this came in.

She frowned, lining up her thoughts on an imaginary page.

She now had money.

Good thing.

Alan had ended up paying off his own damn debt.

Very good thing.

If she wanted, she could now buy pretty much any house she wanted.

Whenever she wanted.

So she wouldn't have to live under the same roof as Blake.

Like pulling a dog into the vet's, she tried to force the words *good thing* into her thought. They absolutely, positively refused to come.

Because, much as she hated to admit it, this wasn't as simple as "Now that she had money, she could do what she damn well pleased." There was Shaun to think about, who was obviously enjoying having his father *be* his father. And Lucille, too, for whom that mother-in-law quarters was barely one step removed from The Promised Land.

And the fact that—okay, she might as well admit this, too—she didn't want to leave.

Which was not a good thing. At all.

As if someone had pulled the plug, she suddenly felt so tired she could hardly move. It hurt to think. It hurt to *be*. All she wanted to do, she realized with the an almost vicious intensity, was to crawl into Blake's arms and never come out. There were no answers there, she knew, no solutions. More likely, she'd only find more trouble.

She didn't need a man, she told herself. She could take care of herself, her children, Lucille—

Oh, hell—this had nothing to do with being able to take care of herself. This had to do with needs far more visceral than even food or shelter. Needs she could deny to the death but she could no longer ignore. Her head dropped to her hand as tears of weary frustration slithered over her bottom lashes.

A blur in a soft-rose crepe pantsuit zipped into the office, grabbed something off a shelf, whizzed back out, popped back in ten seconds later. More hair down than up in her top-knot, Dana dropped into the chair across the desk from Cass, fixing her with ambery eyes.

"Sweetie, you look about ready to keel over," she said, making futile efforts to tuck errant strands of hair back into place. "Go home. Please."

Barely hanging on to her control, Cass shook her head.

"Why not?"

Because going home will only remind me what a sorry mess I am.

"Wanda's doing a major clean today," she lied. "And she hates having bodies cluttering up her workspace."

"Hey. You forget, I've met Wonder Wanda. No way is she gonna keep you out of your own house when you don't feel well. And you don't, do you?"

She really didn't. And that made her feel even more helpless, which made her angrier. She'd felt fine the whole time with Shaun. This go-round, howeve, she felt as though she'd had a run-in with a semi.

As if reading her thoughts, Dana said, "You're not twenty this time, honey. And you've been under a lot of stress. We can handle things here. Really. Go home. Crawl into bed with a good book—" she grinned "—or whatever, and just take it easy."

Cass managed a wan smile. "So you're saying I'm not indispensable?"

"I'm saying—" Dana pushed herself out of the chair, adjusting her necklace so it lay between her full breasts "—I don't want you having the baby in this back room. Unless you're planning on having it standing up."

That got a laugh, feeble though it was. "Speaking of which…" Now Cass, too, got up, trying not to wince. "What do you say, after the baby comes, we sit down and seriously consider finding a larger place?"

Dana gave a short laugh. "I don't think we have much of a choice. Six more months, and the shop's gonna explode, *kapooey!*" Her hands flew into the air. "Sleepers and stuffed toys dangling from tree branches!"

Cass grinned for her partner, then gathered her purse. "I guess I do need a nap…ouch!"

"You okay?"

"This has got to be," she said, trying to dislodge some appendage or other from underneath her ribs, "the longest baby in history. And I clearly am not providing ample enough quarters for him—"

She caught the wistful expression on Dana's face and cut herself short.

"Oh, God, I'm so sorry, honey! I wasn't thinking…."

Wordlessly, Dana walked around the desk and put her hand on Cass's belly. "Now you listen to me—my situation has nothing to do with yours, so don't you go getting all sappy on me. Maybe I won't have the pleasure of throwing up every morning for three months or going to the john every fifteen minutes—" she let out a little "Ohh!" when the baby kicked her palm "—or feeling my baby kick, but I'll have my child one day. When it's time." Then she removed her hand and parked it on her rounded hip. "Now you get your carcass out of here, and I don't want to see it again until the baby's on the outside, you hear me?"

With a soft laugh Cass drew Dana into a brief hug, leaving before either of them turned into blubbering twits.

Amazing. She had the house all to herself. Wanda had taken Lucille to the doctor and then on to the grocery store, according to one note tacked to the refrigerator, and Blake would be back "soon," according to a second.

Ah, bliss. Shaky, maybe, but bliss all the same.

Cass changed into white shorts and what looked like a tablecloth with armholes, poured herself a glass of juice and wandered out into the garden, which involved a brief skirmish at the patio door to ensure the kittens stayed in and the dog stayed out. Feeling like a piano being lowered from a third-floor window, she clumsily settled into a glider on the patio. Only she'd no sooner elevated her poor doughy feet when the cordless phone burred on the glass table beside her. A young, secretarial-type voice asked for Blake.

"He's not available at the moment. May I take a message?"

"Yes, ma'am, this is Southwest Title? I tried reaching Mr. Carter on his cell, like he asked, but his service was down. So would you mind telling him we had to move back his closing on Friday from two to three?"

"I'm sorry—did you say his *closing?*"

"Yes, ma'am, on the Deer Dancer property? The buyer had to switch their appointment, so he needs to come in later—"

"Yes, yes, that's fine. I'll give him the message. Thank you."

It took all of ten seconds for Cass to put two and two together and come out with one man who was going to be skinned alive the next time she saw him. Appropriately enough, the baby walloped her a good one, a well-placed hook right to the bladder.

From the other side of the house, she heard Blake's Range Rover pull up, the car door creak open, slam shut. Dude bounded to his feet to whine and dance at the screen door, his entire back end shimmying in excitement.

"Hey, guy," she heard from the darkened interior of the house. The door screeched on its runners as Blake opened it to step outside, squatting by the dog before he noticed her presence. His huge smile pierced her heart, almost—almost— overriding her pique. "Hey, honey, I didn't expect you to be home." Instantly his brows dipped. "You okay?"

"I'm not sure. You have a message."

"Oh?"

"Mmm. From Southwest Title."

Every muscle in his face instantly hardened, as if he'd been flash frozen. "Oh?" he repeated on a short breath.

"Your appointment on Friday has been moved back from two to three." She considered rising from the glider, thought better of it. Instead, she hooked the bottom of her bare foot on the edge of the glass table in front of her and began an agitated rocking. "So tell me, Blake—did you make a profit on the house?"

He got to his feet slowly, his breath escaping his lips in a long hiss. "You weren't supposed to find out."

"I kinda figured that."

Contrite, apologetic eyes met hers. "First off, no, I didn't. Make a profit. Secondly, C.J. told me he was concerned the property might not sell as quickly as you needed it to. And I didn't want you moving any closer to the birth—"

"So you went behind my back and simply 'took care of things.'"

"If I'd thought there was any other way, I wouldn't have resorted to subterfuge. But you were being so all-fired stubborn about letting me help you—"

"Because I didn't want you to rescue me!"

"What in tarnation is so damned awful about being rescued?" he bellowed, making her start. "You're the mother of my son, for God's sake! You'd just had a ton of crap dumped on you, and I told you from the beginning I wasn't going to stand by and watch you—"

"Learn how to fend for myself? Grow up? Solve my own problems? Which is it, Blake? What is it, exactly, you weren't going to let me do?"

"End up on the street, you blasted woman!"

"You just don't get it, do you? *I don't want to be obligated to you!*"

His eyes darkened. "This isn't about obligation. It's about common sense. And responsibility. A concept that's taken me far too long to figure out, I grant you, but—"

"And how do you figure *you're* responsible for the mess I got *myself* into?"

"The same way you figure you're responsible for Lucille and Towanda, I imagine!"

"It's not the same thing! Lucille's family. And Wanda's as good as. You're not."

"Not for lack of trying, dammit! Believe what you want, Cass, but I didn't ask you to marry me again out of pity. Or simply to solve a problem. I asked you because I love you. Because I've always loved you."

She refused to let his words, the fire in his eyes, derail her. "*Why*, Blake? Why would you want to marry me again when all we do is fight?"

"People fight, Cass! Then the air is cleared and you move on."

"And you know all about moving on, don't you?"

"Damn it to *hell*, Cass! Why is it the harder I try to prove to you I'm not that jerk who walked out on you twelve years ago, the more roadblocks you throw up between us? Why does my trying to make things *better* for you threaten you so much?"

"Stop it!"

They both yanked their heads around to find Shaun standing in the patio doorway, fury contorting his features. Cass's stomach torqued as she literally felt the blood drain from her face. "Oh, God, honey…how long have you been there?"

"Long enough." The kid hurled at her, his hands fisted at his sides. "God—why do you two *do* this? So he bought the house from you, Mom—so what? Dude—it's just a *house!* And Dad's got, like, more money than God, so it's not like it's even that big a deal to him or anything. I mean, Alan left you with this huge debt and everything, right? So Dad tries to take care of things so we don't starve—"

"We wouldn't have starved, Shaun—"

"—and you, like, keep acting like he's doing something terrible to you." He barreled over her objection, his voice rough with pain and confusion. "I don't get it, Mom. I really don't. Maybe you think because I'm fifteen I can't see what's going on between you two, but let me tell you, the room heats up twenty freakin' degrees every time you guys look at each other. Why can't you just admit you still love each other and get on with your lives, already?"

He gave a frustrated jab at the air, then pivoted so fast his rubber-soled shoe squeaked on the cement. Blake took off after him.

"Where are you going?"

"Just out," the kid slung over his shoulder, lobbing a wounded glance at Cass. "You promised you'd try to make it work. You *promised!*"

"Shaun!" Blake grabbed for him, but their son dodged his grasp and disappeared into the house.

"Let him go," Cass said softly, getting to her feet. God, her back was killing her.

"He can't talk to you like that—"

"But he's absolutely right. I did promise him I'd try to make this work." She paused, frowning, as one might to ascertain whether or not that really *is* the ground moving underneath your feet.

"Is he right, though?" Blake asked softly. Still frowning, Cass looked at him. "*Do* you love me?"

If she had any sense at all, she'd deny it. Then again, if she'd had any sense at all, she wouldn't be in this predicament to begin with. "This isn't about my loving you. It's about…oh, *hell!*"

A jolt of white-hot pain tore at her crotch, her muscles locking with such force she could barely catch her breath. She grabbed for Blake's arm, trying desperately to breathe, to get on top of the surprise contraction.

"Let me guess," he said. "Not a Braxton-Hicks?"

She let out a swear word she *never* used. Except when she was in labor.

"Nope, guess not," he said, then made her meet his eyes. "Okay, breathe with me, honey, come on…good, good…let it out, long breath… Done?"

Still stunned from the contraction, she nodded. Then said, "I can't go into labor right now."

"Because…?"

She bequeathed him her most exasperated look. "Because we're in the middle of a fight, because Shaun's upset, because…*dammit!*"

"Good job, sunshine!" Blake said as about a million gallons of amniotic fluid splashed all over the cement. "Outside and everything!"

Leave it to a baby to interrupt a moment of crisis, she thought. Then she caught the cowering puppy's bug-eyed "I didn't do that, I swear," look from underneath the glider, and she had to laugh, at herself, her life, at Whoever plans these things. "I'm irrigating half of Bernalillo county," she muttered, "and he makes jokes. Um, I could really use a towel here?"

"Right."

After Blake left, she tried walking, only to discover her bones had apparently washed out with the fluid. So he returned to find her clutching one of the metal supports for the patio cover, shaking so badly her teeth were rattling.

"Wh-what t-took you so d-d-damn long?" she said, unceremoniously stuffing the towel between her wobbly legs.

"I called Angie. She said call her back once the contractions reached—"

Cass sank ten claws into Blake's forearms and tried not to pass out. He eased her through it again, getting her seated when it had passed.

"I think I'll call her back."

"Good plan." When he turned to go back into the house, however, she snagged his arm, smacking the cordless into his palm. "Leave me and you're a dead man." When he had the nerve to tilt an amused smile at her as he punched in Angie's pager number, she glowered in return. "Not one comment, do you hear me? Not one single solitary comment. We will continue this conversation after I have this…"

She sucked in a breath, clamped onto his arm, and wondered if the kid was trying to blowtorch his way out.

Every time Blake glanced up at the clock, it seemed as though another hour had passed. And with every hour Cass became more exhausted and more discouraged. The way things had started, everyone including Angie had expected the birth to progress quickly. But for some reason the contractions petered out over those first two hours, and now, some ten hours after Cass's water had broken, she was still only five centimeters dilated. Angie finally suggested she stop walking to conserve her energy. No one had yet said anything, but it was pretty clear that Cass's hopes for a natural birth were quickly fading.

She wasn't fighting Blake at all now, about anything. He sat on the edge of the bed, cradling her, her head resting on his shoulder. It had been a full five minutes since the last contraction, and she was close to tears. Angie had left them alone for a few minutes so she could grab a bite to eat.

"You know," he whispered, "this isn't supposed to be an endurance contest."

"I know."

"So if they suggest a C-section…?"

She scrubbed her hand across her cheek, sniffed. "It's okay. I just want whatever's best for the baby."

Angie returned a few minutes later with the resident OB on duty that night, a middle-aged woman of Japanese ancestry with a quick, kind smile. She examined Cass, then folded her arms across her white-coated middle. "Listen, I've got an idea. You think you could get some sleep?"

Cass's smile was weak. "I don't know. Although God knows I'm pooped."

The doctor laid a gentle hand on her belly. "I bet you are. Angie and I have discussed various options, and this is what we came up with. Since the baby doesn't seem stressed, and since your water only broke this afternoon, if you can catch a nap and build up your energy reserves, we thought we might hook you up to a Pitocin drip in a couple hours, see if we can get those contractions back up to speed."

Cass's eyes went wide, but the doctor headed her off at the

pass. "It would be a very weak dosage, I promise. And the baby's in perfect position to slide right out, soon as the door's open. Unless you'd *rather* have a section…?"

She gave a vigorous shake of her head.

"Somehow, I figured that. So…you game?"

Cass let out a weak laugh. "It's not as if I have a pressing social engagement to get to."

"That makes two of us," the doctor said with a grin. Then she looked up at Blake. "How about you?"

"Nope, my dance card's filled for the foreseeable future, too."

"Good. Okay, then, we'll let this woman catch a few winks, then we'll play it by ear, how's that?"

Blake hung around after the doctor and midwife left, almost afraid if he went away, Cass wouldn't be there when he returned. To his surprise, she lifted her hand to his cheek and said, "I'm such a pain in the butt."

"S'okay," he said with a smile. "We're a matched set."

"What we are is a lousy combination. Still…" Her mouth flattened. "I'm glad you're here right now. And don't go getting a swelled head, okay? Put a woman through a thousands hours of labor and she'll say anything."

His heart aching, he bent down to kiss her on the forehead. "I'll remember that," he whispered in her ear, and she almost chuckled. "Get some sleep, honey."

"After this is all over," she said, her eyes drifting closed as she shifted over onto her side, "we have to talk."

His temples began to throb.

Rotating his shoulders in a vain attempt to loosen a few kinked muscles, Blake wandered down the hall to the waiting room. Shaun popped to his feet, worry etched in his features.

"It's—" Blake tried to focus on his watch "—after one

in the morning. I thought you went home with Cille and Wanda ages ago?"

The kid shook his head. "I couldn't…I have to stay, okay?"

"Anything to get out of school, huh?"

That got a fleeting smile. "You got it." Then the worry settled right back in. "How is she?"

"Tired," Blake said as they both sat back down. "But as fine as she can be, under the circumstances. They're going to let her rest, then maybe induce labor in a couple of hours."

The boy bobbed his head, then briefly cut his eyes to Blake. "I'm really sorry I yelled at you and Mom earlier. I mean, if that's what got everything started…the labor and all…"

"Babies come when they're ready, bud. Believe me, you had nothing to do with it. And forget it. About being mad at us. We had it coming."

After several seconds he said, "It's just that…I want…" Obviously fighting tears, he swallowed, unable to finish his sentence.

Blake slipped an arm around Shaun's shoulder. "Yeah. Me, too."

Then, looking like a big blue teddy bear in her scrubs, Angie suddenly appeared in front of them, startling him. "Maybe the two of you should try to get a nap, too," she said, "since Cass is going to need you once those contractions kick in again." She nodded toward a door down the hall. "Go on into the lounge, lie down for a bit. We'll call you," she added with a grin, then swayed back down the hall.

"Whaddya say?" Blake asked, pushing himself up, but Shaun shook his head.

"S'okay, you go ahead. I was kinda dozing earlier. Hey— you got any money? Maybe I could hit up the cafeteria or something."

Suddenly aware of how unsteady he was on his pins, Blake

pulled a twenty out of his wallet and handed it to the kid. "Here. Live," he said, then watched Shaun lope off to the elevators before dragging himself toward the lounge. He was dead to the world within seconds of laying his head on the pillow.

When Angie gently shook him two hours later, he sat bolt upright. Through sleep-blurred eyes, he saw an enormous smile.

"She just woke up," the midwife said as Blake scrambled to his feet, "and damned if she isn't gonna do this all by herself. I figured that would happen. As soon as she relaxed a little and stopped worrying so much, nature took over. She was already at nine centimeters when I checked," she said as they both pushed through the door, "and ready to push."

"Blake!" Cass screamed when he barreled into her room, nearly skidding on the tile floor in his haste to get to her side. "He's coming! Ohmigod! He's co-co-*cuuuuuuuuuhming!*"

He braced her in a one-armed hug, his cheek on her temple, having no idea what he said to her as they worked together to push her baby into the world. Less than twenty minutes later, Jason belted out his displeasure at being so rudely catapulted from his nice, warm bed.

She couldn't have done it without him.

No, that wasn't quite true. She could have done it without him. But she hadn't wanted to. And still she couldn't figure out if that was a good thing or not.

It was nearly dawn, if the raucous birdsong outside the window was any indication. Unlike those legendary peasant ladies who pop out their babies, then get right back to harvesting the crop, Cass wasn't about to harvest anything anytime soon. Except some sleep, if she was lucky. If she could take her eyes off her new son.

At a shade under seven pounds, he seemed impossibly tiny. And incredibly dear, for all the grief he'd given her for the past eight and a half months. For all the grief he would inevitably give her for the next eighteen years, she thought with a wry smile. Cass vaguely wondered what Alan would have made of him, only to realize playing the "what if" game was a waste of energy.

"He looks just like me," Lucille declared, the be-hatted infant clutched to her shriveled, T-shirt-covered bosom.

"No way," Shaun put in. "He's totally got that whole cool thing going with his eyebrows." He waggled his for effect. "Like me."

As tired as she was, Cass had to laugh. "Honestly, you two. He's your basic red, wrinkled, too-early newborn. He doesn't look like anybody yet. Except Mr. Magoo, maybe."

"Well, whoever he looks like," Lucille said through lips trembling underneath haphazardly applied lipstick, "his *bubby* is going to spoil him rotten, and there's not a damn thing you can do about it."

Cass leaned back against the pillows and smiled. "I don't intend to. Though I imagine you'll have to stand in line."

It was true. Mercy and Dana, who'd arrived together at five in the morning, both looked like raccoons from their streaked mascara, which they kept smearing with each swipe of their hands. Shaun's grin when he first saw his baby brother had been so wide his eyes had disappeared, and Towanda…well, one look at the woman's face when she took the tiny infant into her arms, and Cass knew she'd have to fight to get time with her own baby.

After a bit, though, Angie shooed everyone out of the room, leaving Cass with her new son, her ex-husband and about a zillion ambivalent feelings. Blake stretched out beside her on the bed, skimming his finger over the baby's minuscule knuckles, and she thought, oh, hell—he's fallen in love with the baby. And then she thought, *And this is bad why?*

Stop fighting, something inside her urged. *Stop fighting and listen to something besides the fear.*

Blake nestled his index finger in Jason's tiny palm, smiling when the spidery fingers instinctively closed around it, then looked up at Cass.

"What?" she said.

"Never mind, forget it."

"Spit it out, Carter."

His lips were curved, but there was a dead serious cant to the smile that made her want to look away. "I was going to say, it almost reminds me of after Shaun's birth. But then I thought, that's probably not someplace we want to go right now."

Maybe it was something in his voice or his eyes, or maybe it was simply because she was too damn tired to keep her own defenses propped up anymore, but finally she heard him. *Really* heard him. That he was truly, deeply sorry for what had happened. And that, if he could turn back the clock, he'd do things entirely differently.

The problem was, would she?

Could she?

Having zilch energy left for sorting out her cluttered head, Cass let her eyes drift closed, the baby suckling at her breast. A small smile curved her lips when Blake pressed his to her forehead.

Then he stood, slipping his loafers back on. "The nurse said they were going to take the baby away for a couple of hours so you could get some rest, so I thought I'd go home with the others, get cleaned up, then come back later this morning. That okay?"

And there it was, that ridiculous, completely irrational urge to grab him by the front of his shirt and beg him to stay, a direct—and decidedly annoying—byproduct of the apprehension that, despite everything she'd done to banish it, still clung to her a whiny child.

"Of course it's okay," she said, forcing a smile. She even lifted her face when he bent over, accepting his kiss the way one might gingerly test a griddle to see if it's hot. When he pulled away, however, she caught the puzzled look in his eyes. She opened her mouth to speak—although she had no earthly idea what she would say—but he shook his head.

"Later," he said, then strode from the room.

The others had already returned to the house, so Blake drove home alone. Just as well. Between the long night, his adrenaline's rapid retreat after the birth, and Cass's obvious ambivalence about the whole situation, conversation was the last thing he was in the mood for. Maybe he'd felt bonded to little Jason, but that didn't change the fact that he and Cass still had a boatload of issues to sort out. He didn't doubt she was still ticked with him about the house—not that he particularly cared, he'd done what he had to do—but even if she got past that, there was the much larger problem of sorting out their "temporary" arrangement. And the fact remained that, his manipulating the situation aside, he was hardly going to fight her if she really wanted out.

If he couldn't convince her she could trust him now. Completely and without any reservations.

Lucille and Shaun had already crashed by the time he got home. Wanda, however, wired as ever, handed him a mug of coffee before he was all the way into the kitchen. One thing about polyester, he noted, scanning her outfit—it was definitely wrinkle-proof. Her Shirley MacLaine-hued wig, however, sat slightly askew.

"You want breakfast?" she asked.

He slumped down into a kitchen chair and aimed a struggling grin in her general direction. "I think what I want goes way beyond breakfast."

With a silent, sharp nod, she began whisking pans and bowls and assorted utensils out onto various surfaces, keeping up what Blake realized was a one-sided conversation.

"I said—"

He jerked awake.

"—Cass called right before you got home, said she realized she'd picked up the wrong purse, she needs the one hanging on the knob to...*her* bedroom."

He didn't miss her pointed inflection. Surprisingly, neither of the ladies had grilled him about the events of "that night," although he seriously doubted they couldn't surmise what had happened. And that it didn't take. With a nod, Blake dragged himself away from the table, figuring if he didn't get the bag now, Cass's request would slip right out of his brain. Yawning, he made his way down the hall, sighted his quarry hanging over the knob, just like Wanda had said, and made a grab for it. Except somehow he didn't get a good grip on the stupid thing and it flipped over, puking its guts all over the hall floor. And Cass was not one of those rare women who only carried her wallet and lipstick in her purse.

Too tired to even cuss, Blake got down on his hands and knees and began shoveling the contents back inside, which is when he noticed the check. Before he could remind himself this was none of his business, he turned it over, noting the jeweler's imprint...and the preposterously large sum written out after the dollar sign. A tiny flashbulb went off in his brain as he realized—*hello*—she hadn't been wearing her wedding set in the hospital. And that she hadn't been able to get the rings off.

He sat back on his haunches, staring at the check, frowning. Would she even sell her wedding rings in order to be free of the debt Alan had left her?

Or what she saw as her debt to *him?*

Chapter Fourteen

Three hours later, after a much-needed shower and an even more needed nap, Cass rolled onto her side, her back to the door, and settled Jason in for his feed. The baby latched on like a starving piglet, making her chuckle. And wince. Then she decided to try something out.

"Wait till you see the room Daddy fixed up for you," she whispered. "It's like being inside a bowl of orange sherbet."

She waited a second or two, but when her head didn't spin around three times she figured, okay, maybe—deep breath—this could work.

If she let it.

Jason's itty-bitty eyes opened, looking vacantly, if trustingly, up into hers as his fist ineffectually beat the top of her breast while he noisily suckled. On a sigh spawned equally from contentment and anxiety, Cass rested her head on her pillow and decided it was high time she faced a fact or two, the main one of which was—she smiled down at the baby, who'd conked out with her nipple still in his mouth—that she knew, without a shadow of a doubt, that Blake had truly changed. That he wasn't about to bolt at the first—or second, or third—sign of trouble. Which meant she could no longer use Blake's past actions as an excuse to keep him at emotional, if not physical, arm's length.

But more important, she didn't want to.

However, it wasn't that easy. On the surface, all she had to do was reach out and accept what he was offering. Only, it was kind of hard to reach for something, no matter how much you want it, when your hands were already full.

Behind her, the door swung open. The carpeting in the room muffled Blake's footfalls as he came around the bed, pulled up a chair. She looked up into his eyes, expecting to see the smile she fell in love with all those years ago.

It wasn't there.

For a moment the fear tried to sneak back, to again lodge in her very core, where for most of a lifetime it had chipped away at her wholeness. But only for a moment. Because no longer was she going to let someone else's perception of her color her expectations…or drown her hopes before they'd even been fully realized.

This time, dammit, she was going to fight for what she deserved.

And to do that, she was going to have to trust Blake with her very soul.

Seeing Jason snoozing in the crook of Cass's arm, Blake turned to mush all over again. And the thought of giving up full-time fatherhood with this one, as he had with Shaun, stole his breath. It made him dizzy, how much he wanted this second chance. With Cass, with Shaun, with this little guy who'd already stolen his heart. That Cass hadn't told him about the check reminded him he might not get that chance.

Hell, he'd used up every weapon in his arsenal: he'd rail-roaded; he'd manipulated; he'd seduced. He'd even grov-eled—oh, how he'd groveled!—to no avail. What Cass didn't want to do, Cass wasn't going to do. And God love her for it. But damned if he was going down without a fight.

Or at least an explanation.

Questions danced in her eyes at his silence. "I brought your purse," he finally said, setting it on the table next to her bed.

"Oh, thanks. Stupid of me to pick up the wrong one, when this one had my wallet and everything in it...Blake? What is it?"

"The purse dropped and everything spilled out of it when I went to pick it up." At her blank look, he added, "I saw the check."

"The check? What? Oh, no! I'd forgotten it was in there, I just got it yesterday—"

"You sold your wedding rings, didn't you?"

"As a matter of fact, I did, but—"

"Why?"

Her eyes widened. "I think that's pretty obvious, don't you? Because I needed the money. I didn't need the rings."

"Because you didn't want to be obliged to me."

"No, Blake. I didn't. And I'm not going to apologize for that."

"You don't have to," he said, clearly surprising her. Then he sighed. "But I do. For pushing you in directions you clearly have no interest in going. Yeah, I only meant to help, but I was so hell-bent on my own agenda that I refused to consider that maybe my forcing myself back into your life wasn't the best thing for you. If you really can't forgive me, if there really is no possibility of fixing this between us—" he swallowed past the fist in his throat "—I'll accept it. But no way in hell am I leaving this room until you tell me *why*."

Their gazes tangled for several seconds before she said, "Here. Put Skeezix in his bassinet. Then come sit. We've got some serious air clearing to do here. Or at least—" she pushed out a breath "—I do."

He did as she asked, then perched on the edge of the bed, facing her, one foot hooked over the chair rung while she carefully pulled herself up into a sitting position. "Did you ever wonder why I never talked much about my parents?"

Blake had only met the Whitleys a couple of times, once at his and Cass's wedding, another time shortly before Shaun's birth. They'd seemed like a fairly normal couple, the handsome Air Force pilot and his sweet, doting wife. Telling himself to be patient, he said, "Occasionally. But you never talked much about your past at all, so I guess I stopped thinking about it after a while."

"Yeah," she said, an unmistakable edge sneaking into her voice, "I thought I had, too. Just goes to show that you don't have to think about something to let it muck up your life." She was quiet for a moment, then said, "I'm not going to give you some song and dance about having a horrible childhood, because in many ways it was fine. More than fine. But my father—" her mouth twisted "—well, let's just say Dad had some pretty strong ideas about men's and women's roles. Ideas my mother was only too happy to reinforce. Don't get me wrong, Dad adored Mom. And me. Oh, yeah, I was Daddy's little girl, all right," she said on a sigh, not looking at him. "And he took his obligation to take care of us very seriously. Made all the decisions so Mom wouldn't have to worry her pretty little head, came to my defense every time some kid taunted me or I had a run-in with a teacher. Because that was his job, see, to protect his womenfolk. That's what a *real* man did."

As Blake's breathing grew more and more shallow, Cass smoothed her nightgown over her knee, not looking at him. "Only, when he had to be away on maneuvers, both of us turned into piles of helpless goo. Mom, especially. So no strong role model, there. But, boy, didn't it make Dad feel good when he'd return and both of his 'girls' were all over him, so grateful to have our big strong protector back?"

The bitterness in her words catching in the back of Blake's throat, he reached across the bed and wrapped his fingers around her too-cold hand. "A little codependency thing going there?"

That got a short, dry laugh. "Ya think? What really sucked, though, was that even as I got older and was around plenty of other women who more than disproved of Dad's outdated women-as-weaker-sex view of the world, the damage was done. Intellectually I knew it was bunk. In practice I was a mess. Minor decisions could give me hives, major ones could make me sick for days. Frankly, I'm not even sure how I got up the courage to go to college at all, let alone one with thirty thousand students."

Now she met his gaze. "Dad approved of you, you know? When he told you, on our wedding day, to be sure and take care of his baby girl, he wasn't speaking metaphorically."

Muttering a curse, Blake looked away as Cass continued. "I knew it was dangerous, letting myself love you too much, letting myself lean on you. But as long as you were there for me, I convinced myself it was all good."

Heartsick, Blake returned his gaze to hers. "Only I wasn't."

Her eyes glittered. "I hated it, Blake. I hated being left alone with the baby, I hated that you seemed as clueless as I was. But most of all I hated feeling so damn *helpless*. And alone. Like my mother must have felt, I realized. I may not have fully understood what was happening to me, but I think on some level even then I was petrified of turning into her. And I had no idea what to do about it. All I knew was, I wanted you too much, and it scared the hell out of me."

"So you threw me out," he said softly.

"It was my fear I was trying to throw out. Not you. But I didn't know how to separate the two. And afterward I realized I had two choices. I could either shrivel up and die, or not. Since I had a child who desperately needed a mother with her act at least reasonably together, guess which I chose?"

Guilt lanced through him, the pain so deserved as to be almost welcome. "And that included a complete moratorium on relationships."

"Well, that was the plan. Except, the one thing I hadn't counted on was that this…this whatever you want to call it is almost like an addiction. Because deep down I'm still a leaner. Maybe the bulk of the wussiness is dead and buried, but—" she sucked in a deep breath "—let's just say I'm not above temptation."

"Alan?"

"Not just Alan, obviously," she said with a small smile. "But I did at least think *that* was safe. Because our relationship wasn't about passion. Yes, I genuinely cared for him," she said at Blake's raised eyebrows. "But there were no fireworks. I'd had fireworks, and they'd nearly killed me."

He had nothing to say to that. But it sure wasn't looking good for the conversation to start turning in his direction anytime soon. A realization only reinforced when Cass glanced down at their linked hands, then slipped hers out from underneath Blake's, folding it with her other one in her lap.

"Of course," she said, "the irony is that for someone who craved protection, I seemed uncannily adept at making horrible choices in that department. Which is why I decided that it was just easier to not trust at all."

"So you wouldn't get hurt?"

A pause. Then: "I think, for people like me, maybe the hurt is worse? Because we're programmed to trust, to depend on somebody doing what they promise, and when that trust is broken…" She shook her head, then looked toward the window, her hair glinting in the sunlight angling through the slightly streaked panes. "It's devastating," she finished on a broken whisper.

Blake lifted himself off the bed, walking over to the window to stare unseeing into the parking lot. Well, folks, that was that. Somewhere, a fat lady was singing her heart out. "So I was right yesterday," he finally said through a tight throat. "When I said it seemed as though the harder I tried to fix things, the more threatened you felt?"

And with every second that passed without an answer, the lady shrieked a little louder. Then at last Cass said, "I couldn't decide if I was more afraid that you'd leave again, or that you'd stay. Either way, I was screwed."

Blake stilled, then turned, his heart breakdancing inside his chest, to find her smiling at him. "And?"

"And I finally decided that maybe I've been going at this the wrong way," she said softly.

And held out her hand.

An instant later Cass was in his arms, her mouth smiling under his. Then he held her back, trying for a stern look. Judging from her twitching mouth, it wasn't working.

"You *deliberately* made me squirm!"

"Yes, I did," she said without a shred of remorse, then grinned. "And I enjoyed every minute of it." Her smile softened, however, when she framed his jaw in her hands and whispered, "I don't want you to go, Blake. I want this second chance as much as you do." Then she dropped her hands to his shoulders and touched her forehead to his. "But that doesn't mean I still don't have major issues with the idea of your rescuing me, or that I'm not still afraid of falling back into old habits. That's why I was so upset yesterday when I discovered you'd bought the house, that you simply took over as if I couldn't possibly handle any of it on my own."

Blake placed a kiss in her bangs. "Please believe me—that wasn't my motivation."

"I know that. Now. What you did was not only smart, but kind and generous. Oh, Blake…you *have* been busting your buns to prove you've changed. But I've been so busy nursing the past…" She sagged back against her pillows, weariness and apology swimming in her eyes. "I'm so, so sorry for putting you through this. For putting all of us through this. Even so, that doesn't mean this is all tied up with a pretty bow. This is something I've lived with since I was a little girl. It's not going to go away overnight."

"No." Out of Blake's lungs poured the biggest breath he'd expelled in months. "No, I know it's not. But for God's sake…why didn't you just *tell* me what the problem was?"

Her mouth pulled tight. "And admit you had that much power over me?"

"Me?" Blake pressed one hand to his chest to feel his heart bumpin' and thumpin' like a stripper on a caffeine high. "Power over *you?* Yeah, that'll be the day."

She actually laughed; a second later, her mouth was once again soft and willing against his in a kiss more of promise than passion, although there were enough flickers of that to keep things interesting. And definitely hopeful, if the thudding of his heart was any indication. When he finally, reluctantly, broke the kiss, he locked their gazes.

"Now you listen to me, woman," he said, which got a raised eyebrow. "You are one of the strongest, most resilient, most self-reliant women I've ever met. What you've accomplished on your own would put ninety-five percent of the world to shame, you hear me? But being independent doesn't mean you still can't need someone. Or want to be with them—"

"I know that—"

"Hey, I'm on a roll here, don't interrupt me." He blinked. "Where was I?"

Amusement, and something else that made his heart swell, twinkled in her eyes. "Something about…needing someone?"

"Right." He took a breath. "I need *you*…so much it hurts. And I love you so damn much my heart comes close to bursting whenever I see you, or even think about you. What does that have to do with my being able to function on my own? Not a damn thing. But honey—" He cradled her cheek in his palm. "What you wanted from me was perfectly legitimate. You had every right to expect me to be around, to be there for you and Shaun. It was *my* fear that hurt you, Cass, not yours. If anything, *I* was the weak one."

He got up to stand in front of the bassinet, looking down at the baby, chuckling as Jason's intense little frown vaporized into a trembling, gassy smile. *And so was Alan,* he thought but kept to himself. What he did say was, "But when our marriage ended, you weren't the only one who hurt. My world shattered when you asked me for that divorce." Turning to face her again, he said, "No one likes to feel like a failure, Cass. No one."

Tears glistened again in her eyes. "Then why didn't you fight, Blake? Why did you just walk away?"

"Because I thought that's what you wanted. Because…because I was too young and inexperienced to hear what you *really* wanted. Really needed. And I thought you were saying…I wasn't enough for you. Then later I used work to avoid dealing with how much I hurt. How much I missed you. How much I regretted how badly I screwed up. On the surface I suppose I thought I'd moved on. And then Shaun told me you were getting married again, and I realized just how big a line I'd been feeding myself. The thought of seeing you married to someone else…I couldn't handle it. And every time I saw Shaun, it just reminded me of what I'd lost." A smile pushed at his lips. "I never thought I believed in the only-one-true-love thing. Guess I was wrong."

"Yeah," Cass said. "I know how that goes."

"Oh, God, honey…I'm so sorry. Especially for letting Shaun get caught in the crossfire."

"Tell him that," she said gently. "Not me."

"I know. And I have." He pushed out a breath. "And we're working on it."

"Good. But you know what?" she said, almost wonderingly. "As hard as it was after you left, as hurt and angry as I was…well. Your leaving certainly forced me to grow, didn't it? Otherwise, I wonder if would have ever found the courage to crawl out from under all the crap my father had dumped on me." She smiled. "But it wasn't until you wormed your way *back* into my life that I realized how far I still had to go."

"So…my being obnoxious and pushy was actually a good thing?"

The smile melted into a liquid chuckle. "Yeah, Carter. A very good thing."

"Well, there ya go," Blake said, sitting beside her once more. "Guess that makes us living proof that there's a bright side to everything." He slipped his hand underneath her soft, shiny hair and kissed her again, inhaling Pantene and baby and that unique scent he'd carried with him in his heart from the first time he'd held her in his arms.

"So tell me something," he said when he realized the kissing had gone on probably longer than was going to do anybody any good, considering the woman had just given birth and all. "Did you sell my ring, too?"

She giggled, a sound he hadn't heard for more than fifteen years. "Are you kidding? For heaven's sake, I wouldn't have gotten enough for that ring for a meal at Mickey D's."

"So you've still got it?"

"Yeah," Cass said softly. "I've still got it."

"So we're good?"

She smiled. "Sure looks that way from where I'm sitting."

He kissed her again, then said, "My heart is yours, lady. Always has been, even if I had a lousy way of showing it. Always will be."

Cool assessment washed over him from those sharp blue eyes. "Just remember that. 'Cause I really don't want to have to shackle you to the bedpost to keep you from leaving again. Then again, maybe that's not such a bad idea—"

"Okay, Mrs. Stern," a nurse broke in as she swept into the room. "You and Jason have been sprung, if you feel up to it. Ready to go home?"

Heedless of the nurse's watchful gaze, Blake swept a knuckle across Cass's jaw. "Are you?"

"You bet your cute little tush," she said.

There had been the requisite Welcome Home signs and about a dozen It's a Boy! Mylar balloons floating in the living room when they got back to the house. There were what seemed like a thousand people and a thousand questions to answer, and Cass kissed and answered them all. Blake called everybody who wasn't actually present, including his parents, whom he'd ensconced in a lovely condo in Tulsa several years before. Cass heard him say he'd send them plane tickets next week to come out for a visit, and she wondered with a chuckle what Blake's plain-living folks would think of Lucille and Towanda.

After a half hour of this madness, however, Lucille sharply told everyone who didn't live there to get the hell out, the new mother needed her rest. As Cass lowered the sleeping Jason into his grandmother's arms, the old woman raised a precisely penciled eyebrow. "So…how is everything?"

"I take it you don't mean how I'm feeling?"

"You hear this silly woman?" she cooed—actually, growled was a more apt term—to her infant grandson. "No, sweetheart, I don't mean how you're feeling. I know how you're feeling. Like you just pushed King Kong out of your crotch."

"That's a pretty fair assessment, yeah," Cass admitted on a half laugh. "Other than that, though…" She leaned over and planted a kiss on a cheek as soft and withered as the skin of a one-day-past-prime peach. On the drive home from the hospital, she'd finally come clean with Blake about Alan's gambling problem, the true size of the debt, the diamonds, all of it. And soon, she'd have to come clean with Lucille about everything, too. Including Cass's conviction that, had Alan lived, she doubted she would have stayed married to him, baby or no baby. Because it wasn't any more right for Cass to keep the truth from the old girl than it had been for Blake to go behind her back about the house. But like Cass, Lucille was strong enough to handle whatever she needed to, with a little support from the people who loved her. Maybe even stronger. "Everything's just fine."

And her mother-in-law beamed. "Mazel tov, darling," she whispered. "It's about time. Now go spend a few minutes with that cute guy who brought you home from the hospital." She glanced over at Blake, beamed a little more. "Alone."

"But the baby—"

"Is mine for the next hour. So get out of here, already."

The ceiling fan whirred softly overhead as Blake shut the door to her—um, *their?*—bedroom, the breeze caressing them as he drew her into his arms and claimed her mouth. Reclaimed what would always be his. Her fingers teasing the ends of Blake's hair at the nape of his neck, Cass laughed softly against his lips.

"What?"

"It's nice to be able to do this without feeling like I'm standing in another room."

He grinned, bussed her lips again. "I have something for you." Slipping out of her arms, he crossed to the closet and pulled out a white upscale-department-store box.

"A present?" A pleased chuckle rumbled out of her throat. "When did you—"

"Last week. Open it, goof, and stop yammering."

So she did. Opened the box and stopped yammering, both. Inside was a beautiful, light-as-air nursing gown, pure white cotton batiste with delicate tucks and satin ribbons, utterly feminine and lovely.

"Oh, Blake…" she started to say, but he shook his head.

"Go further," he commanded. Puzzled, she batted aside the tissue paper she'd assumed had lined the bottom. A slash of red caught her eye; she lifted out a sliver of crimson satin and lace barely large enough to cover a Barbie doll.

She gave him what she hoped was a cutting look. "Blake…?"

"The first is for now. The second, um…" A sheepish, completely adorable grin traipsed across his jaw. "A guy can hope, can't he?"

The wisp of lingerie fluttered in the fan's breeze as she dangled it from one finger, deliberately withholding her answer. Then she lifted one eyebrow and said, "Incentive for a quick postpartum recovery if ever I saw it."

Relief swirled in those luscious brown eyes. "You mean that?"

"Hey. I wasn't kidding about the shackling-you-to-the-bedpost comment." Enjoying the hell out of his blush, she released the teddy to let it float back into the box, then walked—gingerly—over to her jewelry case. "Actually—" she plucked her "gift" out of its slot, palming it before she turned around "—I have something for you, too."

She smiled as recognition bloomed in his eyes at the circle of gold glimmering in her hand. "Your old wedding band?" he asked on a whisper.

"Scratches and all. Come here."

He went; she placed the ring in his palm, then closed his fingers around it, keeping his hand in both of hers as she whispered, "Blake Carter...will you marry me again?"

His gaze slipped into hers, deeply, completely. Forever. "Are you sure this is what you want?"

"Yes," she answered immediately. "Because I'm sick to death of being held prisoner to my own fears. And if I don't do this—" she kissed the tip of Blake's nose, making him smile "—how am I ever going to learn how to trust?"

"Me, you mean?"

She shook her head. "No. Myself."

Blake wrapped his arms around her, gathering her close. "So is next Saturday good for you?"

His chest smothered her chuckle. "I'll pencil it in."

"Pencil, nothing. This is written in ink. Hell, this is written in *stone*." Then he let go—just one hand, the other one didn't seem interested in leaving anytime too soon—to lift the thin circle of gold to the light. "I don't know, though...this seems kinda plain and boring. Maybe we should think about getting a new one, whaddya think?"

"You even think about replacing it, and you'll be sleeping out on the cou—"

His mouth crushed down on hers, his fingers sizzling against the back of her neck.

"Shaun Carter!" Towanda boomed from down the hall, her voice easily carrying through their closed door. "You get your sorry self back in here and wash up your lunch dishes, you hear me? You think I'm your maid or what?"

The kiss dissolved into laughter, laughter that only increased when Blake assumed a Fred Astaire position and started to "dance" in place with her. And sing. Horrendously. Pleading with her to never again take his sunshine away.

"Deal," she said into Blake's wicked, wonderful eyes, thinking that Shaun was going to be one happy dude, even if Towanda did make him do his own dishes.

* * * * *

Silhouette®

SPECIAL EDITION™

HOLIDAY HEARTS

Because there's no place
like home for the holidays...

UNDER THE MISTLETOE
(SE #1725)
On-sale December 2005

by

KRISTIN HARDY

No-nonsense businesswoman Hadley Stone had work to do—modernize the Hotel Mount Eisenhower and increase profits. But hotel manager Gabe Trask stood in her way, jealously guarding the Victorian landmark's legacy. Would the beautiful Vermont Christmas—and meetings under the mistletoe—soften the adversaries' hearts?

Also in the series...

WHERE THERE'S SMOKE, November 2005
VERMONT VALENTINE, February 2006

The colder the winter, the sweeter the blackberries will be once spring arrives.

Will the Kimball women discover
the promise of a beautiful spring?

Blackberry
WINTER
Cheryl REAVIS